C000212789

Jaime Jones Stars in...

THE ANTIGUAN AFFAIR

An Up in the Air Mystery

Figgy Mack

An Up in the Air Publication

ISBN: 978-1-7393527-0-7

For Phil,
With love.

Chapter 1

"Cabin crew, twenty minutes to landing."

Jaime Jones glanced around the galley with an appraising eye. Trolleys still needed stowing, canisters securing, used headsets collecting, and there was the final run-through with the trash cart. The chaotic flight had kept them on their toes, she could almost taste her first sip of chilled white wine.

Her fellow crew were scurrying around: Mario was already dragging the bin from its stowage, Gabi and Max were dealing with the canisters.

"I'm going to help Jean with the landing cards," said Karen, their immediate supervisor and sky-class purser. "You guys know what you're doing." She headed towards the front of the aircraft to assist the cabin service director, Jean Blackthorn.

Mario raised an eyebrow. "Catch you later," he mouthed at Karen's retreating figure.

Gabi laughed. "I know. *We* could do with the help right now, no? Not the lazy cow at the front." She was referring to the big boss, Jean, who had not bothered to make her way down to the back of the aircraft during the long-haul flight.

"Exactly," replied Mario. "Then again, it's not like Karen had a choice. If Jean calls, you go," he relented.

It was true, thought Jaime, Jean had not been supportive, instead choosing to swan around the first-class cabin with the

1

purser, Tony Hayward. Karen ought to stay and help her team. There were only four of them to take care of the majority of passengers. Still, Gabi didn't hold back when it came to her feelings.

Max offered no opinion on the subject, head down, concentrating on the task at hand: but after nine hours, the others had come to expect this from him. He had barely spoken.

"Keep picturing the palm trees, the ocean, the white sandy beaches. Channel your inner Antigua." Jaime was thrilled to be returning to the Caribbean island.

"Give me New York or Tokyo anytime over a sandy beach," retorted Gabi, her lip curling.

The crew of DebonAir were spoilt for choice when it came to exotic and interesting locations.

"Love New York," chipped in Mario. "But can you beat a cocktail with a tropical breeze blowing through your hair?"

"Er, yes. By shopping in Macy's." They laughed at Gabi's passion for retail therapy.

"There's only so much shopping you can do. And I love it. But I'm over it after a few days. It's all about the scenery for me." Jaime had travelled far and wide. She didn't think she'd ever tire of it.

Gabi dismissed Jaime's comment with a flick of her hand.

Mario continued, "The ravioli at Scarpetta's is hard to beat. Even in Sicily." He was referring to his favourite Manhattan restaurant.

Jaime's stomach growled. She could almost smell the garlic and basil. Then her mind wandered to thoughts of fresh seafood, melt in the mouth steaks and the local fish sandwiches. *Not long to go now*, she gave herself a quick pep talk. "Anyone got anything special planned?" Anything but talk of food, she decided.

"No," Gabi answered quickly. "I've been busy at home. I need to relax."

"Are you and Tony up to anything special?" Jaime was referring to Mario's partner of many years, who was also the first-class purser.

Mario was releasing the brake on the trash cart, pulling it out towards the cabin. For a few seconds, Jaime didn't think he'd heard her. She was about to repeat the question when he mumbled, "Not much. Eating and sunbathing, I guess." He disappeared behind the curtain.

Jaime turned to Max, who was heading into the toilet, slamming the door behind him. *Okay then,* she thought. *There's always Karen, and the flight deck might be fun. A long shot, though.*

Remembering seeing the possibility of a storm on her weather app, she frowned. That would put paid to sitting on the beach or by the pool. At least she had plenty of reading material. This trip looked very much like it was going to be a four book one. Thank goodness she'd packed that many.

A lurch of the aircraft had her grabbing onto the counter and there was a collective gasp from the cabin, the passengers assuming every jolt meant they were crashing to the ground.

Jaime busied herself with the job at hand.

Chapter 2

"Did you put them all back in the travel wallet?"

"Of course I did. Don't I always?" snapped Carol Carfax. Even though they sat at the front of the rear cabin, and it was the luxury airliner, DebonAir, it still wasn't first-class. Why the hell Caleb's firm couldn't splash out on an upgrade she would never know.

Stretching out her legs, she sighed. The landing announcement had been made. Thank goodness they would soon be touching down. She was excited to see her best friend, Maggie. They would catch up over cocktails, she would fill Maggie in on Edinburgh life, and Maggie would update Carol on life in the fast lane of politics on the small Caribbean island. They would compare notes on their irritating spouses and put the world to rights. It was always the tonic she needed.

Glancing over at her husband, she noticed he had his notes out again. God, he was on edge. Whatever business he had was important. It was getting harder and harder to convince the family Antigua was where they should spend the first week of summer every year. Christy and Connor were getting older and wanted to go on separate holidays with their friends, but Caleb's firm had some deal out here they wanted him to broker, so here they were again - which suited her.

"Can I switch it on yet?" The whiny voice of her youngest reached her ear. She knew what Connor was referring to.

4

Bloody phone. He couldn't live without it. At fifteen years old, it was his whole life.

She reached out and patted his knee, "Soon, love. As soon as we've landed. They'll announce it. You know that."

"Jesus, I'm so fucking bored." Connor's tone was petulant and louder than Carol would have liked.

She felt her husband's eyes glued on her, waiting for her to reprimand their son for his foul language. Jesus, how she disliked Caleb right now. Since when did he think it was okay to take such a back seat on bringing up the kids? Okay, he was the one who worked, she had given up her promising career in publishing to be a full-time mother, but that did not mean he could 'opt out'.

She stared at Connor who was sitting with his phone in his hand, ready, waiting. She gave him what she hoped was a 'look'. Connor turned away.

A cabin crew member approached, and Carol glanced at the smiling face. "Not long to go now," she said. "I need to check your seatbelts are fastened."

Carol sighed, running her hands through her spiralled red hair. Her thoughts went back to her son. Little shit. Since they had sent both kids to the new, private boarding school, it was as if they had gotten worse, not better. Connor was rebellious. And Christy, well their relationship had fizzled out. There was a time when mother and daughter would talk. Now, at seventeen, when she should be asking her mum for advice, she had become distant. Carol saw the glances her daughter got when they were out and about. Did Christy notice? She wasn't sure, giving no sign she was aware of any attention from the opposite sex. Thank goodness she was in a girls' only boarding school, although that didn't mean much these days.

"I need to finish one more page. We're not landing for another fifteen minutes." Caleb was holding up his hand in a placating gesture to the stewardess, who, for her part, stood her ground - smiling and waiting.

5

Carol glanced at the woman called Jaime (according to her nametag), admiring her 'no-nonsense' attitude. Caleb, realising he was pushing his luck, snatched up his papers and shoved them into his new 'man bag' resting on his knee.

"Bag in the overhead locker," the stewardess continued, not budging. As Caleb stood to store his bag, the stewardess moved on to the next row, smile still stuck in place.

Carol Carfax could not wait to land on Antigua. It was the perfect destination to kick back and chill out. No worries. No stress.

Chapter 3

The last few DebonAir crew suitcases were lined up next to the carousel. Gripping the handle of her Samsonite, negotiating the packed terminal, Jaime tried not to trip in her three-inch heels - one of the more impractical aspects of the uniform. Outside, in the balmy heat, she spotted their usual bus driver, Thomas. Her face lit up. She squeezed his shoulder.

"How're things with you?" he smiled.

"Not bad. Nothing exciting to report even though it's been months since I was last in Antigua," she replied.

"Well, it isn't a bad thing. No one wants too much drama in their lives, right?" he chuckled. "Now pass your bag for me to load." He reached over for Jaime's suitcase. "Hop on and get out of this sunlight. Mind you, there's a storm brewing. You'll be lucky to escape it."

Glancing at the unblemished sky and brilliant rays of sun, it was hard to believe, although Jaime had been in the Caribbean before when the weather had made a rapid about turn. When it did rain, boy, did it bucket down.

"C'mon Jaime, grab a seat." Gabi's strong French accent was bordering on impatient.

Realising she was blocking the entrance to the bus, Jaime climbed the steps. She squeezed down the narrow aisle to the back into one of the few remaining seats.

"Take it off me, Jaime. And have a slurp before we move. You'll spill it if you don't." Tony Hayward, first-class purser, reached back to hand her a plastic glass filled to the brim.

Thanking him, Jaime took a large glug. "Ooh," she murmured, appreciating the Champagne with a hint of fresh orange juice. "Yum." She was just in time as the bus rolled forward on its way to the resort.

Clutching her drink, Jaime's head jigged around like a ragdoll, the bus bumping up and down on the gravel tracks. The nine-hour flight out had been tough going with only a couple of hours rest in the crew bunk area. Daytime flights were notoriously busy on holiday routes with passengers in party mood the second they got on board. Now it was the crew's turn to have fun, and Tony's cocktails were doing the trick.

Jaime enjoyed the view: palm trees swaying in the ever-present breeze, the sparkling coastline to her left, mountains looming to her right. This island had it all.

Karen Jeffries had everyone's attention. "So, I said to her, *do you have a visa, madam?* And she looked at me blankly, so I explained you needed a visa to be allowed into the country. She still looked puzzled at this stage, but reached into her bag, pulled out her purse and handed me her bloody Visa credit card." Her broad, Brummie accent added to the humour.

The remaining eight crew members burst out laughing, although Jaime didn't miss Karen's quick glance across to the cabin service director, a bit like a child seeking the approval of a stern parent.

Replenishing her drink, Jaime relaxed, looking forward to the next four days. Apart from Karen, Tony and Mario, she had not met the other crew members before. She had taken an instant disliking to Jean Blackthorn though, who was less than friendly.

"Apparently, *he* was on the flight," piped up Captain Rob Bannister when there was a gap in the anecdotes. He was greeted with blank stares.

"Beg pardon, Captain?" queried Tony Hayward.

"Our elusive boss," replied the captain, relishing his piece of gossip.

The cabin service director, Jean Blackthorn, could barely stop herself from choking on the drink she was swallowing. "What? Where?"

Ignoring Jean, Rob continued, "The man himself." He was in his element now, all eyes on him.

The barrage of questions flew at him like bullets from a machine gun.

"Where was he sat?"

"Why didn't you say something?"

"What was he on our flight for?"

"When did you find out?"

Rob held out a restraining hand. "You all know the rules. If he's ever on board, the captain is told as a courtesy and to be honest, I shouldn't have even mentioned it now."

So why did you? pondered Jaime. *Now everyone's worried about how they performed.* She noticed Jean blanch under her orange skin, probably racking her brain to remember any of the first-class passengers, wishing she'd been in the cabin more.

Charles Debon, owner of the airline, was rumoured to pop up now and then, somewhere on one of his aircraft or down-route. The assumption was he would be checking on his staff and the quality of the service or checking out any issues away from base. Jaime wondered how he had managed to stay anonymous; he must travel under an alias. She had never come across anyone who had ever met him or even seen him. Employees of DebonAir had always been curious about their mysterious leader.

Tony was also looking miffed. As the first-class purser, he was solely responsible for service in that cabin. "You could

9

have at least given us a hint," he whined to the captain, "I might have been able to pick him out."

"Now you know I can't, Tony," responded Rob pompously, his ruddy complexion reddening even more. "I'm sworn to secrecy. You know that," he repeated. "And the point is you're not supposed to be able to pick him out. He wants to be treated like everyone else."

"Oops, we could have a tiny problem in that case," Jaime commented, remembering the idiot with the loud voice sat in 24b who had rang his call bell so many times she'd disconnected it. She hoped he wasn't Charles Debon.

"At least let's hear your version of what he looks like." Karen addressed Rob. "I've heard he's gorgeous. A real silver fox. What I wouldn't do to get my hands on that. And stinking rich. Surely the world's most eligible bachelor."

"I have no idea what he looks like or even how old he is," Rob added. "You've heard how private he is. Reclusive for most of the time. Now stop worrying. I'm sure you all did an amazing job." His manner was condescending and irritated the hell out of Jaime – she peered at his co-pilot, Kate, and felt sorry for her. Lord only knew what he'd been like in that tiny cockpit for nine hours.

As this seemed all Rob was going to say on the subject, the conversation was now focused on speculating why their boss had chosen to be on this flight. Did he have his eye on someone? Had there been a complaint against one of them? Was it a random check of service? Perhaps Charles fancied a few days in Antigua. Why not? He owned an airline, after all.

Chapter 4

At the precise moment of the bus attack, Tony was centre stage (where he appeared to be comfortable by all accounts). "I said to him, *now love, the choices are Sancerre or Pouilly-Fume,* having a bit of banter, you know? Now I'm pooing my pants wondering if -"

But the crew never found out what Tony was wondering because the door of the bus burst inwards, and a tall, bony man fell inside with two other men hot on his heels. The first man had to duck to allow the low ceiling to accommodate his height: his companions had no such issues, both being shorter and stockier. The second man was wearing a yellow vest, whilst the third was older and had decided going bare-chested was the way forward, despite his large, flabby gut hanging over the belt of his jeans.

The first attacker waved a large, gleaming knife in the air, shouting, "Everybody down! On the floor! Hand over passports, money, rings. Now!"

Jaime's first thought: it was an impossible ask. There was no way anyone had the space to get on the floor. The bus was cramped enough as it was.

The second and third men squeezed into the bus doorway, shouting. "Hand it over. Where's the cash? We want the money."

The tall robber wielding the evil knife jabbed it in the air matching the actions of the Crocodile Dundee image on his khaki t-shirt. He was pointing it towards the male crew members and eyeballing them as he threw out his demands. "Open them bags, tip 'em out. C'mon now."

The bus had been waiting at a temporary traffic light. It felt to Jaime as though the next sequence of events happened in slow motion, allowing her to notice several things at once. Captain Rob Bannister yelled at Thomas to step on the gas and move the bus forward. Karen Jeffries was clambering over the back of her seat in a desperate bid to put some distance between her and the knife. First Officer Kate Jackson and CSD Jean Blackthorn ducked, trying to get on the floor under the seats.

Jaime and Gabi Pascal, sitting furthest away from the door, had the best vantage point.

Leaning forward, reaching for her handbag, Jaime lifted the flap. Her hand curled around the small canister of pepper spray, illegal to carry onboard, but she deemed worth the risk. Right now, she was prepared to use it.

Tony Hayward was unclipping his large, gold watch and shoving it in the direction of the three men in a bid to placate them. There was sweat dripping down the side of his angular cheek. Max Kleinbeck, on the other hand, remained rooted, trying to squeeze his bag onto the floor of the bus and away from the view of the attackers.

Mario Vanetti, who was sitting opposite the door, was on his feet. Ducking to avoid the knife, he shoved the first intruder down the steps into his two partners in crime. His biceps bulged beneath the short sleeves of his white uniform shirt. The back two attackers fell out of the bus, but the first man was teetering on the edge of the step until a mighty kick from Mario's well-built leg sent him flying out, well into the road beyond. Jaime was reminded of a Jean-Claude Van Damme movie.

"Mario! My god, get back here. Mario!" Tony wailed, distressed at his partner's bravery.

With a jolt, the bus moved forward. Jaime's fingers unfurled from around the pepper spray as she straightened back up.

Captain Rob Bannister stood and surveyed the scene, attempting to take back control. "Everyone, calm down now. They're gone, they're off the bus." He dabbed his forehead with a large handkerchief.

Kate and Jean emerged from their refuge behind the seat. Jaime wondered how they had managed to squeeze into such a cramped space. Karen, who had fallen onto Jaime, was sobbing - her usually sleek hair dishevelled, and black mascara streaked down her cheeks. She had laddered her tights and grazed a leg in her clamber over the back of the seats.

"Oh my god, I look awful. Shit, the state of me!" she wailed.

Jaime eyed her with surprise. *Strange priorities*, she thought.

"Thomas, radio ahead to the hotel and explain the situation. Tell them we may need a doctor on hand. Oh, and tell them to inform the police, of course." Rob barked his orders.

"Yes sir," replied the shaken bus driver.

"It's okay." Karen's tone suggested embarrassment at the outburst. "It's just a graze."

"Well - if you're sure..." replied Rob.

"I'll see the doctor. I may have injured my wrist," Gabrielle Pascal spoke up.

Jaime turned to her and was shocked at how stark her already alabaster complexion was, emphasised by the jet-black hair that fell in a straight bob on her cheeks. "Are you hurt?" she asked, puzzled, as the two of them had not moved throughout the entire incident.

Gabi held onto her left wrist and merely nodded. Then she turned to look out of the window. Rob conferred with Thomas as the bus continued its bumpy journey towards the safety of the luxury hotel resort.

The golden sunshine disappeared behind a large cloud, and Jaime was reminded of the impending storm.

Chapter 5

Large wrought iron gates swung open, offering the crew a warm welcome. Jaime admired the grandeur of the Reef Royale Resort as the bus wound its way along the drive. It was split in two, joined in the middle by a marble-clad reception. There were wicker cushioned seating areas around large tables, ceiling fans whirred in the partially roofed sections, palms swayed back and forth in the gentle breeze, and the whole atmosphere was of a lazy, unhurried calm. Jaime experienced the feeling she had stepped into an old colonial plantation house. Although not huge, the hotel gave the impression of being vast due to its many secluded alcoves. Walking over to the veranda, Jaime gazed out at the Atlantic Ocean, inhaling the salt-tinged air, her hair ruffling in the warm breeze that was always synonymous with Antigua.

"Jaime, we need to gather on the sofas now, please." The patronising sound of the cabin service director's home counties accent cut into Jaime's moment of peace.

She considered pretending she hadn't heard the command. Then thought better of it. Joining the crew on one of the comfy settees, a waiter circulated with a tray of cocktails. Jaime took one of the large glasses and sipped her drink, which was laced with a strong rum. *Just what I need*, she thought.

Everyone except Gabi was present. She was with the doctor.

Captain Rob Bannister addressed his crew. "We have been asked to gather here and await the arrival of a local councillor, Gregory Dickens, who sits on the Board of Public Safety in Antigua. Some of you might know him. He's often around the resort." As he spoke these words, Jaime noticed his sneer. "He is going to chat with each of us about what happened on the journey here, and there will be the offer of counselling if anybody feels they need it. Please don't rush into a decision. Remember - shock can be delayed."

Jaime surveyed the crew: they had perked up marvellously – no doubt the rum punch had contributed. Still, Rob was right. You never knew when the shock might hit you. She tuned back into what he was saying.

"I know it's tedious, folks - but I am afraid it's necessary. He has promised not to take up too much of your valuable rest time."

"What was the last bit?" Jaime whispered to Tony, who was closest to her. As usual, she had managed to zone out as crucial information was given.

"We have to sit here, hun, and wait our turn to speak to old what's his face before we can get to our rooms. I want to get out of these stinky clothes and into the shower." His voice was bordering on whiny.

Tugging on her damp tights, Jaime nodded in agreement.

"Usual order of doing things," trilled Jean unnecessarily, as everyone knew their place.

"Bloody seniority order," mumbled Jaime in what she thought was a whisper. However, judging by the smirk on Mario's face, it had not been quiet enough. As she was to be the penultimate interviewee, she would be sitting there for some time, and the prospect irritated her. Only Gabi was below her in the pecking order. Jaime glanced towards Jean to see if she had relaxed the uniform rules. Eyeing the woman, she noted the uncreased blouse still buttoned to her neck, her bleached blonde hair still scraped back into a tight

16

ponytail at the back of her head, her lipstick once again replenished, and her back ramrod straight.

"For the love of god, that woman is a robot," Jaime whispered in disgust to no one in particular. Feeling tired always made her throw caution to the wind. Catching sight of herself in the reflection of the glass tabletop, she wondered, not for the first time, why her hair never stayed where she put it. Deciding 'uniform standards' could go and take a running jump, (Karen wasn't bothered, having removed her ripped tights and unbuttoned her blouse perhaps more than was decent,) Jaime relaxed back in her chair and tuned in to the chit-chat around her. The bus attack was taking on the elements of a world war. This would get worse once it hit the rumour mill back at base.

First Officer Kate Jackson was quietly praising Mario for his brave actions, making him seem uncomfortable. Studying him, Jaime thought, not for the first time, how good-looking he was. Smooth, light-brown skin, dark wavy curls, an easy smile. He was quick-witted and, despite English being his second language, managed to not only understand the British sense of humour and innuendo but also dish it out. Glancing over at Tony, thinking he must be happy with his partner, she noted he wasn't showing any interest in his other half. Instead, he sat nibbling on his fingernails, agitated.

An attractive, older lady dressed in a smart business suit emerged and headed towards the captain. Jamie watched her stride across the floor and decided she must be someone in authority. She had an 'air' about her. Approaching Rob, she rested a slim hand on his shoulder and bent in to confer with him. His brow uncreased, and he smiled, making him appear much younger. He stood and followed her across the lobby, disappearing down a hall which housed the offices. *Well, she cheered him up*, thought Jaime.

"Who's meeting for drinks later?" Karen slurped more of her cocktail.

"Definitely. I'm ready for a beer." Mario's eagerness was greeted with a dark stare from Tony.

"You've earned it," Gabi chimed in as she made her entrance. "You were awesome."

"How are you? All good?" Mario pointed towards her arm.

She waved it dismissively through the air. "Oh, fine. False alarm. It felt worse than it was. So, what did I miss? Drinks later, is it?"

"I have a few things to do." Jean's snotty tone surprised Jaime as she thought Jean should be the one rallying the crew after what they had been through. It was her job, as their leader, after all.

Karen shrank back in her seat.

"Shall we say about seven?" Gabi took over the arrangements.

"Absolutely," Jaime replied, giving Karen and Gabi some support. She noticed Jean glaring at her. *What's her deal?* she wondered.

Thus ensued an animated debate about what made the perfect first night down-route snack, with pizza coming out on top.

"I fancy some peanut butter," said Gabi. "Do you think I will be able to get hold of some?"

"Unlikely, until breakfast," replied Jaime, noticing Gabi's efforts to be friendly after her earlier odd episode on the bus. "Do you want it on some toast?"

"Ooh, a baguette with some jam, I think."

"A big juicy burger," Mario burst out of nowhere, causing a ripple of laughter.

"A huge glass of Merlot," returned Gabi.

Max Kleinbeck remained on the periphery. Quiet, subdued and disinterested in the conversation around him, in a different way to the quiet Kate, whom Jaime thought seemed shy. She noticed Max's left leg twitching.

Rob reappeared. He motioned to his co-pilot, Kate Jackson, no doubt indicating she was next up, headed over to the suitcases by the elevators, took his luggage, made no eye contact with the rest of his crew and headed off. Jaime eyed him with interest. *Did he seem rattled?*

One down, eight to go. She blew out a breath. This was going to take forever. Deciding what she needed to keep herself going was a pot of Jamaican Blue Mountain, freshly brewed coffee. She looked around for one of the waiters who loitered in the lobby area.

"Anyone joining me for coffee?" she asked of her remaining colleagues.

Jean, in response, drained her cocktail glass, wiggling it in the air, expecting a waiter to materialise and read her mind.

"Think we'll stick with the cocktails, eh love." Tony nudged his partner, sending his drink slopping over the rim of the glass. Mario smiled good-naturedly.

"I'll squeeze in one more cocktail. To be sociable, of course." Karen chuckled at herself.

"Blue Mountain coffee," cooed Gabi. "Yum. It's so smooth and delicious. I always search for it back in Paris, but it's hard to find."

"Coffee for two?"

"No. Maybe not. I'll have a peppermint tea," Gabi decided.

Jaime hailed the waiter, placing the order before the cocktail crowd could get his attention. The councillor had better hurry with his interviews if he was going to get any sense out of this lot.

Chapter 6

The last of the interviewees, Jaime and Gabi sat waiting. Jaime was enjoying her coffee after the rum punch, remembering the many occasions during her earlier years of flying when she had crawled to her room after drinking too much, too quickly. She liked to think she was much more mature these days.

"Of course, my darling husband would love for me to stop this job. He wants me at home all the time, you know? And I wouldn't mind, especially when you end up on a trip working with a bitch like Jean."

Jaime gasped in mock surprise, placing her hand over her chest for added effect. "Whatever can you mean?" she asked with a devious smile. Jean was not the most likeable boss she had worked with.

However, Gabi was back to talking about her husband. "Working for such a demanding company takes him all over the world, you know? Ever since we were married, it's all he's ever done. Thanks to him, we can afford to live in the heart of Paris."

Their chat was interrupted by the arrival of Max from his interview, who had, by all accounts, been quick.

"Next," he declared, turning and heading towards the reception area.

"A man of few words," remarked Jaime as she rose from her seat, pleased to be off.

"Whom are we speaking to?" asked Gabi.

Jaime realised she had not been present when Rob had made his speech. "Some councillor person, Gregory something, he's often around the hotel, so we might recognise him. See you at seven."

As she turned to go, she was just in time to observe the paling of Gabi's complexion for the second time that day.

The moment the door opened the memory hit her. Jaime knew she had heard the name before but hadn't bothered to give it much thought. It was quite a few months back, and she was with the crew. Most of them had met for a drink, and it was crowded in the bar. The feel of his hand had made her flesh crawl. The presumptuous prick thought he could get away with it by offering to buy her a cocktail. One with a disgusting name. She had enjoyed saying no, and he was fuming. God, the arrogance. Some of the girls loved the attention. *His name is Dickens. I bet most people shorten it to Dick.* Jaime smiled at her own joke.

"Miss Jones, Jaime, how lovely to see you too. Come, let us sit."

With a hand placed on her lower back, he tried to lead her towards an intimate seating area, away from the desk and all that was professional.

"Here will be fine, thank you," Jaime stated, heading back towards the desk, perching on the edge of a wooden upright chair, with no intention of staying long. The expression on his face was one she'd seen before. He reminded her of a great white shark with his predatory expression. Incredibly white teeth shone out from a swarthy complexion: blue-green eyes stared. Why had none of the female crew warned her about him when they had come out of their interview? Kate, Jean, Karen. They'd all been interviewed, and surely they'd all visited Antigua before. Jaime was going to give Gabi the heads-up before she came in. This was a man who

21

was used to getting his own way. Well, she was also used to getting her own way where some things were concerned.

"I assume you want an account of the robbery?"

"If it's not too much trouble, Miss Jones," he leered.

She noticed the accent, which sounded like a mix of American with a hint of Scottish. Walking around to the other side of the desk, he removed his well-cut, navy Armani suit jacket, loosened his tie and unfastened his top button, staring at Jaime the whole time. *He's blatantly trying to make me feel uncomfortable,* she thought. Staring him straight in the eye, she gave a brief summary of the attack. The councillor asked her a few questions, although he didn't seem interested in her response. He wasn't even taking notes.

"You say the first attacker was wearing a khaki t-shirt?"

"Yes." Jaime was becoming more irritated by the questions.

"Any other distinguishing features apart from Crocodile Dundee?" he smirked.

"As I already said, I didn't notice any." Enough was enough of this jerk, Jaime got up to leave. She needed to warn Gabi, who would be waiting outside, oblivious to what was in store for her. "I hope that will suffice. As you can imagine, I am tired and would like to get to my room."

"And where would that be?" The councillor favoured her with his lecherous smile. "I may need to get in touch with you again and inform you of any developments," he added. "So, room number?"

"Contact me through the captain if you have to." Resisting the urge to sock him one, she turned and left the room, banging the door behind her. She headed towards the seating area to warn Gabi to be on her guard but stopped dead in her tracks. Gabi wasn't there. Jaime scanned the lobby, no Gabi to be found. Shrugging, she assumed the other woman had given up waiting. Jaime didn't blame her. Retrieving her suitcase, she noticed it was the only one remaining. Grabbing the handle, she headed to her room.

22

Councillor Gregory Dickens could do his own legwork. It was time for a shower and a change of clothes.

Chapter 7

The cabin service director raised the tumbler to her lips. "Cheers, Jeanie," she said aloud. "Here's to nothing." She took a large gulp of the double gin and tonic and sat at the dressing table of her suite to begin the laborious process of reapplying her make-up, ready for the evening out. She was angry. Fuming, in fact.

"Fuck," she shouted out loud. *Why couldn't that pompous twit of a captain have let me know Charlie boy was on board somewhere?* She glared at her reflection. *I would have at least walked around and poured some wine. Now he's going to think I'm lazy.* "Fuck. Fuck. Fuck." She took a deep breath in a bid to calm down, swallowing another large gulp of her drink.

She had often fantasised about the owner of the airline. That one day, their eyes would meet across a crowded first-class cabin. That he would slip her a note as she passed by, caressing her hand as he placed it in her palm. Written on it would be the name of an expensive hotel, a room number, a time. Wearing a tiny black dress and four-inch sandals, she would knock at his door. He would open it, his eyes lighting up at the sight of her. He would take her hand and guide her over to the balcony, the warm breeze blowing in off the ocean. There, he would open a bottle of the most expensive Champagne, pour her a glass, hand it to her, all the time his eyes never leaving hers…

The clatter of mascara falling over on the dressing table focused her attention back on the reflection in the mirror. Studying the bags under her bloodshot eyes, she was brought back to reality. And her foul mood returned as she contemplated how to eradicate the bloated skin with hundreds of pounds worth of expensive products. She didn't much like looking in the mirror these days. What she saw there shocked her as she still thought of herself as young and slim... She was now in her fifties, the years of erratic sleeping patterns, too much exposure to the sun's rays, too much alcohol and rich food - had all taken their toll. The deep tan and bleached blonde hair were still very much in place, but she no longer had the face and figure to accompany these. This realisation, a few years ago, had sent her into a deep depression and made her drink even more. She found it hard to face her younger female colleagues, the reminder of how she once looked too painful to bear, and she could not help but despise them all.

Her position as cabin service director gave her the power to inflict as much misery on her underlings as she desired. An evil smile came to her lips. There were some possibilities on this trip. She knew a few things about some of these people, thanks to her good memory and finely tuned ear for gossip - of which there was no shortage in the airline industry. And there were always plenty of opportunities to learn more.

Draining her glass, she decided what she wanted, needed, in fact, first and foremost, was a man. Someone to romance her; make her feel feminine and sexy again. It had been too long. If only it had worked out with Roy... Now Roy was perfect – at first. In his twenties, handsome, attentive. She remembered seeing him for the first time. He had brought over her glass of chilled wine. A droplet of condensation had dripped off the base on to her jeans. He had been apologetic, grabbing a napkin and dabbing at it, perhaps lingering a little too long... She had felt a flash of heat run through her body. She instinctively knew he had felt it too.

His shift had ended at two am, and he had turned up at her door. They were inseparable for the rest of the trip. He was thoughtful, romantic. She took him shopping and showered him with gifts. He was a considerate lover. Before long, she was flying him to more and more destinations to spend as much time together as her job and living in different parts of the world would allow. Admittedly, it was always the exotic trips he was more able to make, but he couldn't help his schedule - when he could be available.

It had ended as quickly as it had begun when she found him hiding in a quiet corner of a bar, in Mauritius, with some local whore all over him. Well, she showed him. Turfed him out of her room, cancelled his ticket home, abandoned him out in the Indian Ocean to fend for himself. She smiled. She often wondered how he had made it back to Atlanta - out of curiosity, not because she cared.

Dismissing the thought of Roy, she replenished her drink and decided that was enough daydreaming and dwelling on the past. Now she had to think about the future. New beginnings were in order, and she knew who the perfect fit would be. All the signs were there. She couldn't believe he had not made a move on her sooner. Thinking back, the last time she was here, Roy had been with her. That would explain it. Yes, she was positive he wanted her. There was no denying the flirting that had passed between them. If anyone knew when a man was coming onto her, Jean Blackthorn did. And she was up for it. Why the hell not? She was single and had a lot to give.

With a grim determination, she fished in her hefty Louis Vuitton make-up bag for more concealer. Much more. She had someone in her sights, and there would be no stopping her.

Ready at last, she checked herself out in the floor-to-ceiling mirror. Loving her new linen trousers and white silk blouse - the latter being cheekily transparent, she had opted for a satin gold bra with matching thong. It always paid to match. The pair of three-inch high, gold, strappy sandals purchased from Jimmy Choo a few months ago were absolute agony on the balls of her feet and tired legs, but worth it, adding height and making her legs appear longer than they were. She'd have to perch on a bar stool for as long as possible to take the weight off. So far in life, she had not suffered from varicose veins, one thing for which she was grateful. Admiring the ruffles on the loose-fitting blouse, she chose to ignore the rolls of flab around her waist it was hiding. Her freshly washed hair was down, tucked behind her ears to show off large, gold hoop earrings and a lavishly made-up face.

The gin she had so far consumed was enough to give the edge she needed without slurring her speech, although the quantity needed for that had risen over the years. Later she would switch to a crisp, dry, white wine - much easier to handle. Or maybe even Champagne. Who knew how the evening would progress?

Chapter 8

"Pass me the bottle, Mario. I need a spritz." Tony reached out and took the fragrance, spraying it all over his torso.

Mario coughed and headed for the balcony, gasping for air. "C'mon Tony. Who are you trying to impress? I'm right here. You've got me already."

"Who knows who might be in the bar. I like to keep my options open," Tony teased.

Mario smiled and shrugged. "True, I suppose." He was used to Tony's attempts to wind him up.

"Besides," remarked Tony, "it keeps my mind off things. I'm going to focus on having a good time tonight. We'll deal with tomorrow when it comes."

"That's what I always try to tell you. You stress too much. There's nothing more we can do."

"How can you be bloody relaxed about the whole thing?" Tony's voice rose a notch. He wanted to be the voice of reason, for once, but there was no doubt Mario was the cool, calm, collected one of the pair. "This is our whole life in the balance."

Mario raised an eyebrow. "Really? Our whole life? I think we've done well to date. And you win some, you lose some. Let's dial down the drama."

Tony threw his make-up on the counter in a huff. Mario, recognising the signs of a melt-down, walked back towards

28

Tony. Placing his hands on his partner's shoulders, he gently massaged them, feeling Tony begin to relax.

"You always know the right thing to do. I wish I could be the chilled one." Tony stared at his reflection. "Everybody loves you, you know. You're so bloody nice and helpful."

Mario grinned into the mirror. "Glad to hear you admit it for once. Every relationship has a better half."

Tony pouted. "Alright, don't milk it. Just because you tackled three armed robbers and single-handedly saved the entire crew. And my Rolex."

"All in a day's work, love."

"Seriously, though, Mario. What do I bring to this relationship? Besides the glamour?"

"Hmm… give me a minute." This was not the first time Mario had needed to reassure his partner, and he knew it wouldn't be the last.

Tony grabbed a towel off the dresser and flicked it in Mario's direction.

"Okay, okay. It's not difficult to answer. Honestly, I don't know where we'd be without you. Your business brain is second to none. And how you find these properties and parcels of land and jump on them, is incredible." Mario squeezed Tony's shoulder, watching his face brighten.

"I am rather good at it. That's true." Tony laid a hand on Mario's.

"Our portfolio would be nothing. Non-existent without your skills. Don't you forget it."

"Thanks, hun. I needed that."

"We're a team. That's how we get through life. We always come out on top, and we'll succeed this time. Got it?"

Tony picked up his tinted moisturiser. "Got it," he echoed. "Now, let's get a wiggle on. I've laid out what I'm wearing on the bed. You'll need to complement me, of course. I'm thinking matching jeans, same style shirts but different colours. Okay?"

Mario glanced over to the bed, where most of Tony's wardrobe was laid out. He smiled. He knew he put up with a lot, but he also knew it was worth it. Heading to his suitcase, he finished unpacking. When he got to his white jeans, he pulled them on, noticing Tony studying him through the mirror.

"Our minions await us," Tony chuckled. "And I've got my legendary acting skills to assist me this evening. What are you going to do?"

Both men knew they'd need to quell their nerves. Put on a good show.

"I guess I'll have to rely on the cocktails," responded Mario, winking.

Chapter 9

Karen Jeffries sat in a booth, staring at the empty glass. Her forehead felt damp from the still-warm temperature: she prayed her armpits weren't wet. *Shit. It's not even seven, and I'm already pissed. How am I going to get through the night?* She'd come down early: her mission was to find him in the bar before meeting with the crew.

At first, she hadn't seen him, standing there in all his magnificence, then her heart had missed a beat. *Yes! He does want to see me again, despite everything he said earlier. I knew it. I knew he couldn't resist me.* Then she'd spotted his mates - loud and obnoxious, surrounding him, laughing at his jokes. *Bugger.* Was it them he'd come to the bar to meet, not her? Had she got it completely wrong?

The place was filling with couples of all ages, families – some with quite young children and a few singletons savouring their drinks. The staff behind the long horseshoe-shaped bar were busy juggling bottles of spirits, filling gleaming cocktail shakers, and flipping caps off chilled bottles of beer.

She'd decided not to approach, unsure now. Taking a table and waiting to see if he came over was the best plan, then she could pretend she was waiting for the crew. He had spotted her arrival. He was probably just having a quick catch-up with friends, killing time. It would look rude if he walked off as soon as he saw her.

Trying to remember how many cocktails she had consumed was difficult. There were three before the interview. Yes, three had seemed a good amount to face him with. To take the edge off her nerves. He was like a drug to her. No matter what anyone said, she had to have more of him. *Jesus, why do I get so anxious? It's been four months now. Four glorious months together.* And the last time they met was magical. A simple picnic on the beach… perfect weather… he had brought a bottle of rum this time, and they had drunk shots. He had led her to a small clearing behind some rocks, not even bothering to lay down a blanket, overcome with desire. He hadn't been able to hold off any longer.

The waiter made her jump, which in turn irritated her. She glared at him.

"Drink for you, miss? Sex on the Beach, perhaps?" he asked with a dead pan face.

Cheeky little shit. He's coming on to me. Well, two can play that game. "I think I'm ready for a Screaming Orgasm if you can manage that," she replied, equally dead pan.

With a smirk, the waiter moved away and headed back to the bar, desperate to share his anecdote with his colleagues, no doubt. Well, what did she care? Where was she? Oh yes, the beach. Her fuddled brain tried to recall the reason he had given to leave. An emergency at the council office. It must have been urgent, judging by the speed he was out of there, leaving her to collect the remnants of their brief lunch and get herself a cab back.

She'd been thrilled to see him. They hadn't had a chance to get together again on the previous trip, what with his work commitments. It had felt like an eternity. She wasn't allowed to contact him. His rule. But the incident on the bus earlier, although scary, had provided the perfect opportunity for them to meet up without any suspicion being aroused.

The waiter returned and placed her 'Screaming Orgasm' in front of her. "Anything else I can do for you right now?" he asked, leering.

Yes, you can bugger off, you little perv. "I think I'm sorted," she replied, smiling sweetly. What was it about men? Why did they think she would appreciate that sort of humour? How about some goddamn respect? Leaning forward to take a sip from her straw, she reached behind her and tried to pull up the waistband of her jeans, which kept slipping, revealing the top of a red lace thong. The thick, sweet creaminess of the Baileys made her feel sick. She hadn't remembered what was in the drink when she had ordered it and now regretted the rash decision.

Her mind went back to a few hours earlier, the frosty reception she had received from him. It had shocked her. There had been no warmth in his eyes, no spark of desire. He had quashed all hope she'd had of them spending any time together, citing his wife as being suspicious - he had to cool things down. It had been difficult to hide the pain she was feeling. The hurt. He was ushering her out of the door before she even had the chance to tell him how much she had missed him. How much she loved him...

Learning back in her chair, straining to catch a glimpse of him, still laughing with his mates, fresh beer in hand: deep down, she knew. He had no intention of coming over to her table. She'd hoped he'd change his mind after the interview. Desperate to see her. But it turned out that she was the desperate one. The one sat alone, being treated like a slut by the waiters.

A tear rolled down her cheek, and she brushed it away. Why did this always happen? Three times in her life now. Three times she had endured an indescribable feeling of being discarded by men. She may as well face it and say it as it was. Used. Perhaps it was true. Perhaps she was cursed in love.

But someone was looking out for her because two of these low-lifes had ended up getting what they deserved. Remembering hearing the news about Dirk's car crash, recalling the emotions she had felt, she smiled. He'd been her first true love all those years ago. He was an experienced driver, so the accident had been shocking. Fortunately, no one else had been involved. There had been reports earlier, an alligator had been seen on that stretch of road, which, of course, was not unheard of in the Florida Keys. Anyway, he'd deserved it, and she hoped he'd suffered. But not the alligator. It had all happened quite soon after their relationship had ended.

Then there was Simon. Some two years later. His accident was no less freaky and had occurred within days of him dumping her. How many people were unlucky enough to get struck by lightning? And die? On a golf course playing a game they loved? Well, Simon, for one. And good riddance. She pictured him, mid-swing, club behind his back, about to launch at the ball…

Well, who knew? Perhaps she would get lucky for a third time. Perhaps *this* jerk would get his just desserts. The idea cheered her.

Slurping the remnants of her cocktail, she found herself hoping, once again, for him to walk over, smiling, arms outstretched. Ready to rekindle what they once had.

Chapter 10

Stepping out of the shower in her large bathroom suite, Jaime towel-dried her shoulder-length hair. Grabbing another towel, she wrapped it around her as she walked into the bedroom. The floor felt cool under foot, and the ceiling fan created a gentle breeze. Looking longingly at the king-sized bed with its bright white comforter and mountain of pillows, she sat on the edge of it, picking up each book she had brought, one by one, scanning the blurb. Laura Childs' *Postcards from The Dead*, set in New Orleans and featuring scrapbook shop owner Carmela Bertrand, was a particular favourite of hers. The hilarious Agatha Raisin never failed to make her chuckle, along with the escapades of Anne George's Alabama sisters. She had a particular fondness for Carolyn G Hart's Annie Darling mysteries, not least because of the island setting and Annie's to-die-for mystery bookshop, *Death on Demand*. Jaime often felt as though Annie had the perfect life.

Her own recent move to Devon, the home of her most favourite author, Agatha Christie, was proving to be an inspired decision. Not only did she relish the mystery and remoteness of the moors, but she enjoyed the stunning beaches and seafood shacks spanning Devon's miles of stunning coast. She didn't think she would ever get tired of finding new and interesting places to visit. Smiling, she thought about her renovated houseboat moored on the banks of the Dart, with the picturesque town of Dartmouth to her right, and she could make out the top of Greenway across the river. Never in her wildest dreams, growing up, did she think she could ever be lucky enough to have such a view.

Placing the books back on the table, she went out onto her balcony, facing the beach and the ocean beyond. There was a flowery scent in the air, and she could still feel the rays of sun even though it was low in the sky - a burning red ball of flames. This part of the hotel was a brand-new addition to the resort, not anywhere near finished the last time she had visited. Everything in it was new and unused. The flat screen television, the computer (although the internet was dicey) and the fluffy towels.

Staring towards the Atlantic, she noticed how quiet the beach was now, remembering what she had read on the crew brief. It was private – only for those residing in this new wing. How delightful. Peace and quiet, no screaming children. Heaven.

Lounging on one of the steamers, she contemplated the evening ahead, wondering if everyone would turn up. Tony and Mario were certain to show. Tony rarely missed an opportunity to be the centre of attention, she recalled from previous trips.

Rob was not familiar to her. *Pompous prick. Give me a flight deck of Kates anytime over a flight deck of nobs. Oops, I mean Robs, of course,* she corrected herself, laughing out loud, whilst wondering if anyone else was out on their balcony, listening to her strange noises. At home, she would have an attentive audience in the form of Ellery and Wolfe, her dogs, hanging on her every word. How she missed her little babies. Leaving them was the worst part of her job.

Jean was a strange one. Aloof, condescending, not at all likeable. Rob had given her a few strange glances. And Jean appeared to have forgotten her job description. Like taking care of her crew when they've been attacked on a bus. Maybe seeing if they're alright, arranging to meet them all later, have

36

a chat with them. Karen tried to pick up the mantle there until she was stamped upon by Jean. Interesting how she took it lying down. Somehow, she thought Karen had more spirit. Where was it they had flown before? Maybe South Africa? A trip to Victoria Falls from Harare. Yes. Jaime recalled being glad Karen was there on the long journey, upbeat and fun and bringing the refreshments.

Sitting up, she flicked her hair around in the gentle breeze, hoping it would dry enough not to bother using a hairdryer. She had an image of Gabi's thick bob of hair and hoped she hadn't bothered to wash it, or she would never make it for seven.

Time to get dressed. Reluctantly, she dragged herself off the steamer sunbed and into the cool room. Grabbing a pair of jeans, a t-shirt and a pair of wedges, she glanced in the mirror. Keep it simple was always her motto. Not bothering to style her wind-dried hair, she scrunched it into a band, applied a touch of lip gloss and decided she was good to go.

Picking up her room key, she noticed it was rippled, with a small micro-chip built in. Slipping it into her back pocket, she planned on signing her food and drinks to her room. Closing the door, double checking it was locked, she headed towards the outdoor bar, her mind now in full food mode, thinking about the island treats the resort offered.

Chapter 11

Having left her room earlier than the agreed meeting time, Jean Blackthorn was on a mission to get a man and tonight she had her sights set on the hot councillor, Gregory Dickens. She needed to feel desired again, and he was the one to do it. He was a man who could appreciate the slightly older but much more experienced, sophisticated lady. Those younger hussies on this crew had better watch out and stay away, they had no chance. But if they wanted to see how it was done, well, they could always watch and learn.

Swishing into the lounge area, her man radar was on full alert. She had long ago perfected the technique of walking into a bar full of men and getting their undivided attention. She loved it. Thrived on it. Spotting him at the bar, she smiled to herself. So, there he was. She hadn't lost her touch. She had told the councillor she would arrive at a quarter to seven, and sure enough, he hadn't disappointed her.

With a confident stride she headed towards him. He was sat on the edge of his stool, sleeves rolled up, tie pulled down, a bottle of Bud in one hand and a cigar in the other. There were a group of other 'suits' gathered around him, and they were in high spirits. One of them glanced towards Jean as she made her way towards them, leaned into Gregory and said something which forced them all to look in Jean's direction and burst into laughter. Jean's stride faltered. She suddenly doubted herself, and in doing so, almost lost her balance on the three-inch heels. Narrowly avoiding catastrophe, her face felt hot, a bead of sweat forming on the side of her nose. It was a horrible feeling, but all eyes were on her.

There was no turning back now. She must continue the performance. Putting on her brightest smile, she approached the group of men. They were standing in a huddle, not moving aside to let her in. She was used to more gentlemanly behaviour. Dickens was perched on a stool, and he stayed put, not looking her way at all.

Jean tried to regain some composure. "Evening, gentlemen. How are we all doing?" Silence. "Greg, darling, how about a drink?"

"Thanks, sweetheart, mine's a Bud. What about you guys? Sounds like she's buying." This was followed by raucous laughter. They turned away from her and continued to talk amongst themselves as though she were not there.

Jean was mortified. Outraged. She felt the beginnings of an ugly flush spread from her neck travelling to her face. A vein in her forehead began a series of unnatural spasms. She had to leave, get away from this embarrassing situation. As she spun precariously on her gold stilettos, one of the group commented, "Getting desperate, are you, Gregster? Where did you meet her, buddy? 'Grab a Granny' night?"

More laughter. Jean had never been made to feel so low before. Unappreciated. Old. She had put so much effort into getting ready, now she felt stupid. How could she have misjudged the moron? It was not a nice feeling, and she was not a woman to be made fun of. She was normally the one making fun of other people.

Turning to leave the offending area, there was a low growl - a rumble of thunder seeming to go on and on… The night sky turned a shade darker. Storming out of the bar, Jean vowed to get even.

Chapter 12

Humming a little tune her father used to sing to her when she was a toddler, Christy Carfax hung one of her dresses on a hanger and attempted to smooth out the creases. At seventeen, she had packed plenty of outfits to make her appear older. She smiled. There she was, trying to add a few years, and all her mother did was try to remove a few years. How ironic. *Focus, Christy.* There was a lot to do.

Five of her evenings were accounted for, and if she could manage it, she would try to get away during the day too. But she would need to be careful. Her parents may be preoccupied, but they weren't stupid. She would need to check in when necessary. Thank goodness for the privacy of her own room. She was glad she had kicked off last year after they had returned, stating flat-out she would never go on another family holiday again unless she had her own room. Sharing with her little bro, at their ages, was outrageous. Fortunately, both parents had seen sense, and it was arranged for this year.

Assessing the room, she noticed how plush it was. Crisp, cool sheets on the large bed, a small kitchen area and the balcony directly in line with the ocean. *Cool upgrade,* she thought, deciding it was probably because her parents had connections. *Shame I won't be able to spend enough time here to enjoy it.*

Removing a pair of heels from the zip compartment of the case where she had hidden them, she moved on to the rest of her shoes. A mixture of heels and flats, unsure of what her itinerary was going to be. The agency had been clear she should be ready for anything. Sitting on the edge of the bed, twirling a shoe round and round, she thought of expensive yachts, cocktails and sunsets. She had developed a taste for the high life since signing on with 'Angels'. At least one good thing had come out of her new, fancy school. Her new circle of friends had put her onto a good thing. They were more mature than those she had hung around with at her last school. Making money wasn't all about studying and going to uni. No, there were plenty of ways to rake in the cash, and she was doing that right now. The agency was thrilled when they heard she was going to Antigua, asking if she was happy to have a working holiday. Was she ever? The annual family trip was such a drag.

Then the email arrived. What a surprise. He hadn't gone through the proper channels, choosing to contact her directly. He'd specified it would be for one evening and must remain private. She'd bridled at that, being a professional.

Taking the red Dior dress from its carrier, she held it out for inspection. Yes. It would do well for this evening. Along with the black sandals. Sophisticated, yet understated. He hadn't confirmed where they were going. But that wasn't unusual. Somewhere it would give his reputation and ego a boost to be seen with a pretty girl on his arm but out of sight of the gossips. More than likely, a gentleman's club. It was how it worked. For the most part, she had been treated with respect by her dates, like a lady. And if there had been any expectation at the end of the night for things to progress, well, she had never felt at all under pressure to go along with it. Her friend, Cordelia, had hinted the money was fantastic. But what she got, for the little she did, was fine with her. And the clothes allowance was to die for.

41

Sliding the sleek evening dresses to either end of the wardrobe, she finished unpacking her casual wear to hang in the centre. Glancing at her watch, she realised time was running away with her. As usual, her mother had planned for them to meet for dinner at 6.30 pm, not wanting to delay meeting up with her friend, Maggie. The whole reason they were all dragged back here, year upon year. She was such a selfish bitch, trying to keep up appearances with her friends back home – namely, her family loved being together, loved holidaying together. What a crock. Well, this time, it suited Christy fine. Now she had her own agenda.

Pausing once more in her unpacking, she frowned, trying to recollect when things at home had changed. Her dad had always worked a lot but perhaps had not been quite as obsessed with it. Her mother, who had given up her career before it even started, stayed at home to raise them. Which was odd because they were at boarding school and came home on the weekends. What did she do all week?

Remembering a time before they had started their new school, she had asked if she could bring home a friend for dinner. She had been anxious, as it was a boy who'd asked her out. She knew she would have more chance of being able to go out with him if her parents had met him and liked him. Of course, her mother had no problem with her bringing a 'friend' home for dinner and had cooked a meal. Christy recalled the smell of the homemade lasagne and garlic bread as she and Alex had entered the house. She remembered how her mother's jaw had dropped when she had turned to see the 'friend' and discovered they were of the opposite sex.

During dinner, her dad had barely spoken to Alex. It was embarrassing. Her brother, whom she had pinned all her hopes on to help ease the tension, had excused himself as soon as the last mouthful of food had been eaten from his plate. Her mother had taken a phone call from a friend and walked off into the study. Her family had let her down.

She had, until that point, been a model daughter. Worked hard, got good grades, played the obligatory instrument. Yes, she decided. She would never repeat that mistake. As far as her parents were concerned, she had no boyfriend. She was concentrating on her studies and progressing to university. The thought kept them quiet and off her back.

In the meantime, she would be out experiencing life. Making shed loads of money. And there was nothing they could do about it because they would never know.

She smiled, resuming the humming of the little tune.

Chapter 13

Jaime glanced around, looking for familiar faces as she made her way to the bar. It was situated next to the enormous pool, and the wind had picked up, making the palm fronds sway in time to the soft jazz music. Out of the corner of her eye, she glimpsed the retreating figure of Jean Blackthorn dressed in white with gold sandals. About to call out to her, Jaime stopped herself. What was she thinking? She didn't even like the woman. Besides, hadn't she declared she was too busy to meet up?

Jaime perched on a tall stool and ordered a large glass of chardonnay from the attentive bar steward. As she swivelled on her seat to check around for any more of the crew, a hand grasping her thigh brought her to a stop. Spinning round, she found herself uncomfortably close to the smug face of Councillor Gregory Dickens.

"Jaime, how lovely to bump into you again and so soon. Great to see you out of your uniform."

Through gritted teeth, Jaime snarled, "Remove your hand from my leg. Now." She did her best to keep her voice even.

However, instead of removing his hand, the councillor continued, "What is that divine smell?" He bent into her neck as though he was going to bite it.

Jeez, it's Count Dracula. He needs to get his hand off my leg now. How the hell had she not spotted him and his minions before she had taken a seat at the bar? His arrogance was too much to bear, and her right hand was curling into a fist so tight her fingers were turning white.

Had an arm not appeared from her other side and turned her stool away from the councillor, he would have received a crunching blow right to his jaw.

"Excuse me, Miss Jones, may I have a word with you?" It was the deep voice of a tall man with dark eyes, oblivious to the look of fury on her face.

"Really, Fleet. Is that necessary right now? Haven't you got some other guests who need your attention? Jaime is trying to relax," piped up Dickens from over her other shoulder, unaware of how close he had come to a punch in the face. Jaime felt like she was at a tennis match, her head turning from side to side. However, realising she had let her temper get the better of her, and in a public place, she did not need to be asked twice. Uncurling her fist, she turned to the newcomer.

"Of course." She swivelled around to grab her glass of wine whilst seeking out the barman.

"It's already taken care of, miss." The barman nodded in the newcomer's direction.

"My name's Henry Fleet," the man introduced himself as he led her towards one of the many palm-screened, quiet alcoves away from the sight of Dickens at the bar.

"What can I do for you?" asked Jaime after they had settled themselves into a booth.

Henry blushed. "Sorry, but erm… well, nothing. I couldn't stand by and watch that... man." The last word was said through gritted teeth as though he were suppressing what he would really like to call him.

"Oh?" Jaime's eyebrows rose as she studied the figure sat opposite her. Smooth skin, cropped hair and a clean-shaven face. His attire was all business with short-sleeved shirt, green tie and khaki trousers. Mid-thirties, she guessed.

"I hope I wasn't too forward dragging you away. I didn't give it much thought. I stepped into the bar and saw him

45

pawing you. I barged right over there." He paused. "I'm the customer relations manager here at the hotel. I suppose you could say it's my job to help the guests." He smiled.

"Well, a thank you is in order, then," Jaime returned the smile. After all, he turned up in the nick of time.

"Perhaps I can push my luck further by asking you to join me while you finish your drink. Please don't feel obliged. I'm sure your friends will be arriving soon."

"You know, I don't see any of them around. Perhaps a few minutes wouldn't hurt." And, Jaime was thinking, Henry was attractive - in fact, he was quite charming.

"Whereabouts are you from?"

"I live in Devon."

"I've heard of it. But I've only ever visited London. That was when I took a hospitality course there. It was fantastic."

"Are you from Antigua itself?" Jaime took a sip of wine.

"Born and bred."

"It must have been great growing up in such a paradise."

"It is beautiful. But you know how it is, we all want the opposite to what we have. I'd love to move to a big city and experience life there, at least for a while."

Jaime nodded. "You're right. And I would love to experience island living for a while. It's so relaxing."

Before Henry could reply, they were interrupted by a voice calling Jaime's name. Turning, she saw Tony heading her way with Mario trailing behind, both in their designer shirts and tight-fitting jeans, coiffed hair and a hint of make-up. Certainly on Tony, she decided.

"Darling, come and help us find the crew, and by all means bring the hottie with you." Tony eyed Henry.

Henry, to his credit, managed a smile. "Actually, I have to get back to my desk. Perhaps we can catch up tomorrow?" He was addressing Jaime.

"Oh, right. No problem." Jaime attempted to hide her embarrassment at Tony's bluntness - and at Henry's suggestion to meet again. She slid out of the booth, taking her wine with her.

"Wow, you work fast. Or is he your Antiguan playmate? I used to have one in every country before Mario started following me around." He punched his partner lightly on the arm, and they began play fighting.

Cringing, Jaime hoped Henry had not heard the comment. "Don't be crude. We're not all like that, you know."

"Whatever you say, love." They rounded the corner laughing.

Then abruptly stopped.

Chapter 14

Karen Jeffries was sitting alone at a table, hidden from sight, with a large cocktail in front of her, the cloth on the table whipping at the corners. The expression on her face was a mile away from the bubbly, smiling woman Jaime had known before.

Tony spoke first. "Hiya babe. What are you sitting here for by yourself? Where's everyone else?"

Tactful. The woman had obviously arranged to meet someone, had already met them or was a raging alcoholic. *She looks like she's had one too many,* decided Jaime. Karen stood, grabbing the edge of the table. It was Mario who gave her a supporting arm, causing a look of annoyance to flash across Tony's face.

"I was ready a bit early." Karen's words were slurred. "I thought I would wait here instead of in my room. It's so cool out here."

The group moved on in search of more of their party. They headed around yet another alcove of the large outdoor bar, through more palm fronds and bird of paradise plants to find Rob, Kate and Jean. Grabbing chairs, they ordered fresh drinks. Jaime glanced over at Jean. She seemed to have managed to get over whatever had irked her earlier. Although judging by her face, had not regained all her composure.

Max arrived as the drinks were being brought over, a little out of breath and perspiring. He was tall and willowy and

48

tended to favour more formal attire, sporting a starched, open-necked shirt and pleated trousers complete with leather belt. Fetching himself a beer, he seated himself at a slight distance from the others, and Jaime observed the sweat patches under his arms. Talk turned to the only missing crew member, Gabi. Jaime explained how she had disappeared earlier before her interview with the councillor. Karen snorted. There was an awkward silence.

"Maybe the shock of earlier came back to her," Jaime suggested.

However, as if on cue, Gabi rocked up, cocktail in hand and drew up a chair.

"Hey there," Jaime greeted her. "Did you catch Dickens earlier? When I came out, you'd gone."

Gabi smiled. "Yes, all sorted. Must have been when I popped to the ladies' room."

Right, thought Jaime. *With your suitcase?* Turning her attention to Jean, who was seated next to the first officer, Kate, Jaime noticed she was dominating the conversation. Studying Kate, she noted her short, brunette haircut, stocky frame, dated dress sense and a pretty, freckled face, which was flushed. Having not met Kate before, Jaime wanted to know more about her – being the curious soul she was. And in her opinion, no one should have to spend the night sitting next to Jean.

Jaime spoke up. "Who's eating?"

Karen, who was mid-sip of her wine, choked as she shouted, "Yes, deffo. Count me in."

A few hands rose and Jaime glanced at Kate. "Would you help me grab some menus?"

"No problem."

At the bar, Jaime and Kate chatted whilst waiting for the barman to pass them some menus.

They were standing on the opposite side to where the councillor had been earlier, and Jaime saw he was gone.

"I'm glad Councillor Gregory Dickens has left," she commented. "I bumped into him at the bar, and he is such a sleaze."

Kate raised her eyebrows but made no comment.

Jaime continued, "You must have noticed him around here before. He is always after some woman or another."

"I hadn't noticed."

Jaime felt deflated. This was hard work. Some people were so unobservant. She pressed on. "I'm sure he's married. But it doesn't seem to stop him thinking he's god's gift."

"Well, I guess that's men for you," replied the first officer.

Jaime was about to reply when the barman reached over and handed her a pile of menus. Heading back to the table, Jaime spotted that Jean's seat was temporarily vacant and took full advantage of this to ensure she sat next to Kate. She wanted to talk to her some more, feeling she hadn't managed to get underneath the woman's quiet exterior.

After a quick perusal of menus, orders were placed, and drinks were consumed.

"Are you married, Kate?" Jaime was keen to get back to her conversation.

"No. I've not met the right person yet. How long have you been married?"

Jaime's face reddened. She was at a loss for words. Struggling for composure, she managed to stutter, "Oh, erm, I'm not married." Why did that question throw her off guard?

"Oh, sorry." Kate looked embarrassed. "I don't know why I thought you were."

A picture of Ken, her long-dead husband, popped uninvited into Jaime's head. "No problem." With an effort to pull herself together, wondering if she had said or done anything to suggest she might have been married, Jaime attempted to get the conversation back onto a course she was comfortable with. "So, whereabouts do you live?"

"Buckinghamshire, the family home, believe it or not. I guess I've been concentrating hard on my career. I've not had a chance to jump on the property ladder yet."

"You should speak to Tony and Mario," replied Jaime. "That's their hobby. Still, plenty of time, though. The career path is the hardest, and you've done that."

Kate frowned. "I'd say finding the right person to spend your life with is harder."

"Well, true. I can't help there, though. I'm no expert. Ask the captain. I believe he's married." Jaime was used to lying about her married state by now.

Rob, who had been listening in, commented, "No rush, Kate. You need to be sure he's the one for you, married or not, and don't bring kids into this world until you're positive you've got it right." This last part was said with such venom, both women stared at him.

Intrigued, Jaime quickly concluded he must be in an unhappy marriage with a divorce in the pipeline. However, Kate, whom Rob had been trying to advise, had turned an interesting shade of red. She looked as though she were plucking up the courage to say something when the food arrived.

Bugger, bugger and bugger again, thought Jaime. Things were getting interesting. Taking her mahi sandwich and pile of french fries, she added mustard mayo and munched: *these people are not all they appear to be on the surface - although most people never are - least of all me.* She smiled at the irony, her earlier discomfiture at the mention of her married state now abated.

Max had departed upon the arrival of the food, along with Gabi. Neither could have been hungry. *Maybe they were meeting for a secret rendezvous,* Jaime thought mischievously.

Shortly after finishing the delicious meal, the party wound down, tiredness setting in - the five-hour time difference taking its toll. Rob offered to assist Karen as Tony had dragged Mario away a few minutes earlier.

Jaime hoped she could manage a few pages of *Agatha Raisin and the Murderous Marriage* before sleep overcame her.

Chapter 15

Caleb Carfax sat back and sipped on the effeminate-looking pina colada Carol had ordered for him. As a drink per se, he quite enjoyed the taste. It was a first night away tradition they had stuck to for as long as he could remember. But he could not recall how it had started or why they insisted on clinging to it. It was more the adornments in the glass he took objection to. They tended to get stuck in one's nostril if one wasn't careful (and added nothing whatsoever to the flavour of the drink). Still, it was a welcome dose of alcohol after the nine-hour flight.

He had elected not to drink onboard as he'd had quite a few papers to read. A shame, though, as DebonAir served some top-quality wines. He'd make the most of them on the flight home. Observing his daughter's sullen face as she sat doing whatever teenagers did on handheld devices, he acknowledged he'd given up trying to track what she was doing several years ago. It caused way too much friction, and besides, Carol was much better at that sort of stuff than he was.

His wife was engaged in a debate with fifteen-year-old Connor as to why he couldn't order a beer with his meal.

"You're allowed to at fourteen, Mum. How many times do I need to tell you? I'm on holiday, and I'm eating a meal, for god's sake."

53

"Language." Caleb felt obliged to chip in when he remembered to, so Carol didn't feel... what was her buzz word of the month? Oh yes, 'unsupported'. And at least she wasn't giving in this time, he supposed.

Carol ran a hand through her spiralled red hair and threw her husband a reproachful look. She was still an attractive woman, he contemplated. He had chosen well. And she had given up a promising career in publishing to raise the two brats. He was not sure when he had started referring to his offspring as brats, but there it was. Spoilt, sulky and ungrateful is how he described his kids. Only to himself, mind you. To anyone who asked, he would list their achievements and successes from their ridiculously expensive private school in Edinburgh. If they weren't doing well after all the money spent on their education, he would be demanding a refund.

He harboured the hope their annual trip to Antigua would bring the family closer together. Spending more time with each other, really talking. *Yeah right. Like that ever panned out.* Carol would be off doing her thing: lunching, cocktails and goodness knew what else with her university pal, Maggie, and he was working on a deal for his firm. Acknowledging to himself he was a hypocrite; Caleb knew he had to take at least some responsibility for his family's lack of communication.

A long, low rumble made him pause in his ruminations. Christy looked towards the sky with a frown on her face. Connor seemed oblivious. Perhaps he should spend more time with his son. Connor was more argumentative these days, either that or he would not speak at all, shut in his room whenever he was home, like some recluse. His mood swings were getting worse. Puberty. Maybe there would be time later when this deal was in the bag. He had to devote himself to this full-time. He didn't have the luxury of a relaxing holiday. Not yet. Besides, it was in his family's interest he was successful. After all, they benefitted from the fruits of his labour, didn't they?

Christy Carfax yawned in her mother's direction. As expected, it went unacknowledged as her mother was engaged in a phone conversation with her best chum, no doubt. Her father had excused himself, having supposedly spotted some associates he wanted to catch up with, and Connor had taken the opportunity to disappear off to bed. So much for the family vacation. As usual.

Well, it suited her. She, too, had things to do and places to be. Sliding her phone into her bag, she stood from the table and pointed in the general direction of her room. Her mother nodded absently, without a break in her conversation. Christy rose and headed off toward the lifts. When out of her mother's line of sight, she ducked into the lobby, through the door marked 'Ladies' and was relieved to find it empty. She reached into her large leather tote bag and pulled out the tiny red dress, still on the hanger, in its shroud, and the high-heeled sandals. In the confines of a stall, she rapidly changed. Time being of the essence, she was glad she'd had the good sense to bring her things with her. She also figured going all the way back to her room would be taking an unnecessary risk of being seen when she headed back down. Removing the small make-up bag, she applied her usual amount for going out, not the 'acceptable to Mum and Dad' amount.

Satisfied with her appearance, she crammed her other outfit and shoes into the bag and hid it behind the bin for collection later. She'd tucked some cash away on her person, although she didn't expect to be spending any of it. Opening the restroom door, she peered out. The lobby was not too busy, although the receptionist was still present. How long to wait? Or should she brazenly walk out of the hotel? Hmm… Someone might recognise her, and she didn't want word of her nocturnal activities getting back to either parent.

Whilst pondering the best course of action to take, her chance came when the familiar figure of Connor approached the receptionist - holding her attention, causing the woman to disappear into a back room. It was risky, but he had his back to her - Christy had her chance and was through the lobby and out of the door in a flash.

Let the fun begin, she thought to herself as she tottered down the driveway, although the puzzling question of what her little brother was doing out and about after declaring he was going to bed, nagged at her. She'd think about that later.

Connor Carfax stared at his sister's retreating figure. He'd know her walk anywhere. Where the hell was she going? And dressed like that? His attention was brought back by the return of the receptionist, who, without a word, slid a padded brown envelope across the counter towards him. Taking her seat, she resumed typing on the sleek, modern keyboard.

Connor reached out and grabbed the envelope; moving away from the reception desk, he hovered by the door. Glancing at the package, then at the long, lit-up driveway to the resort, he made up his mind. He pushed on the gold-plated handle and headed out into the night.

Picking up the pace, he walked as briskly as he dared, not wanting to attract any attention, heading towards the road beyond the hotel. Emerging onto the pavement, he was in time to see the glimmer of a red dress climbing into the back of a sleek, silver sedan. His jaw dropped, and he stared. As the car pulled away from the kerb and sped off into the night, Connor Carfax was sure he had seen that car before. And he knew exactly whom it belonged to.

Chapter 16

The ship's cabin was large, consisting of a bedroom with ensuite bathroom and a separate living room. Sliding doors were to be found in both rooms leading out onto a slim balcony. They were furnished in a typical Scandinavian style, stark but with all the mod cons. White bedding, white curtains, tasteful paintings of Arctic scenes, a cream sofa in the living area and a dresser housing the coffee filter machine.

She sat on the plump cushion and rested her head back, savouring the peace, the calm before the storm. She needed to get herself together. On the small coffee table lay a pile of books. All belonging to her. All crime novels. Leaning forward, she picked up the top one and flicked it open. It was *The Nantucket Diet Murders* by Virginia Rich. Smiling, she recalled the story so far and the wonderful setting, somewhere she had not visited yet but was on her list. Hopefully, tomorrow would provide some time for quiet reading. It was to be a day at sea, a day to relax and enjoy this little haven with its stunning, ever-changing view.

She knew she would most likely have to move to another cabin, but they all had a view, and it would be worth it. Placing the book back on the table, she sighed, stood and reached for the thick jacket. Zipping it up, she called out, "Ken, are you ready?"

A handsome blonde man appeared around the bedroom door. "Do we have to do this? It's like, minus forty out there." His staccato Swedish accent betrayed his annoyance.

"Humour me, and let's go." The reality was, she knew he was in for a shock.

Jamie sat bolt upright in bed. Trying to calm her rapid breathing, she threw off the duvet and swung her legs over the edge of the mattress. Clicking on the air conditioning, she rose and walked over to the wide French doors, opening them to reveal a clear, early morning sky. Taking in a lungful of fresh air, she watched the lapping waves, trying to bring herself back to the present after her dream. *You're not there, you're in Antigua. This is not the Arctic,* she chanted to herself.

Why had she dreamt about him? Why now? Gazing out at the calm ocean, she puzzled over why she should relive that night when she had not thought about it for years. Was it because of Kate's assumption the previous evening that she was married? Not a great one to dwell on the past, brushing things off, she gave herself a moment to wonder why her last night with Ken would be playing on her mind this much. Sure, there had been the incident on the bus yesterday, but she wasn't traumatised by it.

Shrugging it off, trying not to linger over the memory, she headed over to the small kitchen area locating the filter machine and coffee. Switching it on, she found a mug and, joy of joys, fresh skimmed milk in the small fridge as requested. Listening to the comforting, gurgling noises of the machine, she contemplated how to spend her day. She had her reading material and she wanted to finish her audiobook. A small amount of sunbathing wouldn't go amiss but she needed to be careful not to burn. There was plenty of factor 30 in her toiletry bag.

The last hiss of the machine indicated it was time to pour. Savouring the aroma, Jaime took her first sip of coffee and immediately felt better. Invigorated. Although the positive effects of the coffee reminded her once again of the morning after that fateful night on board the MS Fram. The endless questions, the fruitless searching as the ship circled the area, with no hope of ever finding him, dead or alive. How her first drink of coffee had revived her, the sliding doors of her cabin open, the fresh air of the Arctic, much calmer than it had been, blowing around the room.

She had gotten through the rest of the trip quite well, considering, opting to stay in her cabin for meals but still going on some of the excursions they had booked, not wanting to miss a glimpse of a polar bear in its natural habitat. And the Arctic fox had been mesmerising. The crew had been attentive, and the other passengers showed some sympathy - although she could see in their eyes what others thought.

Finishing the coffee, she threw on some shorts and a t-shirt, brushed her teeth, grabbed the key card and headed towards the golden sand, making a concerted effort to block out any more memories from her past. The past was called that for a reason, and it did no good to dwell.

Opting to give the private beach a try as it was a perk the crew didn't normally have, she approached the tall, iron gate and swiped her room card against the pad. They didn't want anyone sneaking in here uninvited, it seemed. A satisfying click and the gate opened. Watching it close behind her, she began a gentle walk, trying to ease herself in, gradually increasing the pace. Her audiobook was playing *Murder at The Grand Raj Palace* by Vaseem Khan. Enjoying the antics of Inspector Chopra and his side kick, the little elephant Ganesha, she relaxed into the walk, relishing the warmth of the sun's rays.

Deciding to explore the full extent of the beach all the way to the large rock breaker about half a mile down, her pace increased. She felt as though she was covering some ground, stretching out her muscles. As she reached the limits of the beach, the rock formation went way out into the water: impassable. She stood for a while, listening to the story and watching the waves. Although the wind had picked up last night, today, it had abated.

Striding through a clump of seaweed, determined to investigate every inch of the area, she reached the beach limits. There was plenty of beach debris on the sand and she stumbled, losing her balance. Managing to stop herself from falling, she regained her composure, scanning around for the cause of her fall. There were piles of rotting coconut shells, some weeds and a few rocks.

And something else.

A human hand. Fingers outstretched as though reaching for something. Jaime recoiled in horror. Willing herself to take a deep breath, she looked away.

After a minute, she felt her pulse steady, and her capable side kicked in. She turned back towards the gruesome discovery. Tentatively, reaching out her foot and using the tip of her trainer, she moved away the weeds that must be hiding the rest of the body.

And they were. A body dressed in a dark blue Armani suit.

The colour drained from her face as she stared at the awful sight, knowing full-well who this was. Even with the side of the head bashed in, the recognisable profile was of Councillor Gregory Dickens.

Stepping back, she surveyed the scene in front of her, questions flying through her mind. Had he had an accident? What was he doing in this remote spot? Could he have been murdered? Shivering, she glanced around, half expecting a mad man to come flying out of the shrubbery. Noticing the blood around his head had dried, she bent closer, seeing what looked like white mushy pulp in his hair. What on earth? Then she caught the smell; alongside the coppery stench of blood was the distinctive smell of coconut. Peering upwards, she noted the lack of trees directly next to the body, and those close by were devoid of any coconuts. *How had one managed to explode over his head? It couldn't have landed there by accident.* She had been on the beach many times before when a coconut had landed on the head of an unsuspecting person, and although they could cause injury, she had never seen one explode to a pulp. The trees weren't tall enough for one to gain enough momentum.

The authorities needed to be alerted. As she was about to turn and head back to the main resort, she noticed a small card held in the outstretched, rigid hand. Curiosity getting the better of her along with the practical thought - he was dead - no one could help him now, she bent over and peered at it. 'Choices -'. The card was upside down and hard to read at first. Strange. Why was he holding out a business card? Was he handing it to someone? Why didn't they take it? *C'mon, Jaime, you need to report this. Stop messing around,* although secretly, she knew a small part of her was finding it exciting, being thrown into a real-life potential murder mystery rather than reading about them.

Running back along the beach, she realised her audiobook had been playing the entire time: Inspector Chopra and his elephant Ganesha had reached the lobby of the Grand Raj Palace Hotel, stumbling on an equally disturbing sight, only theirs didn't involve a dead body but a monkey wearing a red velvet waistcoat.

Chapter 17

Sipping a freshly made cup of camomile tea, Gabi Pascal stared out at the Atlantic Ocean. A frown played around her full, sensuous mouth. Lazing on a well-cushioned recliner, she had awoken early but had not slept well, deciding she would give her husband a call today. Check in with him. Yes, he'd like that. She needed to time it so she would catch him as he arrived home. Too early, and he would be on the metro. Any later, and he would be eating dinner. The man worked hard, she thought fondly. And he worried about her, a long way from home.

She would entertain him with some stories about the other crew. How hard she found it to understand the one with the bizarre accent they called 'Brummie'; what a bitch the CSD was. Pausing in her thoughts for a minute, she remembered the incident on the bus. No, she wouldn't mention it. He would insist on jumping on the next flight out here. And that was not what she wanted. She would emphasise what a relaxing time she was having.

A movement below the balcony caught her attention, and she glanced down, spying a woman in jogging shorts running back along the beach. Gabi strained to see who it was and recognised the figure of her colleague. Jaime was sprinting flat out, stumbling on a protruding rock as she passed by.

Gabi frowned and called out. "Morning, Jaime."

Jaime slowed and peered along the balconies, hands on her hips, breathing deeply. Her eyes locked on the other woman. "Oh, Gabi." She took another deep breath. "Listen, come to the lobby, will you? Now?"

"What? Why? Is something wrong?"

"I don't want to shout," Jaime almost stage whispered.

"Okay, on my way." Gabi withdrew into her room, seeking out her tracksuit pants and a sweatshirt, then headed to reception, arriving just after Jaime. She walked over to her.

"Well, what is it?" asked Gabi once again.

"A body. On the beach. Dead. Man." Jaime was still struggling to catch her breath.

Gabi's hands flew to her face, eyes wide. "Oh my lord. Sit down, have a minute."

"No, I'm okay. I need to report it."

"Are you sure you're okay? You look pale."

"Come on, the receptionist thinks we've gone mad." Jaime headed over to the desk, where a young woman named Edwina Kershaw was on duty.

Fortunately, the early hour meant the lobby was deserted.

"We need you to call the police," declared Gabi as clearly as her French accent would allow. "My colleague has found a body on the beach."

Edwina Kershaw blinked - her mouth dropped open. "Oh my god. Erm, yes, right, of course. Are you sure they're dead? I mean, what about an ambulance? Do we know who it is? I mean, was?" She pushed a pair of over-sized reading glasses higher on her nose with a trembling hand.

Jaime replied, "I'm pretty sure it's Councillor Gregory Dickens."

Edwina's hand froze on the telephone receiver. "Are you sure? Councillor Dickens?"

"Positive. Please hurry and call. It's… it's not a pleasant sight," she concluded.

"Lord, his poor wife and children." She stared at the two women, eyes wide, tears threatening.

"Tell them he's on the private section of beach, right at the end."

Gabi pulled on Jaime's arm and led her over to a sofa, where they sat to await the arrival of the police.

Chapter 18

The room felt stuffy. Why had she not left the air-conditioning on? She was always chilly at night and too hot in the morning. How Maggie could live somewhere like this, she would never know. Straining her ears, Carol Carfax thought she heard voices in the distance. Had she left her balcony doors ajar?

She reached out an arm with the purpose of prodding her husband awake. Hopefully he would feel too hot and do something about it. Hmm... Carol Carfax sat up in bed at the realisation that what she was prodding was a pillow, not a human body.

Her decision to sit up was a bit rash, as it turned out, and she put a hand to her mass of red curls and held her head steady. Maybe one too many cocktails last night, or jet lag. Yes, that would be it. Jet lag. She glanced to her left, then towards the bathroom. No sign of Caleb anywhere.

She struggled to remember the night before. There had been cocktails by the pool. Maggie had insisted on the waiter bringing them over to their sunbeds, although he had not been happy about it. They had laid there for hours, chatting, plotting. Maggie was in fine form, though. They had spent some time catching up on each other's lives: kids, schools, social activities. Then, of course - the subject of husbands. They had gone through the plot of their favourite Hitchcock movie, *Strangers on a Train*, substituting Guy Haines and

65

Bruno Anthony for themselves. Maggie had gotten into it, pushing Carol to find the most inventive way she could of murdering her husband. At the time, it was hilarious. Now, it seemed a bit tacky. In bad taste.

Carol wondered, not for the first time, why her friend had ever married Gregory Dickens. Well, she supposed she knew the answer. But it was not love. One thing Carol knew for certain: *she* had married Caleb for love.

Staring at the empty side of the bed, she wondered where he could have gone. She hadn't heard him getting up. He wasn't in the habit of morning exercise. Had he already been in bed when she got to the room? Jesus, she couldn't even remember. Did it even look like someone had slept on his side of the bed?

She felt ashamed. Guilty. What kind of wife and mother would dump her husband and kids on the first night of their family holiday? Instead, choosing to get drunk with an old friend, plotting the murder of their spouses? *Bloody hell. What a way to start the trip.* She felt like absolute shit. Why did they put up with her? How had she let this selfish behaviour go on for so many years?

Her mind flitted back to the previous evening. Caleb had made himself scarce by the time Mags arrived. He always tried to avoid Mags, although he was always polite to her when the four of them had dinner, which was a rare occurrence. Just as well, she thought. Caleb and 'the Dick' didn't get on well. She couldn't stand the sight of her best friend's other half either. Sometimes, the way he looked at her... she shuddered.

Carol put her head back on the pillows and closed her eyes. She was not, however, going to fall back to sleep. No. Her mind was going into overdrive. She was now wondering what Christy and Connor thought of a mother who left them to their own devices on holiday, so she could selfishly do her own thing. Still, they were good kids. She could trust them. They had always made good choices. Yes, they were fine.

Chapter 19

Throngs of hungry guests crowded the counters, laden with every type of breakfast item. Plates were piled high with a selection of island fruit, ham, eggs (cooked many ways) and pancakes. Jaime sipped her second cup of coffee as she once again relayed her account of finding the body. The police had arrived on the scene and sectioned off the beach. Jaime had been asked to wait in the restaurant, where one by one, the crew had joined her, desperate to know first-hand what had happened. As Jaime took a break from the barrage of questions, she took a bite of buttery croissant.

In the short time between finding the body and waiting for the police to arrive, Jaime had convinced herself the councillor must have been murdered. It couldn't have been suicide. No one could physically bash the back of their own head in. Accident - maybe. He could have fallen back onto the rocks and smashed his head on them. But what was with the coconut mush? Jaime decided she'd have a hard time ever using coconut conditioner again.

It was weird he was in such a remote spot at that time of night. Murder was a more plausible solution for the circumstances.

"So, you're one hundred per cent certain it was the councillor, Jaime?" Jean's voice made her jump.

"Yes," she replied, not much liking Jean's superior tone.

"Was there much blood?" asked Tony.

"I suppose there was," Jaime responded. "There were dark stains around him."

"Oh, revolting." Kate's face had blanched.

"Well, at least you didn't have to see it, love." Tony's catty tone was not lost on the group.

Mario reached out and squeezed Kate's shoulder. "It's not something we're used to dealing with."

Kate smiled at him.

"I suppose we'll be questioned? I mean, we spoke to him last night, didn't we?" There was a tremor in Karen's voice.

"Don't be ridiculous," chipped in Jean. "Why on earth would we be questioned about the death of a man we hardly knew? We only arrived yesterday. None of us knew him at all". She looked pointedly at Karen, who was now on the verge of tears.

"Oh, we'll be questioned, Jean. You can be sure of it. That's why we're all here. They'll be coming to get us. Ready for the interrogation," added Rob with an evil glint in his eye.

Jean's lined face suggested tiredness, thought Jaime. She was wearing a lot less make-up than yesterday and hadn't bothered much with her hair, which was flat at the back. Karen, on the other hand, had applied make-up. Piled it on - but it was a mess, and it didn't hide the dark shadows under her eyes. Her sundress was rumpled, with one of the straps undone.

Taking the last bite of her croissant, Jaime noticed a man striding towards them wearing the uniform of the local police force: beige shirt and trousers, with a beige hat tucked under his arm. The shirt was open at the top, no doubt a nod to the hot weather they had to work in, thought Jaime with a glare at Jean as she remembered her discomfort in her uniform the previous afternoon. Introducing himself as Officer Kennedy, he asked them to follow him. The crew stared at each other, shuffling to their feet, none of them seeming to want to go first. Mario took the lead, and they all trooped after him like small children following their teacher on a school outing.

Jaime picked up her book and made sure to refill her coffee mug on the way.

Officer Kennedy marched towards the reception area, his starched trousers making a swooshing noise as he went. They followed him through the lobby - where they received curious glances from a few eager tourists who were getting ready for their day out - and along a hallway to a door marked 'Conference Room 1'.

It was a generously proportioned room with an oval table centrally placed and tall-backed chairs tucked around it. A large woman dressed in a cobalt blue trouser suit stood at one end of the table. She had an air of authority, both hands placed on the table as she surveyed their entrance.

"Ladies and Gentlemen, please take a seat." She waved around the table, indicating the waiting chairs. "Sit, please." It was repeated with a smile, but there was a hint of impatience in the tone. "As I am sure you are all aware, we have experienced a devastating tragedy this morning."

They all stared at the woman.

"My name is Inspector Fontaine, and I, along with my partner, will be investigating the circumstances surrounding the death of one of our citizens." Inspector Fontaine gestured towards a corner of the room, where another lady sat at a small table.

Jaime had not noticed the woman was there. She was slight and attractive, also perhaps heading towards fifty, however she was sporting a mint green trouser suit, more tapered and fitted to her figure than her colleague's. She had a laptop in front of her and was frowning at something on the screen. However, she looked up, smiled and said, "Morning, all. I'm Detective Marshall." Then turned her gaze back to the laptop.

"As you are all by now aware," continued Inspector Fontaine, "the body was found at around five o'clock this morning by one of you, who was out walking. We can confirm he has been identified as Councillor Gregory

69

Dickens. He appears to have died from multiple blows: to the top of the head, which, more than likely, was from a coconut, and to the side of the head, which is possibly from the result of him falling on a rock. We will need to wait for the autopsy report before anything can be confirmed. In the meantime, we will be treating it as a suspicious death." The inspector paused and surveyed each one of them.

The crew shuffled in their seats.

"Councillor Dickens was found on a remote, private section of beach belonging to the Reef Royale Resort. We have discovered there are a limited number of rooms able to gain access to that stretch of beach, and many of those have balconies overlooking the first section of it."

Jaime glanced around at the crew. They were giving the inspector their full attention. She was beginning to feel uneasy as a thought niggled at her.

"The resort manager has informed me these rooms are not all completed, which is why they are not occupied by other guests. Just yourselves and one family - until all the wrinkles have been ironed out. You are being used to test them this week." Once again, Fontaine paused, allowing the extent of what she had said to sink in.

"What do you mean?" asked a confused Max Kleinbeck in his staccato voice. "Surely there are many guests staying in this wing."

"Nobody told us we were the only people staying in a whole wing. We should have been told we were isolated and alone," moaned an outraged Tony Hayward, implying he was worried about his own personal safety.

"What I am getting at," explained the inspector, "is how invaluable you are as potential witnesses. Whatever happened to the councillor, one or more of you may have been out on your balcony and seen him walking along the beach. You may have noted the time. He may not have been alone. I am asking you all to think back to last night, later last night, after midnight. Were any of you out on your balcony? Were any of you struggling to sleep? Perhaps you heard something unusual?" Fontaine scanned them all in turn, her red lipsticked mouth set in a grim line, matching red nails tapping on the tabletop.

Jaime decided she was quite an intimidating figure. Rob was staring out the window, perhaps trying to think back. Tony's leg jigged under the table, and Mario reached out a steadying hand, placing it on his partner's thigh. Kate squirmed and Karen stared at the ground, probably uncomfortable because Jean's eyes were locked on her. Gabi stared back at the inspector: unflinching. Max's fingers drummed on the table. Jaime glanced over at Detective Marshall, who was reading something on her screen and taking notes, fully absorbed.

"It's obvious what happened." Tony's red face glared at Inspector Fontaine, who, for her part, remained mute. "Well, a coconut fell on his head, causing him to fall onto a rock. A clear case of an accident. Not suspicious at all." He surveyed the room.

"Thank you for that, Mr…" She paused and glanced over at her colleague.

"Hayward." Detective Marshall's response came without delay.

"Indeed. Mr Hayward. Unfortunately, there were no coconut trees in the immediate vicinity, therefore your… scenario, is impossible."

"He could have staggered for quite a long way before passing out." Tony was like a dog with a bone.

Inspector Fontaine remained calm. "Thank you again. We will, of course, consider it."

"Have you considered Dickens could have approached from the other end of the beach?" Rob suggested.

Crikey, who were these people? They've been watching too many episodes of CSI and not enough of Columbo, decided Jaime. Or they would be aware of the clever tactic used by the dishevelled detective. Let your interviewees do all the talking and they may well just land themselves right in it.

"A possibility," conceded the inspector, "but unlikely. The rocks sectioning that part off and keeping it private are high, inaccessible and go way out into the water. We believe we need to be concentrating on the gate."

"Well, hang on," Kate spoke, "he wasn't staying here, was he?" She was flustered. "I mean, well, I thought you said you can't enter the beach unless you're staying in one of the new rooms?" She looked at Inspector Fontaine, eyes wide.

No one spoke. Her words hung in the air. The thought had occurred to Jaime a little while ago. How had the councillor entered the beach, indeed? Who had swiped him through? One of them, perhaps? One of the family staying in the new wing. There were not many other possibilities. Inspector Fontaine was a wily one. Not spelling it out for them, not being accusatory.

"No," replied the inspector, "he has no reason to stay at the resort. He lives right here on the island."

"What are you saying?" demanded the captain. "Are you suggesting one of us let him through? Why? For what reason? Damn it. Spit it out." His face flushed an even darker shade of red than usual.

"I think you will find, Captain, I am not suggesting anything of the kind. I am merely asking you, at this time, as helpful guests, to let me know if you saw anything pertinent last night." The inspector was in complete control of the situation.

Rob turned away. Jaime couldn't help but admire how Fontaine handled the churlish captain. She sneaked a peek at Detective Marshall, engrossed in her work, and was convinced she saw the woman's lips twitch. Without accusing the crew of anything at all, Fontaine had inferred the potential suspect list was small and should it be declared a murder, they would be right at the top.

"Couldn't he have maybe sneaked in behind someone when they opened the gate? Without them realising?" Kate chipped in, perhaps thinking she had been the one to open Pandora's box and wanted to make amends.

"Possibly, although the gate does swing closed quite quickly. Did anyone access the private beach last night? Did anyone see someone try to sneak in behind them?"

Silence. No one moved. In fact, it seemed as though no one breathed.

After an uncomfortable minute, Jean broke the silence. "I suppose if one of us had happened to be out on our balcony or taking a late-night stroll, we could have seen the councillor entering the beach with someone. It is stunning here at night, with the lights twinkling in the distance."

"You can't say any of us knew the man. We spoke to him yesterday because we were the unfortunate victims of crime on your island. What are you doing about that, by the way?" Tony piped up.

Jaime thought some of the crew were acting like children and doing themselves no favours at all in the manner they were speaking to the inspector.

Ignoring Tony's question, Fontaine said, "We would like to have a quick interview with each of you this morning. If you would be so kind as to wait in the restaurant, where Officer Kennedy can find you and we will be as brief as possible. We don't want to take too much of your morning." She turned to Detective Marshall.

"Captain Bannister, please," the detective responded.

Although the detective had been absorbed on her computer, she must have been following every word said and instructed Fontaine whom to interview first. Was it something to do with what she had discovered? Was she examining their backgrounds? How much could she find out in such a short space of time?

Jaime instinctively knew these women were no fools. They were calm, in control, in receipt of the facts, and interviews were about to begin. They were an indomitable duo, Antigua's answer to Cagney and Lacey. Jaime smiled to herself, remembering the pioneering American police drama of the eighties. She wondered which one had the soppy husband and menagerie of children and which one was the glam singleton. They both fitted that part well.

Officer Kennedy and his swooshing trousers ushered them out of the door and through the reception, back to the restaurant, which had emptied out. Here, he indicated an area for them all to wait. As he walked away, Jaime waited for the backlash from the crew she was sure was brewing. She was not disappointed. There was indignation at the inspector's apparent suspicion, and there were denials at seeing or hearing anything at all from their rooms or balconies.

"Surely the hotel staff can access the beach at any time. And who knows whom they might have let into the area." Tony's smug expression showed him to be pleased with his theory that cast the net wider than just themselves and one other family.

"She wasn't accusing us of anything," noted Gabi. "If you recall, it was Kate who brought it to everyone's attention the councillor couldn't have accessed the beach on his own."

Kate blushed; she was on the verge of tears.

"Like the inspector hadn't thought it, though, just because she didn't say it. She's not stupid, don't make the mistake of thinking she is," warned Mario.

"Well, it was someone from that other family. I bet they knew him. She should be focusing on them. I can't believe they stuck us with a family of killers." Tony's thought processes were all over the place.

Jaime decided to help herself to a tiny bit more breakfast before it was cleared away. She could be sat here a while, and despite everything, her stomach was grumbling.

The omelette was delicious, melted cheddar, sautéed mushrooms and a sprinkle of fresh parsley. Tempted to go for yet another cup of coffee, she noticed a slight tremor in her hands - an indication she had perhaps had too much caffeine - so reluctantly decided against the idea.

As she sat there, listening to the moaning crew, she wondered if it were possible one of them was a cold-blooded killer.

Chapter 20

Captain Rob Bannister sat back in his chair and took a deep breath. He was determined to calm down and not have a repeat of his earlier outburst of temper. He realised his defensiveness did him no favours.

"Captain Bannister, it would be helpful to us if you could please run through your movements last night, and through doing so, it might spark off a memory of something relevant."

"I thought we weren't suspects," he snapped back, then thought better of it. "From when until when?"

"Let's take it from when you left your interview with the councillor until breakfast this morning."

"Fine. I went to my room, unpacked, took a shower, watched some television, dressed and went to the bar. Drank three bottles of Bud, ate a pizza, chatted, went to bed, woke up, showered, dressed, went to breakfast."

"Well, thank you, how informative." The inspector's voice held a tinge of sarcasm. "Who was in the bar with you?"

"I arrived first and took a large table, Kate Jackson, my co-pilot, was a few minutes behind me, followed by Jean Blackthorn. A short while later, Karen, Jaime, Tony and Mario arrived, Max a few minutes later, followed by Gabi."

Detective Marshall tapped away on her keyboard in a corner of the room.

"Were any of them upset or acting out of the ordinary? Was there anything unusual at all?" asked Fontaine, once again tapping her blood-red fingernail on the mahogany tabletop.

"Why are you asking me? You do think it was murder and you do think it was one of us, don't you?" He couldn't help himself.

The inspector regarded him before she spoke. "You know as well as we do, Captain, someone opened the gate for the councillor to pass through. Now that does limit the number of people. We will keep an open mind, but I do need to ask the questions, however uncomfortable they may be."

Rob stared at her. "Well," he paused, "I suppose Jean was acting strangely."

"Jean Blackthorn, the CSD?" Fontaine needed confirmation and Detective Marshall nodded. "In what way?"

"She was flustered, angry. It took her a while to calm down. Of course, no one asked her why. It didn't seem... appropriate. No one likes to get their head bitten off." Rob laughed.

"Can you think of any reason why she should have been angry?"

Rob shook his head.

"Any other observations?"

"Max was one of the last to arrive. Max Kleinbeck, one of the cabin crew. He was agitated, sweating. Who knows what he was up to?" Rob waited for the inspector's response.

"Interesting, Captain. You think he was 'up to something'?"

"Let's say he's not the most forthcoming, sociable chap I have ever met."

"You say you went straight to your room?"

Rob nodded, adding, "Helping Karen Jeffries, who was hammered."

Fontaine raised a quizzical eyebrow but made no comment on the state of Karen Jeffries. Instead, she asked, "When in your room, did you have the balcony doors open or perhaps sit out? Perhaps something or someone caught your eye?"

"No. The doors were closed to keep out any insects. I watched a film and fell asleep. Sorry, I can't help you."

Fontaine waited.

"For goodness' sake," Rob exclaimed, "a thriller with Anthony Hopkins. Fracture, I think it's called."

"Well, if you think of anything, I must remind you it is vital you inform us immediately. We will be based in this room during the investigation."

Rob scraped back his chair. "Will that be all?"

"For now. Send in First Officer Kate Jackson, please."

Rob turned and headed for the door. As he made his way to fetch Kate, he wondered how much digging these two would do on each of them to get to the bottom of the mystery. He frowned. Not too much, he hoped. No, it would not be good for them to dig into his personal life. Not too good at all.

Chapter 21

11:22

Walking back into the conference room a while later, Jaime noticed this time, Detective Marshall standing by the window and Inspector Fontaine perched precariously on the edge of the large table, one low-heeled tan pump on the floor, the other swinging backwards and forwards.

"Miss Jaime Jones. Let me begin by asking if you remember seeing anything unusual last night? Perhaps on the beach outside your balcony?"

Jaime gave this some serious thought, determined to be as helpful as possible. "I cannot say I did, although I do sleep quite soundly after a long flight."

The inspector nodded. "I suppose it was too much to hope we would have a witness to explain any of the goings on last night," she lamented, the suggestion being no one had admitted to seeing anything useful. "Well, perhaps you can talk me through your evening?"

Jaime obliged by telling the inspector about the attack on the bus, the interviews with Dickens (leaving out her personal point of view on the man), going out for drinks, speaking to him briefly in the bar, meeting the rest of the crew. "We all turned in about the same time, around ten o'clock. Oh, wait a minute, Max and Gabi left before as they were not eating." Jaime wasn't comfortable telling the inspector about her exchange with Dickens in the bar, although she knew she should.

"How well would you say you knew the councillor, Miss Jones?"

Jaime squirmed under the intense stare. Why did she make her feel as though she were guilty of something? "I didn't know him at all, but I had seen him around on previous visits. We'd exchanged a few words, at best." (Mentally, she was crossing her fingers, knowing she had refused to have a drink with Dickens in the past and this had angered him.)

"What was your opinion of him?"

Bloody hell, she was pushy. "I'm not sure I had one," she hedged.

"Come on, Miss Jones. Let's be honest here. We have a dead body. You found him. And you did not like him, did you? Not one bit."

Oh crap. How could she know? After a brief pause, she responded, "Actually, you're right. Don't misunderstand, though. I didn't 'know' him, but any exchange I had with him, showed him to be unpleasant." She hesitated.

"In what way?" inquired the inspector.

Jaime felt a stab of irritation. Why had she got to spell out the obvious? "Well, he was sleazy. He leered at women and tried to make us feel uncomfortable. I, for one, don't appreciate that." She tried to keep her voice level.

"And he came across to you that way last night in the bar?"

"Yes, he did, as a matter of fact. He was forward, overly familiar and vile. But nothing I couldn't handle," she felt obliged to add. "I'm sure I'm not the only person to say this."

However, the inspector was not to be drawn into sharing any information she may or may not have on the subject. Instead, she responded with, "And how did you handle the situation?"

"I decided to move away from him, and Mr Fleet's timely arrival helped."

"The customer relations manager?" Fontaine looked alert. "What did he want?"

"Just checking all was well with the room - doing his job." She was trying not to sound frustrated by what she saw as pointless questions. Pointless because she knew any feelings she had about Dickens had nothing to do with his death. And she was being as honest as possible without admitting she was about to punch Dickens on the jaw, and Fleet's arrival stopped her.

Fontaine considered her without speaking for a while. "Do you think any of your colleagues shared your opinion of the councillor?"

"They must have done. Although no one said as much," she added.

"Any of your colleagues acting strangely last night?" Fontaine pursued.

Well, quite frankly, they're all a bit weird, Jaime wanted to say. Instead, she responded in the negative. It didn't feel right to speculate on these people with the inspector, especially when she knew she was quick to jump to conclusions about other people.

"Tell us about Ken Sundberg." The request came from Marshall, who, until now, had remained mute.

Jaime's blood ran cold. Her mind raced. *What? Ken? Why would they ask about him? What did he have to do with Dickens?* She felt her face drain of any colour at the mention of her husband. She struggled to respond. The silence went on and on. Neither woman spoke, just stared at her. Jamie knew she would have to speak. But what to say?

"Ken?" she asked.

"Ken." Detective Marshall did not blink.

"Yes. Well, Ken was my husband. Over ten years ago." She paused. "I'm sorry. I'm struggling to know what he has to do with this situation."

"I suppose you could say most people never find themselves embroiled in the investigation of a death in their lifetime. Yet here we have you, and this is your second time."

Jaime couldn't help but be impressed at the speed with which Detective Marshall had managed to do her background checks. Of course, Jaime should have known her name would crop up in any police checks. Her husband's death had been initially thought suspicious, and Jaime was questioned at the time.

"You must know the circumstances surrounding Ken's death remain a mystery. His body was never recovered."

"You were with him at the time of the fall?" Marshall pushed.

"We were both out on deck. I didn't see him go overboard. One minute he was there; the next he was gone." Jaime could not believe this was being brought up. *How could it be relevant?* she wondered. And how odd she had dreamt about it for the first time in ages the previous night.

The two detectives exchanged a glance Jaime could not decipher. It was Fontaine who took back the reins.

"That's all for now. We'll be stationed here in this room for the duration of the investigation. Don't hesitate to get in touch if you remember anything you think might be important."

Jaime nodded and rose from her chair. Both women stood now, arms folded. The difference in their heights was quite marked. She turned and headed for the door, trying not to rush but desperate to get away. She was no longer sure she would be able to watch another episode of Cagney and Lacey ever again.

Chapter 22

Heading towards the beach, Jaime brooded over the events of the morning. She appeared to be embroiled in a murder mystery. In fact, she was smack bang in the middle of one, assuming the autopsy showed it was in fact, murder. But the lead detectives were treating it as suspicious, and she had been the one to find the body: she couldn't think of a reasonable explanation as to why the councillor's head was covered in coconut pulp, unless someone had smashed one over it. She remembered the time in Amalfi when she had bought a giant lemon, ripped it in half and rubbed it all over her hair. She had read it was good for the roots. However, she had been left with lemon mush all over her head. It had been an embarrassing walk home.

There had been questions when Ken had gone overboard into the freezing waters of the Arctic Ocean, off the north-eastern shores of Greenland. But she had not been asked anything too invasive. The maritime police were not interested in her marriage. They wanted to complete their paperwork and leave the harsh conditions of the Arctic Circle. She had been a mere twenty-one. She'd married too young, but Ken had swept her off her feet. Charming, good-looking, the promise of an interesting life, travelling all over the world. And at first, it had been everything she had hoped for. The travelling remained exciting: Ken had not. He became moody, possessive, always wanting to make the decisions, not liking it when she disagreed with him. She should have realised the nineteen-year age difference mattered. Well, she would never fall into that trap again. At thirty-two, even now, she couldn't contemplate the thought of being tied to someone.

After a short amount of time, she had gotten her job with DebonAir and travelling to exotic places was back on the agenda. But this time, without a moody man calling the shots.

She wondered as she strolled along, how the detectives had found out about her exchange with Dickens in the bar. Karen might have seen something. She was nearby. Kate knew she didn't like the councillor. She had told her whilst they were waiting for menus. Any one of them could have witnessed the scene and passed on the information. Someone had thrown her under the bus. Perhaps she should try and get some information of her own on the crew. See if she could find out anything interesting. She was not comfortable with how her interview had gone. The detectives were shrewd, and she was on their radar. She knew she should have been honest with them straight away about her encounter with the councillor at the bar. Now she'd given the impression she was hiding something. Perhaps if she could find anyone with a motive and somehow pass this on, it would take the heat off her. It was time to stand up for herself. One of the crew could have accessed the beach with the councillor… and it seemed probable it was one of them, or a member of the as yet unidentified family, also in residence in the new wing.

Turning the idea over in her mind, she strode on with a determined step.

Chapter 23

Christy Carfax bobbed around in the waves, enjoying the weightless feeling it gave her. Thirty laps of the roped-off section completed, she thought back to the previous evening, determined not to let any tears fall. She was stronger than that. The Dior dress was ruined, of course. She would never be able to wear it again. Not only was it beyond repair, but it also now brought her bad luck. She would not be able to put it on again without feeling as though something bad would happen. And it would be a constant reminder.

Should she inform the agency? No. He hadn't gone through the proper channels, and they would reprimand her for going along with it, accuse her of going behind their backs to make some extra cash, strike her off their books. Of course, this wasn't true. She was respecting his wishes for privacy. Now, she wondered. Was it only because he was married and held a high social standing within the community that he had wanted to keep things off the radar? Or was it because he had an ulterior motive? Was it because he was a monster? An evil man who liked to get his own way. *Shit, shit, shit.* This was the first time she had been made to feel cheap. And it didn't feel good. *The bastard.*

Ducking her head underneath the salty water, she let herself go. Down, down into the blue abyss... then she swam back up - headed for the shore with a confident, powerful, front crawl stroke. He may have ruined her dress, he may have ruined her faith in men, but he hadn't gotten away with it. No, she had shown him. Her lips pulled up into a small smile as she recalled the grimace on his face when her knee had connected with his groin. It was a satisfying feeling, inflicting so much pain. Thank goodness she had been sensible enough to take some cash for the taxi fare back to the resort.

Reaching the shore, she pulled herself to a standing position and fought against the tide to stride onto the beach. Noticing the lone figure perched on the end of a sun lounger, she faltered.

"Hey, sis." Connor stared at his elder sibling.

"Hey," she replied, at a loss as to what to say. They didn't communicate much anymore, and to find him here, waiting for her, was a bit disconcerting. It also reminded her she had seen him in reception last night. She had forgotten in the midst of everything else. "You alright?"

"Yeah," he replied, adding, "I was going to ask *you*."

There was an uncomfortable pause, neither one knowing how to proceed. Christy couldn't help but wonder how they had drifted so far apart. How could it have happened without her even noticing? She felt a pang of guilt. "I'm fine."

"I was looking for you last night," said Connor. "Wondered if you fancied a movie. Turned out I wasn't as tired as I thought I was."

Christy felt the blush rising in her cheeks and her heart beating faster. She had become quite a convincing liar of late. Through necessity, of course. But lying to her little brother was something new. And she wasn't sure if it felt quite right.

"I didn't hear you knock," she countered, not deeming it to be a lie, as she hadn't heard him knock.

"Maybe you weren't there." Connor stared at her, his eyes dark and fierce.

"What?" She gave a silly laugh.

"Maybe you popped out? I needed to go to reception and I'm sure I saw you pass through." It was more of a statement than a question.

Shit, what does he want from me? She couldn't admit what she was up to. He would be horrified. She was sure he wouldn't snitch on her, but he was the last person she wanted to know how she was earning her money. She kind of wanted him to admire her. The realisation dawned on her: she was not proud of her career path.

"Right. Oh, right, yeah. I needed a bit of air before bed." She held her breath, realising too late what a ridiculous lie it was, and if he had seen her, he would have noticed the change of clothes.

Connor stared at her. Then he stared at the ground for a long time. Christy plopped down in the sand, not sure what to do, what to say.

Eventually, Connor looked up. "I followed you out, checking if you were okay. I saw you get in that car. *His* car…" His voice trailed off.

Christy felt the hairs on her arms stand on end. She had no words. He had discovered her secret, and in the worst possible way. With the worst possible person. Why hadn't she been more careful? Connor stood. *When did he grow so tall?* she thought irrationally.

"How could he? How could you let him?" His fists were tight, ready for action. He was full of pent-up rage.

Christy was filled with fear. What did he know? How far had he followed her? Had he seen her arrive back? She was sure no one had. She thought she had been careful. "No, Con. No way would I ever let him near me. It was just a bit of fun, honest. I can see now how stupid it was. I wanted to get back at Mum and Dad, y'know - for dragging us here every bloody year. It's fine. It won't happen again. I'll say no next time."

Connor looked at her. "Next time?" he queried. "What do you mean, next time?"

Christy remained quiet.

"Shit. He's *dead*, sis. Someone's found him. With a bashed in head. Somewhere on the beach." As he spoke, his eyes bored into hers, in challenge. His voice had lowered to a whisper.

Christy's jaw dropped. She didn't dare to speak. Didn't know how she was supposed to react to this news. And how had Connor found out?

"The police want to talk to us. The whole family. You'd better change."

She didn't have time to ask him anything else as he spun around and marched away.

Christy sat in the sand for a long time, grateful for the sun warming her back. She was remembering the loud tone of the phone ringing after she had returned to her room. The grating voice with that bloody annoying accent. Why had she not found it irritating before? The pleading with her to come and meet him for a few minutes. He wouldn't keep her. How sorry he was. Then, at her refusal to acquiesce, that she owed him. Of all the bloody cheek. Well, he'd got what he deserved. And good riddance.

She stood and headed back to her room. She needed a shower. And had an email to send. And, apparently, the authorities to talk to.

Chapter 24

Strolling along, the grains of sand felt warm beneath her toes. Reaching into her crocheted shoulder bag, Jaime pulled out her mobile phone, disconnecting the earphones. What she wanted to do was google the word 'Choices' written on the card in the dead man's hand. It couldn't hurt to do a bit of investigating. She needed to get herself off the detectives' radar. This was a solid, tangible clue and was a good place to start. It was quite a generic word. Tapping her phone into life, the sun was far too bright to make anything out on the screen. Shielding it with her body, she typed in the words 'Choices, Antigua'. She waited. And waited. The signal was weak. *Bloody internet...*

Feeling something rub on the lower part of her leg, she jumped. Swinging around and peering down, she saw a wriggling body with toffee-coloured hair, two tiny ears standing to attention, piercing dark eyes and a tail wagging ferociously. Bending down, Jaime reached for the back of the dog's ears and gave them a tickle.

"Hey there," she said. "Aren't you the cutest. Yes, you are." The dog ran around in circles, chasing his tail, his excitement at the attention reaching fever pitch. Whilst scratching his head, she felt around for a collar. Nothing. Hmm... he seemed to be well-fed and clean. There was a problem with unwanted dogs on the island and many had to fend for themselves. Reaching into her bag, she exchanged

89

her phone for a water bottle, pouring some into her scooped hand and offering it to her new friend. He lapped up a small amount of water.

Sitting in the sand, she stroked him some more. "I don't know what your name is, but you remind me of a 'Basil' I know. Mind if I call you that?"

The dog did not mind at all, jumping into her lap, he circled several times, settling with a grunt.

"I'm Jaime. Got time to hang out for a bit, Basil? If you're not too busy."

Basil cocked his head and licked his paw. Jaime took it as a 'yes' and decided to verbalise a few thoughts.

"To sum up, there's a dead man, probably murdered, and someone had no problem telling the police I'd exchanged words with him in the bar."

Basil stared straight at her, placing a paw on her forearm. Encouraged, Jaime continued. "You see, Basil, Cagney and Lacey, which is my nickname for the detectives, don't worry, they're before your time, well, they have uncovered some of my history and it's quite concerning. It doesn't put me in a good light."

Basil whined in sympathy. "I know. Thanks for the support. But you see, Detective Marshall, whom I've decided is the Christine Cagney of the pair, has discovered that years ago, I was married to... well, a complete arse, and he died in mysterious circumstances."

Basil rubbed his wet nose onto hers. She couldn't help but laugh out loud, tickling his belly while he rolled around on his back.

After a few minutes, she resumed, "I need to try and identify the family staying in our wing. And knowing what the motive is would help, in my vast experience," she laughed at herself. "Which, by the way, comes from reading crime fiction."

Basil grunted in what Jaime perceived to be appreciation.

"It could have been his wife, although I'm not sure how she would have entered the private beach. Or maybe it was a woman he'd dumped, or the boyfriend or husband."

Jaime sat up, a recollection flooding her brain. Jean storming out of the bar last night from the direction of where the councillor was sitting. Could it be a coincidence? Or could there be a connection between Jean and the dead man? Otherwise, what was she doing leaving the bar at the time they had all arranged to meet? Had she deliberately headed down for a drink early to connect with Dickens? And there was something she had said earlier, when they were being interviewed by Fontaine, that had struck a chord with Jaime. *What was it now?*

And of course, she mustn't forget Karen: she looked like a woman who had been stood up, even though she didn't admit to it. Dressed up and stood up. Goodness knew how long she had been sitting in the bar area waiting and waiting. Hmm… some possible options for the councillor's affairs.

"Thanks for listening. Maybe you can be my little Ganesha and assist me like he helps Inspector Chopra." She smiled at the thought. "Fancy a stroll along the beach, and you can help me plan my next move?" She glanced at the dog, but his attention was elsewhere. To her left and behind her, in fact. His body had turned rigid, and she felt the low growl coming from his core.

Chapter 25

12:14

Unlike her companion, Jaime had not heard the muffled sound of running footsteps behind her or the rasp of heavy breathing that had alerted Basil: someone was closing ground on them. Spinning her head around, she was in time to see the sight of Henry Fleet in his running attire striding towards her. She let out a long breath, waving in greeting. He grinned and waved back.

"Sorry if I startled you, Jaime. I didn't have the breath to call out," he panted.

"Forgiven. Bit hot to be out running," she replied, eyeing his impressive physique.

"Tell me about it. It's the only time of day I can ever get away long enough to run any decent length. The customers are happy after their breakfast and are enjoying themselves on the beach or out on a day trip. How are - "His voice stopped dead as he noticed the dog in Jaime's lap.

"Friendly, isn't he?" Jaime ruffled Basil's coat. "We just met."

"Right. Okay. Perhaps you should be careful. We do have a bit of an issue with strays." Henry looked anxious.

Jaime felt defensive. "He's fine. Couldn't be more sociable, in fact." Basil yipped in agreement. "Quite right, too." Jaime said to him. "You stand up for yourself. You're well-mannered and respectful, aren't you?"

Henry let the subject drop. "How are you doing after this morning? I couldn't believe it when I heard the news." He squatted next to Jaime, placing his hand on her shoulder and giving it a gentle squeeze.

"Not bad. It was a horrid sight. His head had been caved in. Clear case of murder if you ask me," she decided to add.

"How so?" Henry's eyebrows rose.

"Well, there was white mush in his hair, which I believe came from a coconut coming down hard on his head. It could be he fell onto a rock, finishing him off. But there were no trees that close to his body. I suppose he could have staggered some distance."

Henry nodded. "How did it go with the police?" he asked.

Henry could prove to be a valuable source of information. He must have access to who the guests were and perhaps how the police investigation was going, depending on how important his role was, thought Jaime.

"It seems as though the councillor needed help to enter that bit of beach. And those who could oblige are limited in number." She paused, interested in his reaction.

His eyebrows rose a fraction. "It's unfortunate the crew are in that small group."

"What about the other family in the new wing?" she asked, trying her luck at getting some information out of him.

"The Carfaxes? Nice people, from Edinburgh, I believe. Come here every year. Mum, dad, two kids."

Bingo. The Carfax family. At least she had a name - now she needed to identify them. Perhaps they had been on the flight out.

"Come on, let's walk along the beach. Fancy a trot, Basil?"

Basil fancied it: he jumped to his feet and raced around in excited circles. Jaime laughed at his antics. Henry raised a quizzical eyebrow but said nothing.

"You know, from a selfish point of view, the location of the body does not do the resort much good in terms of publicity. Murder or accident, both could keep people away.

For a while, at least. Our security will come into question," Henry commented as he also stood.

Jaime realised this thought had not occurred to her. Could it be a possible motive? Someone who wanted to harm the reputation of the resort. A rival, perhaps. But why target the councillor?

"I assume the hotel staff could all access the private beach?" she pressed on as they walked away from the hotel.

"Few of them have access to the keys. It's a small team who clean those rooms and the key cards must be signed out of m… the manager's office."

The slight stutter didn't go unnoticed. Jaime continued, "I suppose it's easy to check if any of the cards are missing or if any were used last night?"

"Should be straightforward enough. They're strictly monitored." He paused for a moment, adding, "You know, our staff are like family. They've pretty much all been here for years, and any new additions tend to be family of current staff. It's a small island."

He doesn't want it to be any of the staff, thought Jaime. Understandable, she supposed. And the location of the body could mean the business taking a dive, as he pointed out, meaning his job could be in danger.

They paused in their walk whilst Basil investigated a piece of seaweed in his path. She couldn't help thinking the two of them were alike. Suspicious and quick to judge.

"What are you smiling at?" asked Henry.

"Oh, nothing," she replied, not sure Henry would appreciate the observation.

Henry looked at her. "One of your colleagues could have lost a key or had one stolen. We are having a staff meeting soon, to be brought up to date."

Jaime acknowledged someone might have misplaced their key or had it stolen. However, they were not coming clean about it and would not be able to get into their room without asking for a replacement, so attention would be brought to the loss.

They moved on - the offending seaweed having been dealt with. Henry chatted about Dickens, his various roles on the council, his wealth and status. He had left behind a wife and two young children. Money was always a good motive, they agreed, and Dickens had plenty of it. Henry needed to check out the other staff and their opportunity to access the beach, although common sense told her she ought not to trust him. He had shown how much he disliked Dickens the previous night, and he would be able to access the beach. But it came back to why he would choose a spot that put the resort at risk? Still, for now, he was a good source of information and showed a willingness to share what he knew with her.

Walking along in silence for a while, they came upon a little alcove made by some fallen rocks close to a clump of swaying palm trees. As they approached, they caught the soft sound of voices floating over from the other side of the group of rocks. Jaime's hand, which was stroking Basil's back, felt a low growl building inside him. She gave him a reassuring squeeze whilst glancing at Henry, feeling like an eavesdropper. Henry pointed back in the direction they had come, mouthing the words *let's get out of here.*

But they both froze when they overheard the name 'Dickens' mentioned. Remaining rooted to the spot, they crouched down. Basil's ears pricked, understanding the importance of the situation. The voices, although soft, sounded masculine.

"Dickens was the main instigator in the 'against' camp," whispered one voice.

"Rodriguez is for it," whispered the other.

"I know, but until it's official, there's no way I'm celebrating."

"Relax, we're home free. Dickens can't get in our way anymore. It's all good from now on."

"I guess the deal is as good as done. Rodriguez gave us his word he would back us if he could - if Dickens wouldn't find out, and he's not going to now."

"C'mon, it's lunchtime. Let's go and eat and await the good news. Though I don't know how I will keep anything down, I'm too nervous. Those two detectives give me the creeps."

"There's no way they'll find anything out. Now, we have to keep up appearances and do lunch."

There was a shuffling sound and the three eavesdroppers ducked out of sight just in time to avoid being seen by the recognisable figures of Tony Hayward and Mario Vanetti.

Chapter 26

12:15

Margaret Dickens grabbed her mobile phone for the umpteenth time and stared at the screen. No communication from Carol – all her texts unread. "Shit," she shouted, nearly toppling the coffee cup sat by her elbow. "Shit, shit, shit." She could not understand what Carol's problem was. Why would she blank her now when everything was coming together? Greg was dead, for Christ's sake. Now she was free. Totally and utterly free of that disgusting, cheating shit. She needed to celebrate.

The visit, early this morning, from the police had awoken her. Apart from a slight headache though, for which she had taken a couple of paracetamols, she didn't feel too bad. The coffee was helping, along with the gradual, euphoric feeling of freedom. The two female detectives had been sympathetic, and their questions had been routine enough, although the smaller one in the mint green trouser suit had stared at her a bit too intently for her liking. The other one had asked her whereabouts the previous evening. She had been with Carol, and the bar staff could verify it. That little mousy receptionist with the big glasses had called her a cab around midnight.

Maggie knew the police checked out the spouse first. And in her case, there was a possibility they would find out what a cheating prick she was married to, giving her a motive. But she wasn't worried. They would soon find plenty of other people with motives: mistresses who had been cheated on, because he wasn't faithful to anyone; husbands and boyfriends who found out about the affairs. She was going to play the role of the poor, little, unknowing wife. And, of course, there were his business dealings. Lord knew how many enemies he had made through those.

The questions about her husband's life had become more intrusive than she had expected. Especially the one about how much time he'd spent at the Reef Royale. She had answered: it was where he chose to conduct most of his meetings, being a pleasant setting with all the amenities provided. They asked if either she or Greg knew any of the flight crew that were staying there. Of course, she'd denied it. Technically, she didn't know any of them, just *of* them. She was playing the part of the victim who knew nothing of her husband's affairs. And she was sticking to it. Let them find out a different way, because it was not coming from her.

Greg was shagging the airline whores. Had been for years. How many? Well, that was anyone's guess. A pair of navy-blue stockings she'd discovered in his car said it all. A rare slip-up he didn't know he'd made. Who wore navy blue stockings, for goodness' sake? The female crew of DebonAir. Sluts.

Carol's answer to all Maggie's problems was divorce. Maggie had tried to convince her divorce was frowned upon in the uptight world of politics. There was no way Greg would ever have divorced her, nor would she have wanted him to. They would never have survived the scandal unscathed. Being widowed, on the other hand…

Lifting her phone, she was frustrated to note nothing had changed. Carol had still not responded to her messages.

"Faith!" she screamed at the top of her voice. "Get in here, now." She waited a beat then shouted again. There was the sound of footsteps shuffling down the stairs, and an elderly lady with greying, frazzled hair and an oversized smock entered the kitchen. Upon seeing her, Maggie

98

congratulated herself once more on her choice of nanny-cum-housekeeper. She smiled as she recalled her husband's face when she had introduced him to the new help. *That's right, darling*, she had wanted to say, *no worries about you dipping your toe in that water.*

He had been cheating since their honeymoon. For all she knew, he could have shagged the chambermaid in their luxury suite on Mustique. She had soon come to loathe him. Ambition fuelled their marriage. She had the breeding; he had the gift of winning people over. For some reason, they loved him. All those stupid little cretins out there worshipped the ground he had walked on. She could not recall when she had first fantasised about killing him. When she had first decided he was no longer needed. Now he was dead, she would get tons of sympathy...

"I need you to stay over again, Faith. When you pick the children up from school, make sure they get straight in the car and don't speak to any other parents. I don't want them finding out about their dad from anyone but me. I'll break it to them tomorrow. When I'm feeling more ready," she added.

No response.

"Bring them straight back here, give them a healthy dinner, help with their homework, bath and bed. No tv. No radio. No technology. Take the four-wheel drive. I don't know when that storm is coming. Got it?"

Faith nodded wearily. When there were no additional instructions, she turned and left the room.

Maggie watched her leave then stared into the enormous garden. The maintenance man was busy covering the pool and the furniture, ready for the apparent impending rain. She felt irritable. And she blamed Carol.

Holding up the phone once again, she noted there was still no response. It stared back at her, unblinking. "Damn you, Carol Carfax. I won't be ignored. Not by you. Not by anyone."

Chapter 27

The restaurant was crowded. No matter what they were doing, most people always managed to tear themselves away for food. Jaime scanned the tables. Basil was worldly enough to know he would not be welcomed in the restaurant area, albeit located outside. Jaime had bid him farewell as he trotted off, who knew where?

Henry had agreed to check which of the hotel staff had the opportunity to access the beach. Jaime told him she would be investigating the crew. He showed himself to be keen to assist her inquiries, although it would not be in his best interests if it turned out to be one of the staff. It wouldn't look good for the resort. It was going to be difficult to know how much value she could put on information from him. And, of course, he had a motive himself. He disliked the councillor. Weak, but still a motive.

Spurred on by the intriguing conversation they had overheard between Tony and Mario, Jaime had her first inkling of a real motive. It was exciting, and she felt justified in her assumption that it was murder. The pair were indicating Dickens' death benefitted them in some way. Could she see them murdering the councillor? Picturing Mario's muscle power, as demonstrated during the bus attack, he had the physical strength. And Tony could be the instigator. The problem was, she liked them. She had been on numerous trips with them, and they were fun and outgoing. But a successful detective could not allow personal feelings to get in the way, and she was beginning to take her self-appointed role seriously. She must remain impartial and investigate the facts. *Now, let's check out the rest of you and see what motives I can uncover.*

Glancing around the bustling restaurant for familiar faces, her gaze lingered on a small table for two tucked away on the outskirts, obscured by a large, potted palm. The occupant of the table had his head down, reading a newspaper. There was something about his countenance that gave Jaime pause. Had she seen him before? Fair, tousled hair with a touch of grey; a tanned, lean face; late forties. Watching him, she noticed his eye line was above the top of the newspaper, as though he was wanting to give the appearance of reading it but was, in fact, watching something in front of him.

Intrigued, Jaime followed his line of vision. Who could he be spying on? A family of five - mum, dad and three uncontrollable little ones, an elderly couple, him with a bright red face and her sporting oversized, dark sunglasses. And Max, sitting alone, book in front of him and a beer he had barely touched. She turned back to the stranger. Is that who he was spying on? Possibly. But why? And who was he?

Realising she had been stood on the periphery of the restaurant for a few minutes now, she moved on before people thought she was acting weirdly. Spotting Rob and Gabi perusing menus, she headed over.

"How are you two?"

"Bearing up, I suppose. This situation is far from ideal." Rob's face creased into a frown.

Gabi sipped her juice. "More importantly, sweetie, how are you, you poor thing?"

Jaime assumed she meant because she was the one to find the body. "Okay." Keen to keep the attention on the other two and eager to begin some detecting, she added, "What about the fact we're part of the minority with private beach access?"

101

"Bloody ridiculous," fumed Rob. "None of us had anything to do with the man. We pop in and out of the country every few months. What motive could any of us have?"

Jaime glanced at Gabi for a response, but she was reading the menu.

"They would be best off scrutinising that family staying in our wing. They could know the councillor. And have a motive," Rob continued.

A young waiter popped up, dressed in his maroon jacket, order pad in hand. Jaime decided on the Salad Niçoise (she would order an extra tuna steak for her new friend).

"Cheeseburger. Fries. All the trimmings." Rob held out his menu to be taken by the waiter, who was still writing down the order.

Taking the menu, he looked at Gabi. She was still studying the options, even though she'd had ample time to decide.

"The chicken breast."

The waiter scribbled on his pad. But Gabi was not finished.

"How does it come?"

"It's grilled in Cajun spices and comes with fries and slaw," he explained.

"Hmm…" Gabi kept them all on the edge of their seats.

Jaime couldn't hide her irritation. *It's all spelt out in the menu.*

"We can adapt it to suit you, miss?" His tone was obliging but belied his need to move on, as did his quick glance over his shoulder.

"Well, I'll have it poached. With a fresh salad. And no slaw. Please do not put that anywhere near my plate. And no dressing on the salad. Okay?" Passing back the menu, she relaxed back into her seat, satisfied.

Jaime resumed her investigations, asking Rob about himself.

"We've lived in Dorset for thirty years now. Both children have left home, and the wife and I are left rattling around."

"Wow, thirty years is amazing." Gabi stared at him.

"Surely retirement isn't on the cards yet?" asked Jaime.

"I can leave in five years; I will have done my time. I started early and married young. We had our first child when Barbara was twenty."

"I am surprised she didn't join you on this trip; it's an ideal destination to bring a cling-on." Jaime used the airline slang for someone who accompanied you on one of your working trips, a great perk of the job.

"I'm glad she didn't."

Jaime and Gabi both looked up, surprised.

"After everything that's happened, I mean." He corrected himself. "Can you imagine? Some holiday this would have been."

"True. Although she must have been here before?" Jaime pressed on.

Rob's face clouded. "Yes, she's been everywhere." He lapsed into a moody silence, leaving Jaime with more questions.

"And you, Jaime? What's life like at home for you?" Gabi enquired.

Bugger, thought Jaime. *She's turned the tables on me. I suppose it'll have to be give and take, or I'll look like I'm digging too much.*

She smiled. "I've recently moved into my dream home. A houseboat on the River Dart. I love it. It's peaceful there. And I have my two little munchkins to take care of."

Now it was the turn of Rob and Gabi to show surprise. Jaime was quick to explain.

"Rescue dogs. Ellery and Wolfe. They have a lot of energy and keep me busy."

Rob smiled, but Gabi's face showed her disgust.

"I know that part of the world quite well," said Rob. "It's stunning. Are you in Dartmouth itself?"

"Just outside. A hamlet called Grouseham. Although it's pronounced 'gruesome' ironically – because gruesome it is not. Thankfully, only the locals are aware of this weird pronunciation."

Laughing, Rob replied, "We've had many a fun time with the pronunciation of places in Devon and Cornwall."

Yawning, Gabi asked, "What about your boyfriend? What does he do?"

Jaime was losing control of the conversation and where it was going. There was no way around it but to answer.

"I'm single."

The other woman's eyebrows rose a notch. "What, no one?"

"Not everyone feels the need to be partnered up or married, Gabi," Rob interjected. "It's not all it's cracked up to be. If truth be told, most married people would say there are times they wish they were on their own." He took a sip of his beer.

Gabi looked unconvinced, as though she could not believe there was anything better than being married to a man who adored you. Jaime couldn't decide if the woman was deliberately being insensitive or if she didn't realise she was doing it.

The food arrived and Jaime noted her tuna steaks were cooked medium rare, as they should be. She moved the extra tuna steak into her napkin, not wanting to get any seasoning on it. As they tucked in, Jaime attempted to change the subject back to the murder, although she made a mental note to try and find out if there was any gossip on Rob or his wife. That was twice now he had inferred marriage was not the be-all and end-all.

"I wonder what motive someone would have for murdering the councillor."

Rob dipped a chip into his ketchup. "Murder hasn't been confirmed."

"Oh, come on, we all know it will be. The police have as much as said they're investigating a murder."

Rob shrugged. "He didn't come across as a nice character. He was big-headed, you know?"

Jaime nodded. Gabi turned her chicken over and examined it. Rob took a large bite of his burger. Jaime was thinking this was harder than she thought it would be.

"Do you know any of the hotel staff?" Jaime asked Rob.

He finished chewing. "Well, I talk to Vanessa Fleet often. She is the hotel manager; we discuss whether the rooms are acceptable for the crew and how we have found the service etc... She's a lovely lady. Always ready to accommodate our every need, especially since there is talk of us moving to the other side of the island." During this small speech, Rob's face softened.

Jaime tried to hide her surprise. Mrs Fleet? Henry had not mentioned a family member or wife. "I know the customer relations manager, Henry Fleet." Jaime paused.

"Yes, Vanessa's son. A nice chap."

Now that is interesting, thought Jaime, although wasn't it odd Henry had not mentioned his mother at all during their earlier chat? She was the hotel manager, and she would know most of what went on.

Recalling what the captain had said, Jaime continued, "Moving to the other side of the island?"

"Our crew contract comes up for renewal periodically, sometimes there is a bit of a bidding war to give us a better deal than we already have, you know, like bigger rooms, better views, cheaper rates. The number of times we come here, it's good business to have us. Although we get a much cheaper rate, we are the bread and butter of anywhere we stay, guaranteed income all year round."

"Wow, I never knew it was such a cut-throat industry. I suppose Mrs Fleet has been working hard to please?" pushed Jaime.

"I think it would be pretty bad for her if she lost us."

"Is that likely? I mean, who decides?" Jaime was intrigued.

"The tourism council, I think, along with our unions and other interested parties, depending on the country."

"That wouldn't have anything to do with our dead councillor, would it?"

Rob raised his eyebrows. "Well, it might. In a country this small, a leading councillor would be on most committees."

"How can we find out?"

"You know, Jaime, it's not our job to be finding stuff out." Rob's tone was condescending.

Jaime realised she may have come across as too eager. She must rein it in a bit. "I suppose I was trying to think of people who might want Dickens out of the way so the police don't focus on the crew. You know, the councillor could have been taking bribes from other resorts to recommend them."

Gabi had stopped nibbling at her food, now interested in the conversation.

"I suppose it's possible, Jaime. Oh, look who it is." Rob's tone had become frosty.

Jaime and Gabi looked in the same direction. Jean was heading their way. Jaime was happy to have another person to question without having to actively seek her out. Rob had called her out on her investigative spirit, and Gabi had nothing of value to say. She didn't feel as though she was doing a very good detecting job.

"Afternoon Jean. I'm afraid you're a bit late. We've finished." Rob was abrupt.

Jean, however, was unperturbed. "Not to worry, I'm happy with a drink for now." She scanned the area for a waiter and spying one, she waved in his direction. The man hurried over, attentive as ever.

"Large glass of Pinot Grigio."

The man nodded and hurried off.

"That salad looks delicious, Gabi. And the chicken is perfectly poached. Have you lost your appetite? You're not eating it."

Indeed, Gabi had stopped eating, placing her cutlery on the plate and moving it away. "It's not cooked properly," she responded.

"Really?" Jean said, staring at her.

Jaime, watching the exchange between the two, thought it appeared strained. She knew, of course, Gabi wasn't a big fan of the CSD. She had said as much the previous day and it was evident here. The waiter returned with Jean's glass of wine, placing it in front of her. As she sipped, Jaime noticed how Jean stared at Gabi.

Rob had popped in his last mouthful of food. "Tennis lesson for me. Perhaps a cheeseburger was a bad move. Did I mention I've booked us all into Ricardo's tonight? I think it's a good idea to stick to our usual routines. We'll meet in the bar." He scraped back his chair, waved to the waiter and gave him the international sign for his bill.

Gabi apparently decided she would capitalise on this and followed suit, mumbling something about getting out of the hot sun.

Jean looked at Jaime, picking up her glass of wine, she stood.

"I'll leave you in peace, dear. You finish stuffing your face. I have a few things I need to do." And she headed off in the same direction as Gabi.

Jaime watched her walk away. She swallowed the piece of tuna steak and took a sip of water. *Had Jean said that? What a bitch. What a strange lunch.*

The restaurant was quieter now, most guests heading back to their sunbeds, keen to soak in the rays that were still strong. She remembered Thomas' forecast of a storm. There was no sign of it right now.

Max had departed the restaurant, as had the man who appeared to have been spying on him: The Stranger. She hadn't seen them go. *Dammit,* she would need to be more observant. Seeing The Stranger depart would have given her some indication of whom he was spying on, as he would no doubt have wanted to follow his prey.

Still, she had learned a few juicy snippets. Henry Fleet's mother ran the resort and he had chosen to keep it quiet. Why? Mrs Fleet had a possible motive for murder. If the councillor was going to back another resort to take over the crew contract, she would lose the all-year-round revenue and possibly her job along with it. Which, in turn, gave Henry a motive. Could they have been in it together? There was also more to discover about Rob. He was hiding something, but was it connected to the case? And Jean, a nasty piece of work. She had driven Gabi out of the restaurant. Then there was the possibility that some mysterious man was tailing Max, but why?

More questions than answers. She would need to do better than this.

Chapter 28

As Jaime wandered out of the restaurant, she was deep in thought. Remembering what she and Henry had overheard earlier - what could the Hayward / Vanetti partnership be up to? It sounded as though they were going to make a lot of money from a potential deal, and that would be made possible with the death of Gregory Dickens. She knew the two were into property - buying and selling, and there was a high chance this was something to do with the deal. A sudden flashback to the flight over popped into her head. She had been asking the crew what they were planning for their time in Antigua, and Mario had been vague - not giving much away, shying from the question. Was it because he didn't want anyone to know about the deal they were working on? One that involved murder.

Shielding her eyes from the intense rays, she spied Karen lying on a sunbed. *Bingo.* She had chosen to lounge around the huge pool area under one of the canopied beds the resort provided. She was wearing a tiny, white bikini that emphasised her dark skin. A notebook lay on the ground in front of her and a pen was poised mid-air. How fortuitous, an opportunity to gather more information. Jaime felt it was important to know who Karen was supposed to be meeting the previous evening. Something had caused her to drink herself into oblivion, alone, unless it was all an act, to appear drunk – in which case, it was a good one. Jaime approached and perched on the next lounger.

"Hey Karen," she said, but not before she had strained her neck to make out what the other woman was writing. She thought she saw the start of a word: 'bast...' The obvious answer was 'bastard', which was interesting, and to whom could she be referring? Unless, of course, Karen was writing about her favourite band, Bastille, or perhaps she was into fortifications?

Karen, startled, closed the book. "Oh, Jaime. Hi."

She's not happy to see me, thought Jaime, noting Karen's puffy, damp eyes.

"How are you bearing up? It's been a weird trip so far." Jaime's voice held a note of concern.

"Yeah, you could say that. To be honest, I didn't sleep well last night, still a bit of shock from the bus thing, I think." The Brummie accent was strong.

"I know what you mean. I didn't sleep well myself." Did the dream she'd had count as not sleeping well? Jaime supposed it could.

Karen was staring at a spot on the ground. Jaime needed to get the conversation moving in the right direction.

"How was your interview with the police?" she asked.

"To be honest, it was a bit intense." She paused, and Jaime remained mute. "Well, I felt I had to tell them about seeing Jean with Greg in the bar."

Jaime nodded but didn't want to interrupt what sounded like it was going to be some interesting information.

Karen continued, "She was pretty much spurned by him. He was drinking with his mates, she rocked up, all dolled up, and put a hand on his shoulder. There was some laughing from him and his mates. She went as red as beetroot, turned round and stormed away. She was pissed off."

Jaime realised this is when she had entered the bar - as Jean was leaving. So, it was after a confrontation with the

'Dick'. How interesting. Also interesting was Karen's eagerness to throw Jean under the bus.

"You must have been sat there for a while, Karen, to have seen all that," Jaime commented, hoping she would come clean about why she was there so early.

Karen didn't take too kindly to Jaime's statement. "Long enough to spot you turn up, Jaime. Jean, followed by you. What a pair. I mean, what would make you think you had a chance with him? Who do you think you are?"

Jaime's mouth fell open. She had not expected such an outburst, and Karen had got hold of the wrong end of the stick.

"I didn't know he was there. I wanted a drink." There was an edge to Jaime's voice she couldn't help.

"Right. What a coincidence. What happened? That hotel bloke come along and ruin it for you? What's the deal with him? You slut." Karen spat out the words.

Jaime was taken aback. "I don't know what your problem is, Karen Jeffries. You seem to have witnessed a lot. I must wonder what you were doing in the bar early yourself. I suppose it was you who told the detectives all about my so-called meeting with that sleaze?"

Karen grabbed her belongings and shoved them into her wicker beach bag.

Jaime had blown her opportunity to pump Karen for information. A good detective should not lose their temper. "Karen, I don't know what's gotten into you, but you need to calm down. I thought you might want to chat. It's healthy to talk." Jaime adopted what she hoped was a placating tone.

Karen's hands were trembling enough to drop her book and some other bits on the ground. Jaime squatted, to help recover them, her earlier annoyance dying down.

"Leave them, and leave me alone, you cow." Karen growled the words at Jaime, storming off, the tiny bikini bottom disappearing as she went.

111

The sun moved behind a dark cloud. Jamie shivered from the lack of heat. If it was a reaction she wanted, she had got one. Surely that was proof enough that Karen had feelings for the councillor. Not only did she refer to him as 'Greg', but she was also spying on him in the bar. She was jealous of any other woman who went near him. Jaime recalled Karen's upset after the bus attack, concerned more about how she looked than what had just happened. She could have been anticipating a rendezvous with Dickens. But the situation suggested that she had been stood up by him in favour of his mates. Why could she not admit it? Was she embarrassed? Trying to protect his family? Guilty of his murder? Which one was it?

Chapter 29

13:42

"Forty love," shouted the coach with a big smile on his face. "C'mon Mister Rob, put some effort into it."

The tennis courts were located to the side of the resort and surrounded by lush green shrubs. The courts themselves were well-maintained, cropped and green. The ocean could be heard but not seen due to the denseness of the foliage. Rob always felt as though he had been transported to the jungle when he played on these courts. They were much nicer than those at his club in Weymouth. Yes, he could hear the sea, and yes, there were trees. But somehow, this spot felt tranquil.

Sweating, feeling the effects of the cheeseburger he had consumed, but enjoying every minute of the competitive game, Rob grinned. The constant goading of the coach was working, he realised, as he stood ready to receive the next, possibly winning serve. He was determined to at least get his racket onto this one. The guy was not going out on an ace. He trained his eye on the ball and jigged his feet from side to side. The ball came flying at goodness only knew what speed. Rob placed his racquet behind him, eyed up the ball and whacked it low over the net. Amazed at how he had managed to get his racquet on the ball and keep it low, placing it beautifully on the opposite side to where his coach was poised, ready. All in all, not bad. Unfortunately for him, it came straight back, low and right at his feet.

"Game, set and match," came the gleeful voice on the other side of the net.

They walked towards each other and shook hands.

"Well done, Mister Rob, great return. But you were not expecting it to come right back. You rested on your laurels for a second too long. Now, next time..." And he proceeded to brief Rob on their goals for the next session.

They were heading towards the locker room when the coach said, "No Mrs Bannister, this time?"

Rob's step faltered, and he turned towards the coach, a deep red flush spreading across his face. The coach appeared not to notice.

"We were saying at the fitness centre, it is unusual for you to be alone."

Rob was about to enquire as to who was concerned at the lack of his wife's presence but found his mouth had gone dry, and nothing would come out. Instead, he marched back to the locker room alone after having an enjoyable session ruined, leaving his coach staring after him, a puzzled expression on his face.

Why is this happening to me? he fumed as he stomped through the door and threw his expensive racquet on the ground. He knew it was his shame causing him to act like this. Taking a deep breath, he tried to calm down – not allow these negative feelings to control him. He would not let this destroy him.

Chapter 30

Back in her room, Jaime opened her fridge door, popped Basil's tuna steak inside and took out a small bottle of sparkling water. There seemed to be much to find out from the crew, and she didn't want to be on the police radar herself. It was an uncomfortable place to be. Cagney and Lacey were a formidable duo.

Observing was not to be underrated. It worked for Miss Marple. The lobby area was the most bustling place to see any interesting goings-on. She changed into a pair of shorts and a t-shirt, placing the almost finished Agatha Raisin in her bag. Pausing for a second, she grabbed the Carmela Bertrand mystery, not knowing how long she would be sitting around, and the thought of having no reading material was... well, unthinkable. She would need to give the impression she was waiting to go on an outing or meeting someone - that would be good camouflage.

Switching on her phone and heading onto the balcony, Jaime was excited: one bar in the top left corner of the screen. A tiny bit of signal. Before it vanished, she typed the councillor's name into her search engine. The little icon circled. Jaime waited. After what felt like a long time, she was about to give up, when a list appeared on the small screen.

Scrutinising it and tapping on different options, she saw images of the councillor at various events. In all of them, there was that huge, white shark's smile plastered on the

115

tanned face. He seemed to spend a lot of time opening new businesses, launching charity events, putting forward his opinion on various matters. It was, thought Jaime, all quite banal. Nothing stood out to her as controversial. In one shot, he was pictured in his large garden, with his wife standing beside him and two little brats, a boy aged 12 and a girl aged 10, sat cross-legged in front of their parents. A cheesy publicity shot if ever she saw one. Neither child looked endearing, but why would they?

Jaime studied his wife, whose name was Margaret, according to the caption underneath the picture. She was a haughty-looking woman with short hair highlighted with blonde streaks. She had high cheekbones that stuck out on her slim face and, from what Jaime could make out, a skeletal figure. If you could take a disliking to someone just from seeing their picture, she did not like Margaret Dickens. The pair were made for each other. It must have been love at first sight.

Tapping on Margaret's name, Jaime wanted to find out a little more about Mrs Dickens. The spouse was usually suspect number one. While the phone buffered, she slipped on her flipflops and placed the bottle of water in her bag. After a few minutes of nothing, Jaime decided not to waste any more time on this and head out for her stint of surveillance. Putting the phone in her bag with the intention of trying it later in the lobby, she left her room.

The lobby was a hive of activity. Couples were indulging in afternoon tea, sat at tables overlooking the ocean. Jaime smiled, loving the bizarre contrast of the quintessential English afternoon tea with the Caribbean backdrop of whirling ceiling fans, sandy beaches and sparkling blue water. It was not dissimilar to her adopted home county of Devon. Others were indulging in cocktails and playing board games, dominoes and cards.

And there was Jean and Gabi. Jaime's heart beat faster. The two women had not seen her, and she moved off

116

towards a marble pillar, letting it partially obscure her as she observed them. Jean was talking. Jaime studied Gabi's face, trying to interpret the exact expression upon it: uncomfortable, perhaps. Sensing if they were to spot her, any interesting conversation would cease, she found herself a comfy sofa with a wide-ranging view of the area.

Sitting, she turned to study the two women again. Jean was still talking. Jaime was intrigued. Surely Gabi had not requested the rendezvous? After all, she had told Jaime yesterday what a bitch she thought the CSD was, and she couldn't get away from her fast enough at lunch time.

Realising if anyone studied her, they would wonder why she was staring at the two women, Jaime opened her book with the intention of reading a paragraph before resuming her spying.

Agatha Raisin had discovered her husband, Jimmy, had been manipulating people with the intention of blackmailing them. He had an accomplice, someone hiding in the shadows, pulling his strings.

Jaime looked over to find Jean and Gabi had gone. *Damn. Pay attention.* How long had she been reading? At least two chapters. This surveillance was not going to work if she got too involved in the book. Perhaps she should try her audiobook then she could still watch while being entertained? But then it would look obvious she was spying, that was why physically reading was a better option.

She sighed. This was not easy. A waiter passing through the area offered her some refreshments, and she ordered a pot of almond rooibos tea.

Three final chapters later, the tea arrived, and it seemed as though Jimmy Raisin had tried to blackmail one person too many, and the killer had not taken it well, strangling him with his own tie. Didn't all blackmailers end up dead?

There was still a gentle thrum of people in the lobby. Guests always needed something. The afternoon tea partakers had dwindled, although the cocktail drinkers were out in force. Jaime signed the check, thanked the waiter and leaned forward to give the tea a stir. A thought was noodling around her brain. What if Dickens was a blackmailer? Could he have arranged to meet someone late last night with the intention of demanding money from them? Although he appeared to be a wealthy man from his business dealings. Or maybe it wasn't money he was blackmailing them for, but sex. Although it didn't appear that he needed to twist Jean or Karen's arms too much.

As she twirled the leaves around the pot, she recognised the figure of Max stroll into the lobby, stop and glance around. Skulking, she decided.

He had not looked in her direction; walking to the reception desk, he stood at the end of it. Jaime continued to lean forward. Max had taken a leaflet at the end of the desk and was flicking through it, but his actions lacked purpose, like a ruse, thought a suspicious Jaime. She grinned to herself, thinking he was acting no differently from her. Both were lurking in the lobby - she was spying, he was... well, she was going to find out.

The receptionist, the young woman with the thick lens glasses, Edwina Kershaw, had just resumed her post and was busy attending to the couple at the front of the queue, which was long and growing all the time. Max kept glancing in Edwina's direction, but Jaime did not understand why he wasn't joining the queue if he wanted something from her. Deciding to pour her tea before it became too strong, she shifted her chair so she could sit back and be out of sight.

Could she have stumbled upon something vital? Reminding herself to breathe, she took a sip of tea, eyes glued on the receptionist. The woman stole a quick glance or two at Max, pushing her glasses onto her nose at the same time, but continued to take care of her customers. Max's fingers drummed on the counter. He shifted from foot to foot, glancing through one leaflet then taking another. Jaime couldn't remember the last time she had been this tense.

118

Then something curious happened. It all might have been quite natural to anyone milling around the lobby and not paying attention, but Jaime was watching every move. The receptionist returned from the room behind the desk holding a bulky envelope. She went over to the printer, placed the envelope on the counter, pulled a sheet from the printer and took it back to her customers, leaving the envelope in the vicinity of the printer and Max.

While her customers perused the sheet and asked a few questions, Max shifted over nearer to the envelope, now holding in his hand an unfolded map of the island. The receptionist glanced over towards Max as he swiped the envelope under his map, and with a glance around the lobby, walked away.

Jaime gasped, causing a few stares from passers-by. It was like something straight out of a spy movie. She turned back towards the receptionist, expecting her to shout out that Max had swiped her envelope. But she didn't. She turned back to her customers, continuing to assist them.

What the hell was that? It must have been a pre-arranged handover. But why the secrecy? The covert operation? There can be nothing good in that envelope, she decided. Her curiosity piqued, she needed to know what those contents were.

Chapter 31

Heading back to her room, Jaime passed two women coming down the stairs. One was older, with red spiralled hair, the other, perhaps twenty, attractive with a long, brunette mane. A jolt of recognition hit her. On the plane - stubborn husband, boy with a potty mouth. There was a high chance they were part of the Carfax family. No other guests would have any reason to be using this staircase. They were on the same flight out.

Entering her room, she threw off her bag, kicked off the flipflops and made her way to the balcony, where the afternoon sun was still blazing. She plopped onto a sun lounger. What an afternoon. What was going on? What she had witnessed in the hotel lobby was weird.

Closing her eyes, enjoying the heat, Jaime reflected on events so far. After years of reading about the anecdotes of her favourite fictional sleuths, she was now becoming one of them, and it made her feel alive. There was no doubt it was invigorating, and in a short space of time, she had uncovered some interesting information. But what should she do with that information?

Her head was in a whirl. Grabbing a notebook off the desk, the plan was to order her thoughts. A list was required. *How could anyone get through life without a good list?*
Okay, here goes. Possible suspects and motives:

-Mrs Vanessa Fleet: could lose the crew contract to another resort. With Dickens out of the way, does the Reef Royale get to keep the crew? Mrs Fleet could find herself out of a job if she lost the crew contract. What will happen now? What would she do to keep herself in the top position?

-Henry Fleet: same as above. Possible he doesn't want his mother to lose the job she loves. Admitted to disliking the councillor. Trying to hide his family connection from her, but why? With the same surname, it wouldn't take long to discover.

-Edwina Kershaw - Receptionist: something dodgy going on between her and Max Kleinbeck - must discover what that was all about.

-Captain Rob Bannister: opinionated about marriage. Could he be having an affair with someone? Or perhaps his wife is? Who? What's the link to Dickens?

Jaime remembered his sneer the first time he had mentioned Dickens' name the previous day. Strange reaction towards someone he supposedly hardly knew. She continued her list.

-First Officer Kate Jackson: a quiet one. Again, struggling to find a motive.

-Jean Blackthorn: acting strangely on the night of the murder. According to Karen, she was snubbed by the councillor and stormed away. A bitch, but murderer material? And what was with the rendezvous with Gabi?

There was much speculation. What did she know for a fact? Not much. She pushed on, her earlier elation evaporating.

-Karen Jeffries: unhinged for sure. Moody and upset after arriving on the island. Possibly jilted on the first night, spying on the councillor, referred to him as 'Greg' earlier. Could she have been in love with him? He didn't seem the type to reciprocate.

-Tony Hayward: at last, something concrete. A business deal. With Dickens out of the way, everything goes ahead as planned, the deal goes through. Financial motives are strong. Agitated when waiting for his interview with Dickens, biting his fingernails.

-Mario Vanetti: Tony's partner, so same as above. Also, strong physically as was obvious from the bus incident.

-Max Kleinbeck: hard to read him, keeps himself to himself. Suspicious incident with Edwina in the lobby. What does it have to do with Dickens? Further investigating needed to pinpoint a motive.

-Gabrielle Pascal: over reaction to the bus attack, perhaps highly strung? Professes to be happy with her marriage but quick to volunteer information on the subject. Her disappearing act before her interview with Dickens, then lying about it, saying she went to the bathroom. Did she not want to see him? Why? Then there was the rendezvous with Jean despite disliking her.

-The Carfax family: investigation needed.

-Mrs Margaret Dickens: probably hated her husband because he cheated on her, but she couldn't have had access to the beach, could she?

Jaime threw down the pen. Did the list provide any clarity at all? One thing her list made her realise was how many of the crew were acting oddly. But that didn't make them murderers. Some might say she was being a bit odd herself.

There were other people with beach access keys. Cleaners, security guards, someone could have had their card stolen (as Henry had pointed out). Although no one she knew of had admitted to that or reported it.

Then she remembered the Mysterious Stranger in the restaurant at lunch time and how he was spying on someone: Max? Who on earth was he? And was he connected somehow to the murder of Dickens?

Chapter 32

"We need tea. Strong, hot tea." Inspector Winnifred Fontaine stood and headed over towards the refreshment trolley the hotel manager had provided for them whilst they had to be on site.

"Put an extra sugar in mine, Winnie." Detective Letitia Marshall told her colleague and friend of the last fifteen years.

"You need to cut out sugar, Letty. I've been telling you for years now. It'll rot those teeth and pile on the pounds. I should know."

Letitia Marshall chuckled. "Pass me a biscuit while you're at it."

"No treats here, my friend. Now take the tea and shush. You need to stay trim until you find the man of your dreams."

Letitia ignored her friend's comment, having heard it many times before - Winnifred was constantly fretting about her single status.

"So, what are we thinking? Interviews done. First impressions, girl. Don't hold back."

Winnifred Fontaine had no intention of holding back. She had never held back in her life, which had gotten her into a bit of trouble on occasion. "Typical captain. Exactly what I would have expected him to be like."

"What a pompous twerp."

Winnifred snorted, and tea dripped out of her nose and onto her trouser leg, causing Letitia to let out a whoop of laughter.

"This is a potential murder investigation. If anyone hears us, we'll be in trouble. Stop laughing so loudly. Shush. Watch this." Letitia proceeded to put her hand over her mouth and titter like a small child. This had an even worse effect on Winnifred, who was doubled over with laughter, tears streaming from her eyes.

"I'm going to wet myself. Letty, stop," she managed.

Both women took a deep breath, a sip of tea and tried to calm down.

"It won't be long until we have the cause of death confirmed. Until then, we'll proceed on the assumption of a suspicious death." Winnifred attempted to find her professional manner.

Letitia nodded in agreement.

"We know our list of possible suspects is limited because of the location of the body. The DebonAir crew and the Carfax family. Some of the hotel staff too, but we're waiting on confirmation. Agreed?"

Letitia nodded once more. "Y'know, I flew DebonAir once to London to visit Aunty Gladys. It was wonderful. Champagne, seafood, fine wine. And the seats were so plush. My one big treat to myself."

Winnifred smiled at her friend. "Yes, I remember. You never stopped going on about it for months."

Both women laughed. "The crew are all vetted, which begs the question, how did Miss Jaime Jones slip through the net? What with her past involvement in a possible murder enquiry?"

"True. I suppose it was out in the Arctic Circle. And it was never conclusive. No arrests made. Perhaps the people at DebonAir missed it."

"Perhaps. But I uncovered it with relative ease."

"Ah, yes, but that's you, Letty. You are one hot detective."

"Yes, I am. But thanks for pointing it out. I discovered the owner of the airline is a bit of a recluse. Never appears in public. Never does interviews. No reports of where he lives but he owns many houses. He does keep a tight rein on his airline, though, hopping on and off flights as and when it suits him, checking on how his business is running. The mysterious Charles Debon. Doubt it's his real name."

"Any idea if he was on this flight out?"

"No. But I have requested the information from the airline's head office. We'll hear soon enough."

"Good work, partner. What else do we know?" Winnifred relied on her friend's legendary research skills.

Letitia sat a little straighter as she replied. "Apart from Jones, all background checks came back clean. We must go on witness reports and any possible motives we can uncover. We both knew Councillor Gregory Dickens well."

Winnifred nodded in agreement.

"We both hated his guts," continued Letitia.

Another nod from her colleague.

"We're both lucky we were at the fundraiser for the Antigua Animal Protection Society last night, till after midnight, with plenty of witnesses, or we might have to go on our own suspect list."

Again, Winnifred nodded. "A piece of work he was. A nasty, womanising, dangerous animal."

"There'll be no shortage of suspects. Thank goodness for the private beach access, limiting it. There were rumours about flings, even though his wife Margaret, pretends she knows nothing."

"I know, right? What's that all about? I often felt sorry for her, then she would make some nasty comment about my figure, or my outfit and I would remember what a bitch she is." Winnifred let out a long breath, trying to calm herself down.

"Yes, it's true it couldn't have happened to a nicer couple. Still, it has happened, and it's our job to investigate it.

125

Margaret should be at the top of our suspect list, but we'll be struggling to find her opportunity. The taxi driver has confirmed he dropped her home at half past midnight, waited for her to go in, sat outside for the next forty minutes waiting for another job. He confirms she never came back out, and she was drunk." Letitia paused.

"It does make it quite tight for her to have killed her husband. How would she have returned to the resort and accessed the beach? It seems unlikely. And the bar staff confirmed she was by the pool with her friend all evening. They kept them on their toes ordering a whole range of cocktails.

What do we know about the Carfax family?" Winnifred looked at her colleague.

"The mother, Carol Carfax, is best friends with Margaret Dickens. They went to university together. Carol's husband, Caleb, is out here doing business, something to do with planning. He might have been involved with Dickens on that front. I need more info on the exact nature of what he does. There are two children, Christy, 17 and Connor, 15. Still looking into those two.

"Back to the crew, we'll have to dig a bit there. Some of these women could have been involved with Dickens. It was written all over the face of Karen Jeffries. The others were a bit hard to read. Jaime Jones was not going to admit to her altercation with him until we prised it out of her."

"What's your take on CSD Jean Blackthorn?" Winnifred pushed.

"Well, I'm glad she's not my boss. She has an evil air about her, and she thinks a lot of herself. Of course, the Jeffries woman didn't hold back on filling us in that Blackthorn had been snubbed by Dickens at the bar."

"Right. What was it she heard one of his cronies say? 'Grab a Granny night'? How bloody rude."

"An English expression I've heard a few times before. *So* insulting. She would not have enjoyed hearing that." Letitia pulled a face.

"I don't think any of us would, but enough to kill for?"

"We've had much weaker motives, Winnie."

"True enough. Okay, we have some digging to do. In the meantime, we'll get Kennedy to hang around the crew and see what he can pick up." Winnifred was referring to Officer Kennedy, one of their team.

"You know, it's going to be a crime with plenty of motives. Remember a rumour a few years back, Dicken's was taking bribes? Manipulating all sorts of issues that he shouldn't have been involved in?" Letitia looked thoughtful.

"Jeez, yes. Of course. It was brushed under the carpet, though."

"That's right. Here we have a man with no shortage of enemies, but we have a limited suspect list. It's interesting - out of all the interviews we have done this morning, only Miss Jaime Jones, when pushed, admitted what a vile person he was. Others must have thought the same, and we gave them all equal opportunity to come clean. Even his own wife professed to being grief-stricken by his death."

"I know. What a crock. Right, c'mon, let's get out of here and back to the station." Winnifred stood.

"Right behind you, girlfriend," Letitia also stood.

"It's Emmy's football night and she needs picking up. I'll have to get off early. Brian's at his scrabble game."

Letitia rolled her eyes.

"I know you're rolling your eyes, Letty. You always do. He's entitled to one night off a week."

"Sure, Winnie. Whatever. Answer me one question before you vanish into the night."

"Anything, my dear."

Letitia pointed at her trouser suit. "What colour are you going with tomorrow?"

Chapter 33

Dressed for the evening ahead and feeling relaxed after getting stuck into *Postcards from The Dead,* Jaime, armed with Basil's treat, pulled her door closed. She checked it was locked and headed off towards the beach, long cardigan in hand. Although the temperature was still warm, she knew from many years of experience, when inside, the air-conditioning could be overbearing, and she hated being cold.

As she neared the beach, she removed her wedges and enjoyed the warm grains of sand as they engulfed her feet. The weather was calm. The kind of calm that comes before a storm. Deciding to take a stroll away from the resort, Jaime went through her plan for the evening. The idea was to set a chain of events in motion that would hopefully result in her finding out what was in Max's parcel. It had to be important. The way he had received it suggested some impropriety.

It was not long, however, before the object of her stroll arrived, tail wagging. Jaime plonked herself down, unwrapped the food and held a piece of tuna out for him to try. As he leaned forward towards the morsel, Jaime noticed something in his mouth.

"What's that? What are you carrying around with you?" she asked.

Basil put his two front paws on Jaime's leg and dropped the item in her lap. He sniffed the food and politely took it from her. As she passed him bite-sized pieces of the tuna steak, Jaime lifted the object from her lap to examine. It was a small, damp card. Turning it over, she gasped. The words on the front read, 'Choices - It's Up To You' followed by a phone number. Basil paused in his chewing to look at her. Realising she was alright, he continued to eat. Jaime stared at the business card, knowing full well where she had seen it before. Well, part of it, at least, sticking out of a dead man's grasp.

"How on earth -?" she said to the dog, who had finished his snack in record time and was now licking his left paw.

There was no doubt in Jaime's mind - this was the card she had seen in Dickens' hand when she'd discovered his body. And what were the chances of there being two of them? "Did you take this from the councillor's hand? I mean, when? Or find it somewhere else?" she asked, and Basil yipped.

Jaime stroked his head and studied the card. At least she could now try the phone number and find out what the card was for. That could give her investigation a huge boost. A thought struck her. Basil must have taken the card after she left and before the police arrived on the scene; otherwise, it would now be locked up as evidence. It was unlikely the murderer returned to the scene to retrieve it, then dropped it somewhere - if it was the same card. And she had to assume it was, as the chances of there being two of these floating around were slim.

That meant she was in possession of evidence Cagney and Lacey had not seen. The last thing she wanted to do was interfere in their investigation. But she couldn't hand them the card now they already suspected her of murder. And they would never believe she just 'came across it'. All she could do was continue her investigation and make sure, if she uncovered anything of note, to tell them.

"I'm grateful you brought this to me, you know. You are helpful. Good boy. Let me tell you what I'm planning to do this evening. See what you think." She proceeded to outline her plan. "What do you think? Will it work?" Receiving no response, she looked down.

Basil had stopped licking his paw and was staring out to sea, for all the world as though he were giving her idea some serious consideration.

"There are no guarantees, but I have to try something."

Basil's tail wagged in the sand, flicking grains in all directions.

"I knew you'd agree." She patted his back. "Well, I suppose I had better go and do my duty. Although I know who I would rather be spending my evening with."

They stood, Jaime reaching for her shoes while Basil stretched one leg at a time. Turning, he headed back in the direction from which he had come. Jaime stared after him, wondering how he knew the business card would be useful to her. He seemed to be taking his role as Ganesha seriously.

Brushing the sand off her cardigan, she strode towards the bar, sliding the piece of evidence into her pocket.

Chapter 34

Approaching the resort, Jaime could hear the upbeat jazz notes from the in-house band. That, alongside the hum of voices, clinking of glasses and lapping waves, made for a seductive blend. She had agreed to meet Henry for a drink and a catch-up before going out to dinner with the crew. Spying him already at the bar, she walked over. He reached over and kissed her cheek, surprising her with the forward but not unwelcome gesture. Ordering a gin and slimline tonic, she followed Henry to a cosy alcove.

Knowing her time was limited, as the crew were heading out for dinner soon, Jaime dived straight in. "Did you find out anything useful?" she asked, crossing her fingers.

Henry took a swig of his beer. "Autopsy results are just in, and murder is confirmed. Bashed on the head, from above, with a coconut. A rotten one, no doubt, hence how easy it turned to mush. The blow as he hit a rock was what finished him off. It won't do the hotel a great deal of good. This kind of adverse publicity could be the start of a slow decline."

Jaime was not surprised at the autopsy result. "Have you been able to shed any light on whether any of the hotel staff accessed the beach?" Her eyes bore into his, watching for any sign he might not be telling her the truth.

"I've spent the afternoon checking into that. Each key has a tiny microchip in it, programmed for each room. If one is lost, it will need to be replaced by the contractor's own

131

security people. They supplied just enough for the number of rooms, no extras. There are two skeleton key cards for the cleaning crew, which are both where they should be." He paused. "Locked in the manager's office. They must be handed over by the manager and handed back in. They were last logged back in yesterday at 3.05 pm."

Jaime sighed. "Who has access to them, only the manager?"

"Right. The office is locked when not occupied. And she has the keys to the lock box. She lives on-site, though, should a guest ever need a key in an emergency." Henry shuffled on his seat. If true, this exonerated most of the resort staff, but it by no means put Mrs Vanessa Fleet in the clear.

"Why so few keys?" Her brow furrowed in puzzlement. "And why so strict with the cleaning team? I thought they had access to all areas at all times."

"We need to tighten security; all resorts on the island do. There have been some shocking crimes against tourists in recent years, and people don't feel as safe as they should on their dream holiday." He paused, perhaps considering the irony of what he had said. "The airline crew are like our guinea pigs in a way, checking out any potential problems with the rooms before we let them out to the important people." He gave her a grin.

"Oh well, thanks a lot." She laughed. "Were the Carfax family guinea pigs too?"

"Close friends of Dickens and his wife. The type of people we are 'encouraged' to upgrade." He smiled. "Well, the wife is close friends with Dickens' wife, I believe, not so much the husbands."

Jaime raised an eyebrow. "Oh? Is there anymore to that story?"

Henry took another long swig of his beer. "I've heard from a few guests there was a bit of an altercation between the two last night in the bar. It must have been after we left. That's all I know."

Jaime digested this new piece of information as she sipped her drink, enjoying the refreshing taste of the cucumber. It appeared the Carfax father disliked Dickens enough to lose his temper in public. Interesting… it seemed as though she and Mr Carfax had something in common.

Some useful information from Henry, but how far could she trust what he said? She had no way of confirming any of it, although he acted sincerely enough.

"How do you like working here?" she asked on a whim. "Do you have any family nearby?"

Henry folded his arms. "That's a bit of a tangent," he hedged.

"I suppose I've realised how little I know about you," she responded, her eyes never leaving his face. *Come on*, she was thinking, *tell me the hotel manager is your mother.*

"I love my job. Although it is not without its challenges. But what job is, right? Do you like your job?" he asked.

Deflated, Jaime answered, "Yes, I do like aspects of the job. I could do without the overnight flights, though. They don't make you feel good the next day."

Why would he not acknowledge his relationship to the resort manager? It was just plain ridiculous. Were they in cahoots to bump off Dickens?

"You know, Jaime, there is this great little restaurant - popular with locals. It's tucked away near the harbour. The views are magnificent, and the seafood," he paused. "There's none better."

Jaime felt uncomfortable. "I made a list of all possible suspects and motives. You're on it." She paused, waiting for him to protest, to be outraged.

"I thought he was a vile man, and I detested him. He made life difficult for most of the people around him, often, it seemed, because he loved his power." His voice was steady, and raising his bottle, he finished off his drink.

Jaime was not sure how she felt about this admission. Should she be disturbed by his arrogance by not wanting to hide his hate for the victim? Was this outburst a ploy to make him appear honest and upfront when, in fact, he was hiding something from her?

Henry resumed his earlier train of thought, not one to be deterred. "How about it, Jaime? I'm sure you'll love it. Tomorrow, perhaps?"

Jaime was amazed by his perseverance after she had told him he was on her list of suspects. However, right now, she didn't feel comfortable enough to go on a date with him.

"Can I let you know?" Now it was her turn to hedge. Afterall, he had his uses, the new investigative side of her thought.

Henry looked disappointed. "Sure, let me know. I'll see you tomorrow, no doubt."

They stood, about to part company, when Jaime remembered to ask, "Have you heard of a place called 'Choices'?"

"There's a supermarket with that name, I think, on the old airport road," he replied.

A supermarket was not what she was expecting him to say, but she supposed it made sense. There would be many choices there. But why would Dickens have a business card for a supermarket? Once again, Henry leaned towards her and his lips brushed her cheek, he turned and strode away from the bar.

Jaime stood where she was, analysing her feelings. Henry had given her some useful information, if it was to be relied upon. But she was not sure how she felt about going on a date with him. Her focus needed to be her investigation, but he could be useful...

Strolling around the periphery of the bar, on the lookout for any of the crew, she stopped in her tracks. There he was again. That man. The Stranger. The one she had been sure was watching Max earlier, at lunchtime. Well, he wasn't watching Max now. No, he was staring at her.

Sat alone at a table, a glass of amber liquid in front of him, his blue eyes locked on her. The fair hair was blowing in the breeze and his cream shirt was open at the neck. Everything about him suggested he was comfortable, relaxed even. She felt hypnotised and knew she should move on, tear herself away from his gaze, but for some reason, she did not want to. Debating whether to seize the moment and walk over to his table, ask him who he was and why he was eyeballing her, the decision was taken out of her hands. Mario's arm slid around her shoulder and squeezed it. She jumped.

"You're lucky you didn't get a smack in the face, creeping up on me like that."

Mario put his hands up in mock surrender. "Only me, JJ. Rounding up the troops. You ready?"

"Yep, sure," she replied as she turned back to The Stranger's table. He wasn't there. All that remained was an empty glass. She sighed, disappointed.

Following Mario out towards the lobby, she had a strong desire to see that man again.

Chapter 35

Nine crew and one portly police officer made their way down the winding hill towards the town. As they strolled towards Ricardo's, they commented on the twinkling lights coming from the yachts and nearby businesses. The air was still warm, but the breeze had gathered some momentum. Jaime was glad of the extra layer she had chosen to wear. The restaurant was busy, most of it situated outside, with a canopy above.

Officer Kennedy chose to remain outdoors, sitting at a small table with his packet of cigarettes. The inside section had bi-folding doors that were fully opened. The crew were led through the building to a large circular table, situated on the back patio. Lighting was by small tealight candles, with a couple of spotlights attached to each corner of the building.

Jaime was glad of the round table; they were much more sociable and would enable her to hear more conversations than she would if it had been a long, rectangular affair. She had, without much difficulty, engineered it so she was sat next to Max. No one else was rushing for that spot.

Rob took charge of ordering the wine, a couple of bottles of red and white and menus were passed around.

"How are you holding up with everything that's happened?" She turned to Max.

He answered in his clipped German accent. "Well, okay. And you?" he appeared to add as an afterthought.

136

"Not too bad, but it's awful to think one of us around this table is a possible murderer." The captain had informed the crew this was now officially a suspicious death. She looked at the man, interested in the reaction it would provoke. She was disappointed. He seemed disinterested.

"I guess," was his response.

Jaime tried again. "Yes, I assume it will affect our flight home. It can't all run smoothly after everything that's happened." Surely she would strike a nerve eventually.

"I am sure we will be fine." He took a long sip of his iced water. He had refused any wine.

Jaime, on the other hand, took a large sip of her chardonnay and savoured it. Glancing around the table, she noticed Jean topping up her wine glass already, taking a giant gulp. She turned her attention back to Max.

"Well, I don't suppose we will be allowed to leave until the police have apprehended their killer." She pursued her theme after noticing Max paying a bit more attention to what she was saying. He was looking thoughtful. "Aren't you curious to know what happened to the councillor?"

"I guess what goes around comes around, and I hear he was not a nice man," he responded.

"You believe in an eye for an eye?"

"More like karma."

"Well, I guess you have a point," Jaime conceded.

Gabi, sitting to Jaime's left side, had been listening. She ran her finger around the edge of her glass. "I think what goes around does come around," she agreed.

"From what I've been told, some of the hotel staff could have had access to the private beach. As I understand it, receptionists have skeleton keys to help guests if they lose one. I'm sure the inspector will get around to investigating them soon." Jaime glanced across at Max.

Sure enough, the deliberate mention of the hotel's receptionist had an effect on him. He reached for his water glass with a trembling hand and took a long sip. Excusing himself, he disappeared in the direction of the restrooms. Little white lies were the way forward. Jaime congratulated herself for channelling her inner Agatha Raisin. But she wasn't done with him yet.

The waiter was in situ and was working his way around the table taking orders. Jaime took another sip of her wine and glanced through the menu. She decided on the fresh, garlic king prawns and would follow with a sirloin steak (Basil would love that), rice and a garden salad. For other members of the crew, it wasn't quite as straightforward.

"I'll need the fish grilling and the sauce on the side. Oh, and skinny fries, not chunky ones."

"Same for me, except I'll have the mashed potatoes. And the sauce on the fish, but not on the potatoes."

"Can we have two more bottles of each wine and some water?" Jean had finished one bottle of wine before the waiter had had a chance to put pen to paper.

Whilst the harried man was making his way around the crew, Jaime listened to Kate Jackson, whose tongue had loosened, talking about how hard she worked to get to where she was. Tony and Mario were, of course, seated together, spending much of the time whispering to each other. Karen, sat to Tony's left, didn't seem to mind. She stared absently around the dining area, not engaging with anyone. Jaime, remembering the uncomfortable episode with her earlier, wondered if Karen would acknowledge her at all this evening. She thought not.

Max had returned from the restroom in time to order a seafood gumbo. After all the orders had been taken and all the questions asked, Jaime returned to her conversation with Max. She had a plan to put into action, she needed him to believe his 'parcel' was going to be discovered, therefore forcing him to move it. She leaned in towards him in a confidential manner.

"I wonder when the police will decide to go through our rooms."

His head flipped around to face her, "What do you mean?" he demanded. There was a real intensity in his face Jaime had not seen before.

Bingo. A reaction. Some emotion. The man is not a robot, after all.

She feigned surprise. "Well, it stands to reason Fontaine and Marshall will want to search our rooms, we are suspects. I think they will take us by surprise and do it first thing in the morning when we are feeling a bit groggy and won't protest too much. Or maybe when we're away on the shuttle."

Max paled. "They can't search our rooms, that's not allowed."

"Oh, I wouldn't put anything past the inspector. She's desperate to solve this case. I bet she is under real pressure, the Reef Royale being such a well-known resort. They won't want the bad publicity to linger on." She was thinking about her conversation with Henry earlier. "They may want to bring in someone bigger, like the Antiguan version of the FBI." She cringed at her own comment. "They're on a deadline to come up with something soon or they'll have to hand over the case." Had she waffled too much? She was feeling more than a little reckless in her desperation to get some answers.

Max relapsed into a moody silence. Jaime was satisfied. She had laid her trap. The reaction Max gave to the news the rooms may be searched was what Jaime had been hoping for. She was glad he had taken on board what she said. She had been worried it all sounded far-fetched, which it was.

The food arrived and the wine flowed (in Jean's direction). To the other patrons, they were merely a bunch of happy, relaxed friends out for an evening of fun. When it was time for dessert, Jean needed her American baked cheesecake to come with vanilla ice cream, Gabi needed a selection of fresh fruit that was not on the menu, Mario had to have three different ice cream flavours with his tiramisu, Tony had to have a slice of pecan pie, but with half a dollop of whipped cream to accommodate his diet - he couldn't order a normal portion and eat half of it. Then there were the liqueur coffees, most, except for Jaime, Max and Gabi had to have.

There had been the usual crew ruckus over the bill and who had had what, resulting in it taking a lot more time to settle than it would if they had been happy to split it evenly.

"So, who's up for Devine's?" Tony asked as he stood from the table. He was referring to a popular local night spot, a few minutes' walk from the marina. "I think we could all do with letting our hair down a bit and having a boogie. And I'm sure Officer Kennedy would love to join us." He grinned.

Jaime was horrified. If there was one thing in this world she would eliminate if she could, it was tacky nightclubs. The truth was, she hated loud music and had no coordination whatsoever, which didn't bode well in a club. Her feelings were visible on her face.

"C'mon, Jaime. Live a little. We'll show you how it's done." And with that, Tony gyrated his slim hips in Mario's direction.

Rob strode out of the restaurant, followed by Max.

"I guess that's a no from you two?" Tony shouted after them.

"Well, count me in. Bring on the totty." Kate fist pumped the air.

Mario turned to Jaime, his eyes pleading with her to come. As much as she found their company entertaining, she was adamant she wasn't going, plus, she had a surveillance mission planned.

Squeezing both Tony and Mario's shoulders, she said, "Enjoy yourselves. You don't need me for that. Or my attempt at dancing, for that matter."

"Oh, that's what I was most looking forward to," Tony replied with a grin. "I'm having flashbacks to a time in... now, where was it? Rio? You were on the dance floor, Jaime, and I'm not kidding..."

But Jaime had decided she did not remember or care what had happened on a dance floor in who knew where. She was leaving, hating people who always managed to remember embarrassing moments and bring them up years later. She waved to a still-talking Tony and walked away, hearing Jean's voice a few octaves louder than normal due to her drunken state.

"Count me in, boys. I'm still good for a boogie, and who knows what eye candy there might be. It could be my lucky night. Hold my hand, Mario, don't let me trip in these heels."

Jaime grinned, resisting the urge to turn around and look at Tony's face.

Arriving at the hotel close to 11 pm, Max departed, followed by Karen. Gabi, at least, said goodnight before heading off. Rob staggered to the bar. Although tempted to spy on him, there was no time. Turning, Jaime headed for the stairs. Her night was far from over.

Chapter 36

Rob knew unless he passed out, there would be no rest for him tonight. The thought of lying in bed awake, with time to dwell, was an unbearable prospect. He parked himself on a bar stool and ordered a double brandy. When it arrived, he took a long sip, then sat staring into it. The gentle hand on his shoulder brought him out of his reverie. Turning, he found himself staring into the face of Vanessa fleet. He managed a smile and pulled out a stool for her.

"Penny for them." Her voice was soothing.

God, how can I unburden myself to her? Aloud, he said, "I'm sorry, Vanessa. I don't think I can talk about it. Please don't take offence. I want to. Really, I do."

"Whatever it is, it's eating you up. I've noticed you have seemed depressed for a long time now. It's Barbara, isn't it?"

Rob was startled. "How did you know?"

"I guess I'm observant. You haven't brought her with you this time, yet she has been a regular feature. I'm assuming you two are having difficulties."

Rob managed a smile. "You could say that. But it's not what I'm sure you're thinking." He paused, debating how far to go. Then he made his decision. After all, what could be worse than his current predicament?

And so, over cognacs, in a secluded corner of an empty bar, Captain Rob Bannister unburdened himself to the sympathetic ear of the resort manager, Vanessa Fleet. She listened without interruption, and when he concluded, she reached out for his hand. Vanessa sympathised with the captain, openly admiring his calmness at his predicament.

As he was talking, Rob realised the relief he was feeling. It was incredible. And to his amazement, Vanessa did not judge him or look embarrassed for him but gave the occasional encouraging nod.

He smiled, feeling happy. Yes, he still had a lot to deal with, decisions to make, but he felt he could do it now. It was good to think he had a choice with which direction his life could go in. He no longer felt trapped in his marriage.

And it was only then he realised he had no love for his wife anymore. He shook his head, taking a sip of cognac.

Staring into Vanessa's deep brown eyes, he made a decision. She had helped him more than he cared to say. He took a chance and, cupping her face in his hands, kissed her on the lips. Embracing the moment, she reached out and clasped his neck, pulling him in closer. It was as though they were the only people in the world. Finally, they broke apart, smiling at each other.

"I haven't felt this good in ages," he laughed. "And I can't thank you enough." He jumped up and put out his hand. "Come on, let's go for a midnight swim."

Vanessa's face showed surprise. She laughed. "Why not?"

Hand in hand, they headed out into the night.

Chapter 37

Back in her room, Jaime replayed the scene downstairs. She had watched as the captain disappeared to the bar area. She suspected Max would not make his move until later, if at all. There would still be a lot of activity in the communal areas, and he would not want to be seen moving the incriminating envelope from his room. And he would wait for the nightclub goers to return and go to bed, and so would she. That would be her cue to move.

Jaime changed into a dark pair of tracksuit pants and a hoodie, mainly for mosquito protection but also to quash the chill she was feeling despite the still-warm temperatures. She armed herself with a penlight and a cushion, cracked open her door and peered out. No sign of the revellers yet. It was half past midnight, and they were doing the shuttle tomorrow.

Surely they wouldn't stay out too much longer.

Settling back in a chair, Jaime continued to read, her ears tuned in to the silence. It was as the protagonists, Carmela and Ava, were rushing to put out a fire in Carmela's New Orleans courtyard apartment that Jaime heard a faint scuffle and giggle. Putting her book down she tiptoed to the door, stuck her ear to it, straining to hear any sounds.

There it was. The unmistakeable sound of a door clicking, more shuffles, and another door clicked. *That must be them,* she thought. No time to lose. She must get into position before Max left his room and saw her.

Mission underway, she crept out of her room, allowing the door to click shut. This was the point of no return. So far, she had engaged in conversations and unobtrusively watched the crew as she attempted to get her investigation under way, but now she was creeping around in the middle of the night. She would find it difficult to explain why she was hiding under a staircase armed with a torch, a cushion and a pair of latex gloves obtained from housekeeping earlier on.

Taking a deep breath to calm her nerves, she crept down the steps and slipped around and underneath the staircase, a hiding place she had scoped out earlier. The lobby was a ghost town. Shifting a few pot plants helped to keep her out of view. The hiding place gave her a partial view of the lifts, which could be interesting if there were other nocturnal activities.

Feeling better now she was in position, and positive she hadn't missed Max – she had been too quick leaving her room - she glanced at her watch. 1.05 am. Max wouldn't have attempted to move the parcel earlier; the chances of being seen were too high – and he would want to move it as far from his room as possible.

The envelope must contain something he did not want anyone else to know about, otherwise, why the cloak and dagger way of receiving it from Edwina Kershaw? And why that reaction to her suggestion of a room search? He was bothered by the idea, leading her to believe she was on the right track. Now further confirmation was needed to prove he was up to no good.

Sitting on the plump cushion, she realised it was a bit on the small side - a pillow might have been better. Bummer, she thought and chuckled to herself.

A small handful of people arrived in the lobby, going up the opposite stairs to the original wing or in one of the lifts, retiring to bed for the night. She tried to think of likely hiding places for the contents of the large envelope. Max couldn't risk anywhere inside, there were always people around, and the cleaners began first thing in the morning. She suspected somewhere outdoors where he could hide and retrieve it.

A thought struck her. Should he make an appearance, how was she going to follow him? He might leave the resort. Oh, bother. She hadn't thought this through. And what if he didn't have the envelope anymore? What if he had passed it on? And where was her flask of coffee and tray of doughnuts, like any organised surveillance expert would have? Feeling like the amateur she was, Jaime now doubted herself, all her earlier confidence ebbing away.

Time ticked. She was bored. Her bum was numb, and her back was hurting since she had nothing to lean on. What if Max hid the parcel over his balcony or somewhere clever in his room. She was considering calling it a night. Admitting defeat. It had gone quiet in general. The evening receptionist was nowhere in sight, although who could blame him if he was taking a nap?

The faint squeak of trainers on the steps above startled her. In fact, they had woken her up. *Damn.* She cursed herself for falling asleep on surveillance and crawled over to the edge of her hidey-hole, trying not to cry out in pain (her rear had also been to sleep). She was rewarded by the retreating figure of Max holding a carrier bag. *Yes*, she mouthed, fist-pumping the air. Maybe she wasn't such an idiot after all. She might be cut out to be a detective. Okay, enough self-congratulating.

Checking her watch, she was startled to see it was 1.40 am. She had only been waiting for thirty-five minutes. How did real detectives do it for hours on end?

Max was headed for the main entrance out towards the front driveway. The reception desk was still empty, and there was the faint sound of snoring coming from the back office. As soon as he was out of sight, Jaime double-checked the coast was clear and proceeded towards the front entrance, her heart hammering. She tried to keep close to the wall, for some reason thinking if Max returned, she could maybe blend into it.

Jaime peeked around the side door and into the driveway, her heart sank. Where had he gone? She'd lost him. *Bugger.* What an absolute waste of time and effort.

Reluctant to give up, she crept out of the door and towards the first flower bed, crouched, lifting her head to scan further down the drive. It was dark except for the areas that contained an uplighter, which materialised at the base of every palm tree. Even the stars seemed to have dulled. Maybe that storm was brewing after all.

Considering switching on her torch, she rejected the idea as foolish. Instead, she stared intently into the blackness, trying to make out any movement. She almost missed the tiny glow of torchlight bobbing around in the distance. He must be searching for a good spot, she thought. Watching the faint glow from the light, she assumed that Max was checking every inch of the front courtyard, then he was in the parking area, then back towards the flower beds that curved around the opening.

He was unsure, she decided. Jaime resorted to sitting on the concrete, her legs stretched out in front of her as she stared at the bobbing light. She had been there so long she feared getting cramp.

Then, there he was. Right in front of her. After all his scouring of the hotel grounds, he had decided to come all the way back towards the main doors. Why couldn't he have decided half an hour ago?

Hardly daring to breathe, she felt sure he must be able to see her. When her eyes adjusted to the dark, Jaime could make out his figure, peering down, scooping soil with his hands to make a hole for his waterproof bag, no doubt. She had no choice but to wait, feeling conspicuous.

147

After what felt like an age, he finished digging. Jaime wondered how deep he had gone. The carrier bag rustled as he placed it into the hole and started refilling it.

The snuffling noise next to her nearly finished her off. Two little paws scratched at her legs in excitement at the nocturnal activities. She reached over and stroked the back of Basil's head in a soothing manner. *I shouldn't be surprised he's here*, she thought. *I mentioned my plan.* The two of them hovered there in the dark, waiting for the activity taking place right before them to stop. Basil managed to contain his enthusiasm, somehow knowing not to growl or bark at the person who was close by. Doggy instinct, she decided. It must be the canine equivalent of female intuition.

Finally, Max was done patting the soil down. He brushed it off his hands and made his way back towards the lobby, passing perilously close to the pair.

After waiting for a few more moments, Jaime exhaled. What a relief to evade being caught. And what an absolute thrill. Basil sensed her relief but mistook it for playtime.

"Shush. We're still on surveillance," she whispered towards the direction of the scratching sounds. Basil plonked himself on the ground with a grunt.

Checking he was heading back to his room, Jaime pulled herself into a crouching position and crawled towards the doors in time to see Max turning onto the staircase. Using the light spilling out from the lobby, Jaime noted it was 2.30 am. Max had taken close to an hour to hide his parcel. She couldn't wait to check what was in it.

After what felt like an eternity of checking in case he came back – which amounted to twenty minutes, she crawled around to the other side of the flower bed, four little paws right behind. Pulling on the latex gloves, she found a stone on the ground to scoop away at the disturbed earth. Desperate for something to do after being forced to lie in silence for ages, Basil jumped onto the bed of soil and frantically took over the digging, showering Jaime with dry earth. She stifled a giggle and turned her head away from the flying soil, spotting some car headlights.

"Basil. Shush," she whispered to the dog, but to no avail. Basil was engaged in his job, and nothing was going to stop him. Jaime ducked as low as she could as the car pulled over somewhere short of the entrance. Strange, she thought. What's wrong with right outside the door? She heard the click of the car door opening and the sound of a low voice.

"Thanks again, Pumpkin. It's been a perfect evening."

Jaime could not hear 'Pumpkin's' reply, but whatever it was, it prompted the response,

"Sure, no problem. Email the agency, and they'll book you in." And then, "Oh, you're generous. You know you don't have to. They do pay me, you know. But, well, thanks anyway."

The sound of clicking heels as 'Pumpkin's' escort for the evening trotted past the pair. Basil paused in his quest to observe the passer-by as Jaime marvelled at the heels: at least four inches. She looked up in time to catch the woman's profile as the light caught her face. Recognition flooded through her. It was the Carfax girl. What on earth was she doing?

However, there was no time for contemplating this, as Basil's efforts had produced a faint rustling sound. She patted him on the back to get him to cease digging, however, this didn't work.

"Stop. Enough," Jaime hissed, but still the legs kept going. The only way to stop him was by lifting him up, legs still digging in mid-air, and placing him on the ground. His doggy frown was adorable. Ignoring this, Jaime retrieved the bag, ducked as low as she could behind the flower bed wall and opened the package right there.

Head-to-head with the inquisitive dog, they peered inside at the envelope she had seen Max with earlier in the lobby. Pulling at the flap, it peeled open to reveal another plastic bag. This one was sealed with clear tape that had to be prised open even more carefully. It was impossible not to tear it. She took her torch and strained to make out the contents.

Lots of tightly wrapped parcels of what she guessed to be marijuana, packed together in blocks. Her breathing became even more harsh and panicky. Basil licked her cheek but was disinterested in the contents as it was nothing he could eat. It could explain Max's odd, withdrawn behaviour if indeed he was using drugs although, she thought, there was far too much here for personal consumption. Jaime had a vision of Cagney and Lacey flying out of a nearby bush, guns drawn, shouting at her to get down.

She needed to get out of here. Rewrapping it and replacing it as she had found it, she used her torch to locate and scrape away any fly-away soil that had been tossed around. Basil cocked an eyebrow. Human beings were odd creatures sometimes, he was no doubt thinking.

Thanking him for his timely assistance and support, promising to meet tomorrow with his sirloin steak, Jaime said goodbye to the dog and tiptoed her way back inside, aware she had to run the gauntlet of the lobby once more.

It was not until she was back in the safety of her own private space she started to breathe normally, her thoughts returning to the main event of the night.

Max, what have you gotten yourself into? And what does it have to do with the murder of councillor Gregory Dickens?

Chapter 38

Sliding open the heavy glass door, the freezing wind smacked her full-on in the face. Although gasping for breath, she was filled with energy. It was well after midnight; the darkness was pierced with light from the stars. Fastening the expedition jacket tightly around her, she grabbed his hand and pulled him out onto the deck, her eyes darting around, checking for any other signs of life. No one in sight at this unsociable hour. Pulling on the reluctant hand, she remembered their earlier conversation over dinner: her gentle persuasion it would be exciting; his reproving look, the look she had been on the receiving end of more and more lately. Battling the ferocious gusts, they held onto the handrail: slowly, carefully, making their way to the stern. She wanted to feel the full force of nature, and what better place than the Arctic Ocean? She had always felt the allure of remote locations, loving the idea you were the only person around for miles.

The spotlights shining from the MS Fram highlighted large chunks of ice floating in the well-below freezing water. Climbing towards the forward deck, a rope barrier barred their way, put in place due to the weather conditions. The crew were rigid in their rules concerning the safety of passengers, and she knew she was bringing them into forbidden territory.

He followed, trying, she knew, not to be the party pooper. Feeling invincible, she climbed over the rope. Ken followed. Still grasping the handrail, they inched forward, the hood of her jacket blowing into her face, blocking her view. Yanking it away from her eyes, she led them to the limits of the ship whereupon she let go of the rail and held her face up to the elements. Turning to her husband of one year, she studied his face, the light from the night sky giving his normally tanned skin a greyish hue: the green eyes appraised her, his square, determined jaw firmly set. She gestured for him to stand beside her, to follow what she was doing.

Marriage to Ken had been exciting at first: different. Then she had felt trapped, as bit by bit, she was swallowed by his overbearing, dominant personality, his increasingly jealous nature and cutting remarks. She turned away from the fierce wind, her foot slipping on the wooden decking of the ship, her heart skipping a beat as she reached out to grab the low rail. Smiling at the irony - this was exactly why the crew had barred this section off. Swivelling her head in Ken's direction, knowing he would be wanting to go back in, she saw he had turned away from her, about to step down from the small platform they were occupying. Yet another extreme gust of wind whacked them, this time from behind. Ken was not holding on as he negotiated the step. His attention was caught in his desire to get away from the dangerous situation. The situation she had put him in.

It was sometime later she forced herself to look down. Down into the deep, dark depths below...

Beep. Beep. Beep. Jaime's eyes opened. Her hand reached out for her phone, and she fumbled to silence the obnoxious sound. 5.45 flashed on the screen, and she moaned. How on earth was she going to get through today's shuttle to St Lucia on a few hours' sleep? At least it was a short service, although she knew from experience the passengers would still be demanding.

Dragging herself to the bathroom, she reached in and switched on the shower - whilst it was heating, she filled the coffee machine with water and freshly ground beans. A hot shower and a strong coffee should do the trick. Recalling her dream, she stared at her reflection in the mirror. For the second night in a row, that dream. That memory of her last night with Ken. So real. So accurate. Why now?

As the scalding water ran over her body, Jaime made a determined effort to cast aside her nightmare. Pondering the discovery of the previous night, she knew she had to inform the authorities, but she didn't fancy revealing to Cagney and Lacey she had been out most of the night, spying on Max. Somehow, it made her feel guilty, that she was in the wrong. The idea of an anonymous telephone call popped into her head. Of course, she wouldn't do it herself, she didn't think she'd be able to pull it off. Her accent was easy to identify, and she was no good at changing it. Henry. Yes, he was a possibility. She would call upon Henry to help her out with this. He would want to know there were drugs on the premises: also, one of his receptionists appeared to be involved. Okay, she needed to get a move on. She would have time to fill him in before the bus departed.

Twenty minutes later, Jaime was dressed, hair tied back, and minimal make-up applied. She had consumed two cups of coffee and was yanking her wheelie bag out of the self-closing door, trying not to let it slam. Turning towards the lift, a movement caught her eye. She glimpsed Tony and Mario leaving from the same room, some distance down the hall. Her first thought was they were both early too. Perhaps they wanted to grab some breakfast before they left the hotel.

Her second thought was much more interesting. They were sharing a room. Of course they were. That's what couples who flew together did. They were always allocated individual rooms, as was standard procedure, but most would

153

want to share, leaving the other room unused. What was interesting to Jaime was it meant they would have a spare key. One they didn't need. They could have lost it. Someone could have found it, used it to access the private beach with the councillor. Did they know they'd lost it? Perhaps they didn't want to admit it, as it could be deemed suspicious. Perhaps they had given it to someone else to allow them access to the beach, so they could kill the councillor. Although that would be a silly idea as it put all the crew under the spotlight.

Tottering into the lift, she pressed the button for reception, her mind racing. Should she ask them straight out if they still had the key? Or tread more carefully? Perhaps she oughtn't to alert them, give them a chance to lie about still having it.

Reaching the lobby, the question of the whereabouts of the extra key would have to wait. There was the more pressing issue of the anonymous phone call. She headed off towards Henry's office. Approaching, she could hear his voice through the open door, although she couldn't make out what he was saying. Tapping on it, she waited.

"Hello." Henry's voice. "Come in."

Jaime peeked around the door, expecting someone else to be in the room. However, Henry sat alone at his desk, phone in hand, a huge smile spreading across his face.

"Morning. How are you? Not too busy, I hope."

"Things get going pretty early in the hotel business," he replied. "But not too busy to see you. Come in, sit down."

Jaime closed the door behind her, causing Henry to raise his eyebrows.

"I need to speak to you in confidence. But I don't have much time. The bus for the airport departs in about fifteen minutes."

"Okay. I'm all ears." He leant forward, giving her his full attention.

Jaime proceeded to tell him what she had witnessed the previous day, the plan she had put into action and her nocturnal activities. Henry's eyes grew wide. Once she had finished, he put his hands to his temples and rubbed them in a circular motion.

"I can't believe you put yourself in the path of danger. Why didn't you tell me what you were doing? I would have helped."

"I didn't think my plan would work, and I would have felt daft dragging you along to witness my potentially monumental mistake."

"Well, as it turns out, you were right. And now we have drugs buried on our hotel grounds. This isn't good. Does it somehow link to the murder?"

"I'm not sure how or if it links, but there could be a connection. Perhaps Dickens was involved somehow. Or perhaps he found out about it and had to be silenced."

"Well, either way, those drugs need to be found by the right people and removed, and Max arrested along with anyone else involved."

"Well, your receptionist certainly is."

Henry looked pained. "She's been with us for several years. Christ, how long has this been going on?"

"Can you make an anonymous call to the detectives? Point them in the direction of the drugs and those involved? I can't tell them I was interfering. They'll arrest me."

Henry nodded. "Yes, it's the best plan. I don't want you getting into trouble over this. I'll do it."

Jaime was grateful.

"I'll wait until you have left, though, when you're on the bus, to keep you out of the picture."

"Perfect plan. And thank you for agreeing to help."

"Those drugs need removing, and this… operation needs stopping."

Jaime nodded and stood. "I'd better go."

"Right. It's fortunate about the CCTV, I must say."

155

Jaime stopped mid-stride, frozen to the spot. Turning her head slowly to look at Henry, she opened her mouth to speak, but no words came out.

"Jesus, don't tell me you hadn't thought about the CCTV before your drug recovery operation?" Henry was dumbfounded.

Leaning on the handle of her wheelie bag for support, Jaime managed, "Of course I did. I know there's no CCTV in the lobby. That would be amateurish if I hadn't checked that first."

Looking at her face, Henry nodded. "Okay then. And there I was thinking this is your first time doing something like this."

"It is, obviously. But I'm not a total moron." She looked indignant and continued to the door. "Thanks again for your help," she added.

"No problem, Jaime. Enjoy the shuttle."

As she was reaching for the door handle, eager to leave the office, Henry called out, "Just for future reference, there's CCTV in the lobby and most of the grounds, but since it's being updated, it's currently out of action. But that's just between you and me."

Pulling open the door, Jaime mumbled, "Right. Thanks again."

Wishing the ground would swallow her up, she clattered down the hall to carry out phase two of the day's plan.

Chapter 39

The crew gathered in the lobby, standing around their wheelie bags, waiting to leave. Captain Rob Bannister was flustered, however, and in a conflab with Kate and Tony. Jaime stood next to Mario, nudging his arm.

"What's he worked up about?"

Mario replied without taking his gaze off the little scene in front of him. "Jean's a no-show. Not answering her phone, not responding to the hammering on her door. They're getting a skeleton key from the manager. She lives on site."

"Crikey. I wouldn't want to be that person." Jaime shivered at the thought of Jean's wrath upon being invaded in the privacy of her room.

Tony's voice came over the gentle din of the lobby. "Let's get ourselves onto the bus, guys. Rob will let us know what's happening soon enough."

The crew obediently filed out into the overcast, cloudy day. There was not a glimpse of sun anywhere. It wasn't the first time someone had been a no-show for a shuttle, in Jaime's experience. They were usually hung over or had spent the night away from the hotel, so hadn't gotten their wake-up call. It landed you in serious trouble. Jaime could not recall a cabin service director ever not showing up for a flight, though. She wondered what the problem could be - a vague feeling of apprehension settling over her.

Jaime ensured she was at the back of the line, enabling her to take the seat right at the front, closest to Thomas, the driver. She needed to pick his brain on the journey to the airport. Thomas himself was finishing loading the last bag into his trailer: he headed over to where Rob was standing. Jaime watched the scene and noted Rob's head shaking in resignation. They both walked towards the bus, and Thomas climbed into the driver's seat as Rob climbed aboard and stood at the front of the aisle.

"As you are aware," he began, "We are having a problem locating our cabin service director. She does not appear to be in her room, nor is she responding to calls on her mobile phone. This is odd." Rob paused, he seemed to be choosing his next words carefully. "In the interest of remaining professional, we will be heading to the airport without Jean. We cannot afford for the plane to be delayed by even a second. Our passengers are used to punctuality. Tony will be stepping up and performing a dual role today, first-class purser as well as cabin service director. We will all need to take some slack wherever we can."

Jaime turned her gaze to note Karen's reaction to Tony's temporary promotion. By rights, she should be the next in line to step into Jean's shoes. Karen, however, was gazing out the window, unaffected by what was going on around her. She looked worse than the day before, with dark shadows under her eyes. Jaime wondered if she had been asked to step up and had refused or had just been by-passed.

"Where can she be?" asked Kate. "She was out with us at the club, and we all came back together. She went to the bar saying she needed a nightcap. Perhaps we should have gone with her?" Kate was directing this comment at Tony and Mario.

Tony bristled. "Yes, we all arrived safely back in a taxi and parted ways in the lobby. We didn't know it was required of us to chaperone her, Kate."

"Oh, I didn't mean —"

"You never do, do you? Why don't we focus on the job in hand and let the hotel staff and the police continue their

158

search for Jean? That okay with everyone?" Tony's tone suggested anything other than silent assent would be unacceptable.

A hush fell over the group. Captain Rob slid into an empty seat, and Thomas took his cue to get moving.

It was about ten minutes into the journey before anyone dared to speak to each other. It was obvious Tony's mood had scared the group into silence. Mario was asking Karen something about Birmingham. Gabi joined in, and Rob leaned over towards Kate to discuss the pre-flight checks. The volume increased until it reached a pitch Jaime was comfortable with to begin the next stage of her morning plan, not wanting to be overheard.

"Can I ask you a question, Thomas?" she asked the bus driver, aware he was concentrating on his driving and the road ahead, the bus attack of a few days ago possibly at the forefront of his mind.

"Anything you like. Fire away."

"Well, it's about a place called 'Choices'. I came across a business card with it written on, and I'm desperate to know what type of business it is." Jaime had not had a chance to dial the number on the card since it came into her possession later last night, and it still being so early in the morning.

Thomas creased his brow and was silent for a few moments. "Nothing is springing to mind. I can hazard a guess or two if it helps."

Jaime nodded. "Yes, please."

"Well, there's the possibility it could be something to do with higher education. That strikes me as the most obvious. Perhaps something to do with a college. I could ask my daughter."

"That would be good. I was thinking about some sort of financial company, maybe," she offered.

"Yes. Yes, could be. Accounting of some kind or a business advisor. To be honest, it's quite open to many possibilities. Tell you what I'll do. As well as asking my Vicky,

I'll see what the wife has to say. She'll have more idea than me. Tisher pays a lot more attention to what goes on around the island than I do. She has a wide network of friends she can probe."

"Fantastic. Thanks so much, Thomas."

"I'll try and have some information for when I collect you guys later."

Jaime sat back in her seat and spent the rest of the bumpy journey pondering how she could have been so stupid as to not check the lobby area for cameras. It was fortuitous that they were out of action. Then again, had they been working, surely Cagney and Lacey would have seen who was with Dickens when he accessed the beach.

Sneaking a glance over at Max, she noticed his, tired face. She felt sorry for what was going to happen upon their return. Then she remembered the amount of drugs in the parcel – too much for personal use. And they could have a connection to Dickens and his murder. No, she shouldn't feel any sympathy towards this man. He had chosen his path and it was leading him down a treacherous route.

Chapter 40

"I could eat twenty of these, they're so damn small," Jaime complained to Mario as the shuttle got under way. She waved a tiny packet of sour cream pretzels in his face.

"I believe you." He raised an eyebrow. "Remember that buffet in New York? Fourth of July? I've never seen anyone go back so many times and clear each plateful."

"I love a roast dinner, and their baked cheesecake is to die for." She attempted to defend herself whilst emptying the packet of pretzels into her mouth.

"I beg to differ. Give me a spicy arrabbiata any time. Think yourself lucky you have a good metabolism, or this plane would no longer be airborne."

His teasing made her laugh as Jaime headed towards what seemed like the millionth call bell. The plane had just taken off, and the crew were trying their best to set up the bar trolleys and commence the service. Across the other side of the galley, Gabi and Max were about ready to head out, but they had an extra pair of hands as Karen had decided to assist them. Jaime wasn't surprised Karen was avoiding her after their exchange the day before.

As she approached row twenty-eight of the sky-class cabin, the current offending call bell ringers, Jaime heard what she guessed was a Texan drawl.

"I saw him. It was soon after take-off, the captain was telling us we were going over central London. He was sitting

161

on his balcony with a cup of tea. I could see the corgi on his lap a mile away."

"Well, you'd need to be able to spot it from further away than that, considering how high we were flying at the time," came the tart reply. The first lady was glaring over at her companion, not liking to be contradicted. They noticed Jaime standing there, a smile fixed on her face. Jaime was wondering how long this argument must have been going on for. The plane had left Heathrow over ten hours ago.

"How can I help you, ladies?"

"Well, Thelma and me have decided to treat ourselves to two large gin and tonics." The woman smiled at Jaime.

"Of course. We are attempting to get out into the cabin and commence a drinks service."

The two women stared at her, and Jaime had to remember the DebonAir way. The customers had paid more than the average fare to travel with the airline, they must be well looked after.

Jaime sighed. "Ice and a slice?"

The women brightened. "Yes ma'am, and plenty of ice. We know how you Brits like to hang on to it. Can you believe when we were in one of your cute little pubs overlooking Hyde Park, we ordered -"

But she was cut off by her companion, who was a stickler for details. "Oh no, nuh huh, not Hyde Park, the other big one, you know..."

As she stood there, Jaime heard a succession of at least another five call bells dinging in the galley.

"Two large gins, coming up, with a *ton* of ice." She headed off back to the relative safety of the galley, cursing the daytime Caribbean shuttles.

She had almost reached the curtain when a hand stretched out and tugged on her skirt. Her stride faltered, and she paused for the briefest of moments to steady her temper at this breach of her personal space. Turning, she looked down

162

at a young woman with a shiny bronzed face. "How can I help?"

"I need a red wine," the woman stated.

"Of course you do," Jaime murmured.

"Excuse me?" the overly made-up woman asked with more than a hint of suspicion.

"I said, of course, right away." Jaime lied.

The woman still eyeballed her, and Jaime yanked back the curtain leaping through, almost knocking over Mario. He managed to hold onto the glass of tomato juice he was pouring without spilling any over his pristine, white shirt.

"Whoa, there, Jaime. What's the rush?" A lock of dark, wavy hair fell over his smooth, olive skin.

Jaime took a deep breath. "Lord, give me strength. Bloody Thelma and Louise out there must have knocked back a litre of gin on the first leg. We need to get out there and commence the bar service before this gets out of hand. The others have already started."

"You know it's the British, right?" Mario laughed as he said it. "We Italians sit back, relax and sleep."

"We mainly have British people on our flights, so not a fair comment. But since we're on the subject, you Italians do like to comment on the food. I don't know why you ever leave home. Nothing's ever as good as your mama does it." Teasing Mario was always good fun, he took it well and could dish it out.

Her mind drifted back to the snippet of conversation she and Henry had overheard the day before, between Tony and Mario on the beach. She liked the pair. She had flown with them on quite a few occasions over the years and had always found them fun. But how well did she really know them? Tony could be quick to flare on occasion, but it didn't last long, and Mario seemed to bring out the best in him. Their conversation was interrupted by yet another 'ding' and the pair, by silent consent, dutifully got on with the task of setting up the trolley and pushing it to the top of the cabin.

The going was slow as they made their way along the rows of seats, trying to catch Max and Gabi, who were flying along. Jaime reached the trio of unaccompanied minors, those travelling without any adults, but would be met by a parent or guardian at the other end. It came under Jaime's remit to take care of them on the shuttle and hand them over to the airline 'nanny' in St Lucia. They were seated together in a row of three, easier for her to watch over. All had their heads buried in some form of technology, engrossed in a film or game. *Well, at least it stops them from bothering me,* she thought.

In what felt like hours, but in fact, was twenty-five minutes, Jaime and Mario reached the galley with their depleted bar trolley, as Gabi and Max were finishing the penultimate row on their side. Not bad, she thought, considering they'd had Karen running back and forth for them and had been ahead. Now began the task of restocking the mobile bar, ready for the onslaught of bells that would begin chiming again as people finished their drinks.

Three call bells later, Jaime headed back towards the galley, accidentally kicking a shoe that had been removed and left sticking out into the narrow aisle. *Bugger.* Managing not to stumble, she watched as the shoe flew away from her and came to a stop next to a dosing middle-aged man. Stepping back into the galley, she placed her tray on the counter and headed back out to return the shoe, noticing with amusement Mario had been waylaid by Thelma and Louise, no doubt 'treating' themselves to another drink. She reached the shoe, stretched out her foot, and, using her toe, slid it back along the aisle. It was a man's loafer, expensive, if not a little worn. Approaching the area she thought it had originated from, she paused, noticing it was occupied by a row of females, probably a mother and two daughters. *Oh, that can't be right,* she thought. Crouching, trying not to stick her backside in some unfortunate soul's face, she searched for the partner of

164

the offending shoe. *Hmm…* She frowned. *Where has it come from? It must be from around this section.* Standing, she studied the surrounding passengers for a likely candidate. Failing to work out who the shoe belonged to, she kicked the loafer under the nearest seat (that happened to belong to an elderly lady) and scurried back towards the galley.

Mario appeared close behind her, swearing under his breath in Italian.

"Don't tell me. Two large G&Ts?" Jaime guessed.

"Worse. Two large G&T's, and they're heading this way to drink them. With me." Mario grimaced.

Jaime's peel of laughter was louder than she intended. "Well, I wish I could help you, but I must head to the front and grab the trash cart. Sorry."

"Hurry up."

Finding the entire situation hilarious, Jaime headed forward, deciding to get herself a tasty snack whilst there. The food in first-class was amazing, and she had no intention of rushing back. Let Mario suffer for a while. That would serve him right for all his teasing, she chuckled.

Tony, sipping from a porcelain cup, looking for all the world like a first-class passenger himself, glanced up.

"Hiya," he drawled. "How's it going back in the zoo?"

"Oh, dandy," Jaime quipped. "Your other half is about to be assaulted by Thelma and Louise. He's panicking."

"Bless him," replied Tony, grinning. "Well, I must attend to my passengers, and I have the paperwork to do, thanks to our missing CSD."

"Anyhow," she remembered the main reason for her visit, "I need the rubbish bin, and I'm famished."

"Help yourself. There are some prawns and scallops and the cheese board."

The first-class passengers were treated to yet more food, even though the shuttle was a mere one hour and five minutes. Jaime busied herself, getting a 'light' snack together while Tony filled her in on the celebrity homes in his magazine (clearly not as busy as he claimed). His eyes lit up as he discussed the style choices of the rich and famous. Jaime desperately wanted to know what he and Mario were up to on this trip, but there was no time to probe him. She rested a tray of goodies on top of the trolley for her colleagues, thanked Tony and headed back down the aircraft.

Within a stone's throw of the galley, the trolley stopped dead, almost causing her to barrel into it and the tray to fly like a missile towards an unsuspecting passenger. Jaime's quick reaction stopped a potential decapitation. After their drinks, most were napping or trying to, unaware of her predicament. Regaining her composure, she tried to shove the trolley, but it refused to move forward, instead pulling to the side. The last thing Jaime wanted to do was bang into a passenger's chair. She felt irritated and bent to examine the wheels.

"Bloody hell," she mouthed. Something was wrapped around the front, right wheel. It looked a bit like a cat. Staring at it, she tried to make out what it could be. Stumped, she stood upright and reached over towards the passenger's seat on her right and pressed the call bell five times in succession in a desperate bid to get Mario's attention from the galley.

Studying the gap between the side of the cart and the armrest of the nearest passenger chair, Jaime's years of experience told her not to attempt to squeeze through. The curtain yanked back, and Mario's frowning face popped out. When he saw it was Jaime who had rang the bell, his eyebrows creased into a questioning look. Jaime, not wanting to draw attention to herself, beckoned him. He pointed at his watch and theatrically tapped it with his finger, no doubt to make a point about the length of time she had been gone. However, he relented and walked towards her as she was pointing to the wheel of her trolley, mouthing the words *Help. Something's stuck.*

Upon reaching her, Mario crouched. He tugged at the offending item. Jaime tried her best to hold onto the trolley and the goodies perched on top. After what felt like an epic battle, Mario arose from his squat, victorious, holding between his forefinger and thumb what looked like a head. She stifled a scream. Mario wiggled the object closer to her, leaning over the trolley. Jaime realised it was not a whole head but part of a head. Someone's hairpiece, in fact. The jet-black curly mass, dancing in front of her, conjured the image of someone relaxing, oblivious to the fact they were without their hair.

Giggling, she heard a grunt coming from in front of her and saw Mario was barely able to contain himself either. As quickly as they could, Mario at one end, guiding, and Jaime at the other, pushing, they shoved the trolley back to the galley and drew the curtain, both collapsing into uncontrollable laughter, made all the worse by trying to be quiet. Thelma and Louise were standing in the galley, drinks in hand, staring at the two as they doubled over. Not knowing quite what to make of it, the two elderly passengers decided the best thing to do was exit and return to their seats straightaway, assuming the flight attendants had gone quite mad.

Gabi, who was tidying the galley, paused. "What's with you two?" she asked. "Share the joke. I've had no conversation all flight with Max."

All Mario could do in response was waft the wig in her direction. Karen returned to the galley and eyed the laughing pair.

"We need to clear the cabin, please, guys. We don't have long." Her tone was sharp.

Jaime and Mario took a few deep breaths, managing to control themselves.

"What the hell are we supposed to do with it?" Mario asked as Karen flounced out of the galley.

"Throw it in the trash," answered Gabi.

"We need to find the person sitting there with no hair and plonk it back on their head." This set them off giggling again.

167

Jaime stood and cracked open the curtain, scanning for any sign of a bald head. The seat backs were too high for this to be helpful. They agreed the only option would be to walk back up the aisle and 'drop' the wig back in roughly the same area they thought it had come from and hope the owner would be able to retrieve it. Mario volunteered. Jaime peeked around the curtain to give Mario some indication of where to put it.

Upon reaching row thirty-one, Mario stooped as though he were retrieving some litter. When he stood, his hands were empty. He proceeded forward, no doubt to see his partner and fill him in on 'wig gate'. Jaime retreated into the galley, still grinning. Moments like these reminded her why she did this job nine years later, despite the unsociable hours and demanding workload. Although the pay, great shopping and beaches helped.

Glancing at her watch, she realised with a start it was time for the captain's landing announcement. Alongside Gabi and Max, they had the bar trolleys collapsed and put away and the galley secured for landing, leaving just enough time to sample some first-class food.

Chapter 41

Still in the party mood as the plane touched down on the island of St Lucia, the passengers cheered the smooth landing. Jaime thought it was like breaking into applause on a bus every time the driver successfully negotiated a bus stop. Making her way to door one to arrange the handover of her unaccompanied minors, she surveyed the left side of the aircraft: just about every person began to stand in the aisle, attempting to grab their bags from overhead lockers. There was the usual mayhem as most ignored the 'fasten seat belt' signs that were still illuminated. Her sadistic side prayed for some oversized wheelie bag to drop onto some idiot's head. One day, she thought, it's going to happen.

Stepping out onto the top of the steps, she saw the 'nanny' for her UMs. Thank goodness. The ground crew scurried around like ants preparing for the deluge of passengers. Marvelling at the colourful houses lining the runway, she couldn't help but feel they were too close for comfort. Small children, playing in their yards, had paused to watch the aircraft landing. This was not a daily flight; in fact, it was scheduled for three times a week, quite a major event, in fact.

"Hello, hi there," yelled Jaime across the tarmac, perhaps a little too enthusiastically. The woman, dressed in the uniform of the airport ground staff waved back, perhaps a little less enthusiastically, and headed in Jaime's direction, paperwork in hand. "How are you?" Jaime continued, not giving the woman a chance to answer. "Good to see you. I have…" Jaime listed the names, matched them to the paperwork, thanked the woman saying a hasty goodbye to the already squabbling UMs and beat a hasty retreat. *Yippee,* she cheered to herself.

"What's made you smile? Share the joke." Tony Hayward had appeared by her side.

"Just lost some baggage," she quipped.

Tony picked up the handset that was nestled between the crew seats and proceeded to make an announcement. "Ladies and Gentlemen, a request from the local authority, please can you all have your passports in your hands as you disembark the aircraft, thank you." More pandemonium in the aisles as everyone tried to open their bags and locate their passports. "Please now disembark the aircraft through the front door. Once again, thank you for choosing DebonAir."

It was Tony's role to stand at door one and say the goodbyes along with the CSD. However, in her absence and in the spirit of teamwork (and because she was stuck by the door), Jaime assisted him in the not-too-small task. Passengers flooded by, eager to disembark and begin their holiday.

"Goodbye, goodbye, thank you, thanks. Have a good trip. Bye bye." Jaime and Tony tried to mix it up, to avoid the monotony. As those from the back of the aircraft made it to the door, Jaime could not help but notice one elderly gentleman, his wife behind him, beaming at her as he approached the exit.

"Thank you, missy. Lovely flight." He grabbed her hand.

Jaime was at a loss for words. Her mouth open, she stared at the man. Not because he had grabbed her hand. No. What had caught her attention and rendered her momentarily speechless was his wonky mass of jet black, curly hair.

Fifteen minutes later and the aircraft resembled a ghost town, albeit a wrecked ghost town. Jaime reached into the overhead locker for her wheelie bag and placing it on the ground, unzipped it to retrieve her heels. Slipping them on, she noticed Karen emerge from the rear toilet, make-up replenished, bright red lipstick glistening. Jaime wasn't going that far with her make-up, she felt quite happy with her dab of peach lip gloss, but she noted Karen was looking more like her usual self.

Chapter 42

In a small room in the heart of the town hall, seven people were gathered around an oval table. This morning, the lights were switched on in a bid to cheer the darkened room and allow those present to read their notes. Angela Montgomery sat at the head of the table, a sheaf of papers in front of her and called the meeting to order. The conversation died down, coffee cups put back in their saucers, and six heads turned towards her.

One chair remained vacant, and all present were studiously ignoring it.

"Number one on our agenda today, as you can see from the list in front of you, is the funeral of our colleague Gregory Dickens. We will be holding a memorial service on Friday to honour his work, and I need people to come forward with a few prepared words and speak."

There was a general murmur around the room, but nobody spoke up.

Angela held up her hand. "Come and speak to me any time today if you can do it." *It will be a bloody miracle if anyone offers to stand and say some good words on the councillor's behalf,* she thought to herself. Oh well, she would have to bully them into it.

"Item number two. It's an appeal on the decision to reject planning permission to build on lot numbers 2968 and 2969 by the owners Haywood and Vanetti. Previously rejected

172

because of its proximity to the ocean front and the effect it may have on surrounding property prices." *A good few of which are owned by the Dickens family,* she thought. "Any questions from the floor before we vote?" She looked around at the bored faces. There were still another fifteen items on the agenda. "All those in favour of the appeal, raise your hand."

All hands rose, including her own. *Well, that was easier than last time*, she thought, *when bloody Dickens manipulated some of them into opposing. He could be such a bully. Things will run a lot smoother with him out of the way.*

"All in favour, motion carried. Now, item number three - the acquisition of land by a foreign investor. Councillor Rodriguez, I believe you wanted to say a few words on this subject?"

In a corner of the room, a young woman typed away on a laptop, recording each word said. She was thinking how boring her job now was without the presence of Greggie. He always used to give her a wink, brush past her leg or put an arm around her when it wasn't necessary. She sighed, shrugged and carried on typing.

"On hold for now. Let's move on to item number four," called Angela as she signalled to the girl to bring her more coffee.

Sheltering under the canopy of a local café, Caleb Carfax glanced across to the front doors of the grand old town hall for what seemed like the hundredth time that morning. They would have to take a break soon. These government officials were not known for over doing it. His stomach felt queasy. So much depended on this. He still couldn't believe that bastard Dickens had shafted him. Every bloody year they came to this bloody island so Carol could spend time with her pompous, stuck-up pal from uni. All the times he had had to sit and endure meals, all four of them, playing like the perfect couples. And the one time he had asked a small favour of that slimy bastard, this is what happened. He thought back to the first evening.

"Carfax. Long-time no-see. Glad you're all back on the island. Where are they? On the cocktails already? Well, I guess I'll not see Maggie until the morning." He'd been ecstatic about that, thought Caleb. And it was obvious why. God only knew why they stayed married.

He thought of his own marriage, and there was a stab of guilt, an uncomfortable feeling adding to the one he already had. He brushed it aside. He had been the one to bring up the deal. Dickens had enjoyed toying with him, making him wait. God how he'd hated having to ask this man for a favour.

"Bad news, Carfax. Couldn't get enough support. I tried. I mean, what are friends for? Not to say you can't try again in a few years, right? Quick beer? I have an appointment soon, but I've time for one with an old buddy."

Caleb remembered the rage that had built from within. He had put himself out there, asked a man he detested for a favour, all to help a company he had been with for years, all to further a career he didn't care about, all to keep his kids in a posh, over-privileged school. All to be dismissed by this prick. All to be made okay with a 'quick beer'.

Taking a sharp intake of breath, he brought himself back to the present, trying to focus on moving forward.

The town hall doors swung open, and a small, dark-haired ferret of a man peered out. Caleb raised a hand. His new contact wasn't much to look at. *Let's hope there's more to him than reaches the eye,* he thought.

The man walked across the square with quick little steps and took a seat at the table.

"Re-presented again, no questions, no issues, on hold for the usual eight weeks. Can't see any objections arising. You should be fine this time." The man waited.

Caleb knew this was good news. The best he could have hoped for, given the situation. Hopefully, he could span it out back at work and still be the hero.

"Okay, great," he replied. "Second half will be transferred when the decision is final."

"Satisfactory." With a curt nod, the man rose and headed back to the offices.

Caleb decided he liked him. Efficient, no extraneous conversation. No messing around. Why on earth had he gone to Dickens in the first place? A silly move.

His mind wandered back to that first night once again. Snatches of what he had said popped into his head. Who knew how much alcohol he had consumed? *No more mistakes now,* he thought. *I appear to have gotten away with this one. No more mistakes.*

Chapter 43

All shuttle days varied. It depended on the length of time the crew would need to spend there as to what they were allowed to do. Jaime had been to Moscow several times but had never been allowed to leave the plane. On other occasions, in parts of Africa, the crew had been taken to a hotel for the day, where they would be treated to lunch and spend their time relaxing by a pool. In St Lucia, there was only time to walk around the airport, pick up any duty free needed before boarding would begin for the return flight to Antigua, then onto London.

Standing in their positions, ready for boarding, Jaime had a chance to observe Karen, who was acting like a total bitch towards her, which Jaime resented. Karen had not been a happy bunny. Her mood had gone sour since they had arrived in Antigua. Jaime remembered how she had laughed and joked on the flight out, all the way from London, had been the perfect team member, always positive and hardworking. And as a leader, she had been fair. Now, she barely looked at Jaime, and when she did, there was an odd expression on her face Jaime found hard to decipher.

Brushing Karen's behaviour aside, she turned her attention to those who were beginning to board the aircraft, thus ending their holidays. There was the usual array of travellers: those who thought themselves well-heeled in their loafers and light-coloured blazers; those who wanted to travel in complete comfort, hence the baggy shorts and t-shirts (without much thought given to the absolute opposite weather when they touched down in London); and there were those who had bought into the local culture and had opted for the braided hair, friendship bracelets and tie-dye garments. It made for an eclectic bunch, thought Jaime, none of whom looked remotely tired.

A little over ninety minutes later, the plane had touched down, the shuttle was over, and Jaime and her crew were handing over to their colleagues, who would take the plane back to Heathrow. There was time to exchange a few pleasantries with the new team, none of whom Jaime knew well and who had been staying in the sister resort. A few of them asked about events at the Reef Royale, but Rob curtailed too much information being passed on by ushering them off the plane.

Heading towards the bus, Jaime knew she needed to be seated near Thomas again, in the hope he would have been able to find out some information for her about 'Choices'.

Once they had cleared the chaotic area around the arrivals section, Thomas shifted in his seat. "Tish spoke to several friends, and it took a while, but someone had heard of a clinic called 'Choices'."

"A clinic?" Jaime repeated.

"Yup. And not any clinic. They specialise in abortions." He said the last word in a whisper, Jaime had to strain to hear it.

"Abortions?" she repeated, feeling like a parrot.

"Exactly." Thomas nodded.

Abortions were not a subject people openly discussed in Antigua. The idea of them was frowned upon by some, like in many other parts of the world. The intriguing question now was why Dickens had been holding their business card. Had he been trying to hand it to someone? Or had he been given it? But why? And by whom? Did it point towards the motive for the crime? Had he finally gone too far with his affairs and needed whoever she was to get an abortion? The question was, who? Was the murderer a woman? Or was it perhaps a husband? Partner? Family member who objected to the way Dickens treated women?

That could point to the captain who had brought his wife here in the past but had not on this occasion. Jaime again recalled the disdain with which he mentioned his name when announcing the interviews when they arrived. How old would Mrs Bannister be? She realised Thomas was talking.

"…some free time this afternoon. I can take you to have a recce?"

"Fantastic." Jaime felt a surge of adrenaline. It was easier to get more information face to face, she thought, rather than over the telephone. Was she making some headway in this case at last? She hoped so. A trip to check out the clinic was the best move; make some enquiries and even find out if any familiar names had appointments there. Realising this was some real sleuthing, her stomach fluttered in excitement. She would need to be on her A-game to find out anything relevant.

Thomas continued, "There's been some activity back at the resort. I had parked in the layby, next to reception when I saw two constables walking out with the receptionist, Edwina. They put her into the back of their police car."

Jaime's eyes widened. Henry must have made the anonymous call otherwise the police would not have known to talk to Edwina. She couldn't help but glance over her shoulder at Max, who was sitting staring out the window at the dark, brooding sky. His days were numbered.

Pulling into the resort, the bus crunched along the gravel driveway towards the glass doors of the reception – and two waiting police officers. Turning to Max, noting his discomfort, Jaime could make out a bead of sweat running down his cheek, despite the air-conditioning being switched

178

on. He shifted in his seat, sliding away from the window. As Thomas slowed to a stop, police officers approached the door and stood to the side. Even though she knew what was happening, Jaime's stomach was doing flipflops. She felt responsible for this situation.

Being nearest the door, she stood, holding her bag in one hand and the handrail in the other. Stepping off the bus and past the officers, she headed towards the glass doors. One by one, the crew followed her, glancing at the waiting police. Max was the last to climb off, and as he stepped onto the ground each officer placed a hand on his arm, asking him to accompany them into reception, as they had some questions. Max walked with them. He looked as though he couldn't wait to get away from the inquisitive stares of the crew.

Jaime caught sight of Henry standing inside the lobby. He turned his head towards her and winked.

Chapter 44

The outside dining room was thinning out, partly due to the late hour and partly due to the dark sky and increasing gusts of wind. The crew found themselves sitting at the same table together, discussing the morning's events. They had all agreed to run to their rooms, change clothes and meet back in the restaurant.

"It must have something to do with Dickens' murder. It can't be a coincidence."

Mario nodded in agreement with his partner. "Hard to believe there's some separate crime occurring at the same time."

Kate's head was jiggling around; she looked like a child who desperately wanted to join in the conversation but didn't quite know how. Jaime thought she was going to put her hand up and wait for permission. However, she managed to jump in.

"Maybe he was having an affair with the councillor, it all turned sour and the councillor dumped him - he was bitter." She paused for breath.

Karen was staring at her. "Are you for real? You think Max and Greg were..." She trailed off, at a loss for words.

Every time Karen opened her mouth to speak now, it seemed to Jaime she further cemented the fact she had been close to the councillor. Glancing at her watch, Jaime knew it was getting near to the time she had agreed to meet Thomas for their recce of 'Choices'. It was a shame she had to leave - the conversation was exactly what she wanted it to be: discussions about the murder and each other. Popping the last morsel of the cheeseburger into her mouth, she pushed back her chair.

"Any update on Jean's whereabouts?" Gabi addressed Tony as she circled her finger around her water glass.

"Not had an update yet," he replied, adding, "I'm leaving that little issue with Rob to sort out. And good luck to him, I say. I wouldn't want to be the one to confront her when she decides to show up."

Rob's face clouded over. Gabi took a sip of water.

"I'm out," said Jaime as she rose from her chair. She was feeling more and more concerned at Jean's continued absence. However, she couldn't focus on that right now. She was off to check out an abortion clinic, and a nugget of an idea was beginning to form.

"I'll catch you all later." She walked towards the lobby in search of Thomas. Scanning the area outside the resort, Jamie let her mind wander to Max, Edwina and their crime. It had to be a separate issue and have nothing whatsoever to do with Dickens' murder. Otherwise, the card clutched in his dead hand didn't fit, and the idea noodling around in her brain didn't work.

She was reminded of the 'dying clue' that was always a feature of the Ellery Queen Mysteries and was of great significance. This spurred her on. What she knew was she needed to go to the clinic as soon as possible, check it out, see what information she would be able to unearth.

Chapter 45

It was 2 pm, there were quite a few guests around; the place was always a hive of activity during the day. Jaime noticed with interest Edwina had been replaced by an older lady with a shock of grey hair and small framed glasses perched on top of her nose. She seemed to be taking the queue in her stride. Jaime guessed she was experienced at the job.

Walking towards the large glass doors, which were open in a welcoming manner, despite the dark and brooding sky, Jaime shivered. A strange sensation had come over her. Pausing and stepping to the side of the open doors to not block the entrance, she turned back, scanning the large indoor space. She could not shake the feeling she was being watched. That there was a presence somewhere in the lobby: lurking in the shadows, waiting, watching. However, no one seemed to be paying her any attention. Was she being fanciful? Although, she knew she was not prone to flights of fancy. Quite the opposite, in fact.

"Jaime. Over here."

Her head spun round. Thomas approached from the direction of the resort car park.

She waved to him and smiled. "Hi there. Long-time no-see."

"All good. All good." Thomas smiled.

As they strolled towards the bus, she noticed a police officer standing guard right next to the flower bed where the incriminating packet of drugs had been buried. They must have uncovered them, she thought. They must have their evidence. Henry had done well in following her information on where they were buried.

Nearing Thomas' gleaming van, he exclaimed, "Hello, who's that?" He was looking at the passenger door, where a dog sat.

"Basil," responded Jaime in delight. "This is Basil, Thomas. He's become a friend since I arrived. He's the one who brought the business card to me."

Basil stood and wagged his tail. Thomas was the first to reach him, and Basil jumped up his leg. Thomas ruffled his ears.

"Aren't you a friendly little chap? Who's a good boy, eh? Who's a good boy?"

Jaime watched, grinning. What was it about animals that made people so soppy? She joined in. "What are you doing here, Basil? Are you looking for me?"

Basil yipped.

"Oh, you are. Well, here I am, and this is my friend, Thomas."

"I think someone wants to come on the trip," remarked Thomas. "He knew where to find you."

"Do you mind?" asked Jaime, aware this was his business vehicle and dogs shed hairs.

"Mind? I'd love it. C'mon, you jump in the front and Basil can sit next to you. He can look out the window. Besides, no one ever sits in the front seat. It's no problem if there are a few hairs."

Jaime remembered the sirloin steak she had for her new friend and checked if Thomas minded waiting whilst she ran back to her room to retrieve it from the refrigerator.

A few minutes later, a breathless Jaime hopped into the bus where Thomas and Basil were waiting. She was anxious about the lack of safety harness for him, thinking of how Ellery and Wolfe always wore their seatbelts in her car.

Thomas assured her he would drive with extreme care, and she could hold on to him. No laws existed on the island concerning pets in cars. Off they went, all three of them, headed towards 'Choices'.

"I guess this could be pointless if Max confesses to the murder," Jaime conceded. "Or Edwina."

Thomas was thoughtful as the bus jigged along the bumpy road. "I never had much to do with Councillor Dickens, myself. But there's always been rumours about his morals, mainly when it came to council business. He made sure he looked after his own interests. He was a wily one. But as far as I know, he was careful, and nothing could ever be proved. Not the type to get his hands dirty with something like drugs. I don't see it."

Basil's head was involuntarily nodding as he stared out the front window, chomping on the pieces of steak Jaime was handing to him.

Thomas continued, "You think there's got to be something in this card business? A reason for him having it?"

"I think it's a loose end that needs checking," she replied. "And since, thanks to Basil here, Cagney and Lacey know nothing about it, we owe it to them to see if it's relevant or not." Jaime knew she was holding back just how important she deemed this line of enquiry to be.

Thomas raised an eyebrow at the reference to two fictional detectives but didn't comment. As they chugged along, Jaime stared out to the ocean on her left. The sand was white, and the waves formed tips as they crashed along the shoreline.

"One of the most beautiful beaches in the world, Half Moon Bay. Although I say so myself." Thomas chuckled. "On a sunny day, that beach would be full of tourists and locals."

Jaime nodded. She'd had the privilege of visiting the beach a few years back when one of her colleagues had hired a jeep for the day. It had been stunning then as it was now.

"We'll be passing St John's before long, and it's not far to All Saints. I know the street."

Jaime loved every second of the drive around the island. Nothing could beat getting out and about and exploring a place. "Is Nelson's Dockyard near here?" she enquired.

"Not too far. I carried out a tour there last week. Popular and crowded."

Jaime was now observing the colourful homes they were passing, with small front yards and banana trees separating them. Every now and then, she caught a glimpse of everyday life, someone sweeping their front porch, a door wide open to reveal a living room or a kitchen. People doing their everyday chores but doing it on this stunning Caribbean island.

A short time later, a dilapidated sign on the edge of the road read, 'All Saints – Population 3,412'. She sat a little straighter, and Basil decided to stretch.

"We're arriving at the old sugarcane plantation now," Thomas informed them. "It used to be the main industry in this town, Betty's Hope, it's called. Now it's used solely for tourism as an open-air museum."

Jaime looked on with interest as they passed the plantation. A pair of sugar mills were in fantastic condition, despite being over 300 years old.

"The Great House was in ruins when the government began renovation in 1990," continued Thomas, in full tour guide mode. "But they managed to get it into a good enough state to allow in visitors. It was African slaves who kept this place running for a few hundred years," he added.

Jaime was in awe of this beautiful old plantation with its ruined buildings still showing signs of the grandeur of the past.

Thomas was putting on his left turn signal as he said, "This is the street."

The road was lined with bungalows, painted in the pretty colours synonymous with the island, most surrounded by

185

tidy lawns and a scattering of vehicles parked on the street. As they neared the building in question, Jaime gave it the once over. It was well maintained, with vertical blinds at each front window. The small front lawn was well-tended, and a variety of shrubs resided there. The opening of the driveway stood to its left, and there was a pair of tall, wrought iron gates keeping out the world. Glancing towards the other houses on the street, Jaime noted this was the only one that deemed it necessary to have any gates at all. Thomas had no choice but to pull up on the street opposite the bungalow and silenced his engine.

"This is the one," he confirmed, scrutinising it.

"Wow, what's with the over-the-top gates?" remarked Jaime, straining to see through the gaps. "No one else has them."

Thomas was staring at the front garden. "Y'know, I think they have one of those electric fences wound through the bushes. You can just make it out."

"Oh," she exclaimed. "Yes, I can see it now. How bizarre. This is a nice neighbourhood. There's no sign outside, no indication as to what this place is." Jaime was feeling more than a little frustrated.

Basil sensed this and jumped on her lap, staring at her face, his nose millimetres from hers, causing her to giggle.

"What do you think you're doing?" she asked the dog, who responded by licking her cheek.

"Hold on," Thomas declared. "Activity."

Jaime gently moved Basil's head to the side and turned in the same direction as Thomas. A sleek, silver car was pulling up outside the front of the bungalow. It angled towards the gates. An arm appeared from the driver's window and pushed the button on an intercom Jaime had not noticed before. After a minute, the gates slowly swung open, and as the car inched forward, a man dressed in a smart white shirt and tie emerged from a small building hidden in the shrubbery of the garden. He stepped out into the path of the

186

car, forcing it stop, and approached the driver's side. Leaning in, there was a short conversation, the guard spoke into a walkie-talkie radio.

Winding down her window, straining to hear anything, all Jamie caught was a crackling noise. The guard returned his radio to his belt, stood aside and waved the car forward. As he headed back towards his tiny office, his glance caught sight of Jaime and Thomas, sat staring at him through their open windows. He paused, reaching back for his radio. Whatever his next actions were, they would never know, as the gates finished closing, and he was out of view.

Jaime and Thomas turned to stare at each other.

"That's interesting," remarked Jaime. "They have tight security."

"I suppose they feel they need it," mused Thomas. "These places often come under attack, and they must want to protect their clients."

"He didn't like us sitting here. How on earth am I supposed to get in there and do some detecting?" Jaime felt more than a little desperate.

"I'd say you're not. I think you might have to rethink that one." Thomas started the engine.

Jaime was not ready to leave. She wondered if there might be anything to gain from driving onto the street behind to see if the back of the house could be viewed.

"Not much more to be learned sitting here. And I think this one needs a drop or two of water." Thomas was ready to call it a day.

Jaime noticed Basil's panting, accompanied by his tongue hanging out of his mouth, and she was racked with guilt. She should have noticed herself. Of course he was thirsty. There may be no sunshine today, but it was still warm and being inside a vehicle, albeit with air-conditioning, didn't help. "I've got some water but nothing to put it in."

"Further along the road is Potter's Village. It's named after the pots they make there. I think you'll like a look around, and we can get this one a water bowl. Sound good?"

"Sounds great," replied Jaime. Although she was happy to be visiting more of the island, she was also disappointed. Her idea of brazenly walking into the clinic to find information on possible patients was naïve, to say the least. This needed some serious thought and a proper plan, not a half-baked one.

The short drive north was captivating, and Jaime's mood lifted. The quintessential township of Potter's Village was just as she imagined it would be - terraces surrounding quaint cottages were laden with the most cheerful pottery Jaime had ever seen. It even beat the Algarve region of Portugal. She felt she would be in danger here of buying far too much and not be able transport it home. Thomas pulled over to the side of the road for Jaime to get out and explore. Basil jumped out with her, wanting to stretch his legs too.

"You two go on. I'll stay here. I have a few calls to make."

"Great. We won't be long. We'll bring you something back."

The two of them trotted to the nearest building, where Jaime bought a set of six bright yellow, orange and green ceramic bowls. Thanking the vendor, she moved on, taking the bottle of water from her bag as she walked. Rinsing out one of the bowls, which was a bit dusty, she filled it and placed it on the ground, whereupon Basil lapped it up. Jaime took a swig herself whilst perusing her surroundings. While she was here, she thought she would treat herself to a set of brightly coloured coffee mugs. It didn't take her long to find what she was looking for. The cheery set would fit perfectly into the snug kitchen of her floating home. Popping into a small shop, she purchased two cans of ice-cold coke and said goodbye to the village. Retrieving Basil's nearly empty water bowl, they headed back to the cool interior of the bus, where Thomas received his cold drink.

"I see you've been busy." He was peering at Jaime's wrapped packages as he turned the ignition key. "Next stop St. John's."

Chapter 46

The two had agreed to make a quick pit stop in the capital on their way back to the resort. Thomas had an errand to run, and she was happy to revisit the colourful, lively town. Finding a parking spot near the cathedral, the three clambered out of the bus. Jaime wondered if Basil would stay with them or wander off on his own. He must know the area well, she thought, what with him being a local.

Once again, the humidity was palpable as they headed off in the direction of Heritage Quay, the grey of the sky ominous and foreboding. An enormous cruise ship was moored up, its gleaming white body looming over the docks. Tourists milled around, taking in the picturesque scene. Basil trotted along with them, and Jaime wondered, not for the first time if he had a home or a family somewhere. Did he get by totally on his own?

Strolling towards Lower St. Mary's Street, Thomas told her about his daughter, studying to be a doctor at The American University of Antigua, and his eyes lit with pride. Jaime was impressed, thinking there must be a lot of competition to get a place there. The throngs thinned out a little as she and Basil waited outside the post office for Thomas to get his supplies. She bent, stroking the dog's head, noting how at ease he acted amongst the crowds.

"Next stop, Hemingway's, Basil. I can't wait to go back there. We'll wait for a seat on the terrace so you can come too."

"Yip," Basil responded, probably suspecting a morsel or two would be coming his way.

Thomas emerged from the dark interior of the post office, calling back to someone he knew. Whatever their response was, it caused Thomas to chuckle. As they headed towards Hemingway's, Thomas told her the traditionally built wooden structure from the 1800s had been the once well-known hotel 'Jardins'. Climbing the stairs, Jaime felt the excitement she always did when entering somewhere so absolutely as it should be. This was how she had imagined the West Indies to look before she had the opportunity to visit for herself.

The polished wooden bar with its high chairs, the whirring ceiling fans, blue and white checked tablecloths giving it a casual, laid-back air. Carrying Basil, they waited to be seated outside. If anyone minded the presence of the dog, nobody gave any indication. After a few minutes, they were guided out to a small table overlooking the street below and with a view of the quay and the cruise ship beyond. Jaime sighed; her earlier frustrations abated.

Placing Basil on the ground, he sat under the table, gazing out through the gaps in the slats to the ocean beyond. Jaime had brought his bowl and ordered fresh water along with some tea for herself. Thomas opted for another coke, and they both decided to order from the dessert menu. Thomas chose the coconut pie, whilst Jaime decided to give the pecan pie a go. Relaxing back into her seat, she gazed down to the street below. Thomas was speculating on what Jaime's next move could be in finding out why the clinic might be important in the councillor's death.

Jaime mulled it over. There was an element of cloak and dagger about the clinic, or was that her imagination? Their drinks arrived, and she poured Basil's water for him and stirred her tea.

"Do you think Tisher might be able to get us any information from someone who works there?"

Thomas frowned. "From what I could gather, her information was not first-hand. I'm not sure how much more she could find out."

Their waitress returned carrying two plates, both containing huge pieces of pie, one of them topped with cream. Jaime's mouth watered. Not normally a dessert fan, she enjoyed a piece of well-baked pecan pie when she could find one. They thanked the waitress and tucked in, Jaime making sure Basil enjoyed some of the filling. A sugar burst was what she needed.

"The cruise ships are enormous," remarked Jaime as she finished the last morsel of pie. "I love going on cruises but can't help but feel a bit guilty when they call in at such small islands."

"The thing to remember is they keep the shops and bars going. These people make mega money when a few thousand holiday makers flood in for a couple of hours, all keen to spend some dollars. And don't feel too guilty, 'cos the normal prices are hiked right up."

Jaime laughed. "True, and why not. The holiday makers don't know or care, it keeps everyone happy."

Some twenty minutes later, the waitress arrived to clear away the plates.

"Tell Chef Angela compliments from her oldest friend. I can tell it's her pie, alright."

The waitress chuckled. "It's hers, for sure. And the praise does come a lot. Still, she never gets tired of it. I'll pass it on for sure. Can I get you anything else right now?"

Reluctantly, Jaime asked for the bill. Not that she didn't want to pay it, but she didn't want to leave the charming café. She eyed Thomas. "Oldest friend? Something you want to share with us?"

"Not a thing. It's exactly that. Angela, Tish and me were all at school together centuries ago."

"Wow. Has she never left the island?"

"Sure. Went off to hone her skills for many years. But she came home. Most of us do, y'know."

"I can understand," replied Jaime, staring at the street below.

As she watched, a figure caught her eye. A tall slim man, in a khaki t-shirt. There was something familiar about him. It was the face of Crocodile Dundee staring out from his chest. A jolt of recognition shot through her, causing her to knock Basil's water bowl over. It wasn't full, but there was enough of a puddle for her and Thomas to grab their napkins and mop the spill, not wanting to draw attention to the mess. Basil wasn't bothered about drawing attention. He sprang from where he had been napping under the table, banging his head on the wooden leg in his rush to escape the disaster. The only saving grace was the café crowd had thinned out - the audience was smaller than it might have been.

"What's that all about?" Thomas huffed from his bent-over position near the floor.

"I've recognised someone in the street below," whispered Jaime, also from her hunched-over position under the table.

Basil's head appeared, joining in the conflab and standing in the remaining puddle of water.

"Who?" asked Thomas, lifting Basil's paws one by one to mop underneath them.

"It's one of the attackers from the bus journey the other day. He's right there." She jabbed her finger in the general direction of the street below.

Thomas' eyes grew wide. "Well, we can't lose him. You'd better go and see if you can find him. I'll settle the bill and be right behind you. Don't follow him without me. Y'hear? Just locate him and wait."

But Jaime was already halfway across the terrace, followed by her faithful companion. Racing down the stairs, she paused at the bottom and stuck her head out the door, checking along the street. There. She spotted him some way off. He had paused, lighting a cigarette. There were enough people around to head towards him without standing out. Following, she tried to form a plan. The police needed to be called, but Jaime knew by the time they arrived, he could have vanished. No, if she could find out where he lived or frequented, they would have a much better chance of picking him up, maybe even his accomplices too.

The man walked at a leisurely pace, not in too much of a hurry, heading into the nearby Redcliffe Quay shopping district. Jaime had visited the area before, so had some idea of what was around. It was a popular place and she felt safe walking through it. Her quarry did not bother to browse in any shops, though, but wandered and smoked. Wisps of foggy grey rose from above his head.

Reaching into her bag, she pulled out her phone, scrolling for Thomas' number, glad she had programmed him in. Except for the odd stop and sniff, Basil stayed right with her, which was comforting. Thomas answered on the first ring, worry tingeing his voice. After explaining where she was. Thomas said he would catch her up but insisted she stay on the line.

After another ten minutes of meandering through the shopping streets, the attacker surprised her by turning into a doorway. She carried on walking, curious to see which shop he had chosen to visit. It was a tiny tobacco store, according to the sign above the door. Reaching down to fuss over Basil, she thought what a great decoy dogs could be, giving you a perfect excuse to linger and be nosy.

The interior of the shop was dark and dusty, and an ancient man sat on a stool behind an old-fashioned cash register. He was reading a magazine, and there was no one inside. The only place the attacker could have gone was behind a brown and orange floral curtain that must have led into a back room. *Ha* - she thought - *this must be his hangout.*

Heavy breathing in her other ear, not the one with the phone against it, caused a minor panic attack until she turned and saw Thomas had arrived. Giving him a minute to catch his breath and allowing her heartbeat to get back to normal, she led him passed the shop and told him what she had discovered.

"We need to call the police and tell them. If they're quick, they'll get him, unless there's a back door."

"Could be, but he's got no reason to be concerned or think he's being followed," Jaime observed. Holding her phone, ready to dial, she paused. Reporting this would no doubt lead to her having to make a statement, which would take time. It would put her on Cagney and Lacey's radar, again, which is not a place she wanted to be. She could imagine the questions. *What were you doing in St John's, Miss Jones? You were seen leaving the resort some few hours ago, where have you been?* Unless she lied to the detectives, she would have to admit to visiting the abortion clinic because she had the business card and had not passed it onto them - she was meddling in the crime. No, there was no way this would pan out well for her. She turned to Thomas.

"I don't suppose there's any way you could call the police, is there? And maybe not mention me at all? I'm not sure I want to draw attention to myself right now."

Thomas patted her arm, already holding his phone to his ear, waiting to be connected. After detailing to the person on the other end what he had discovered, imparting his details and promising not to approach the man, he hung up.

"Shall we wait and watch?" asked Jaime. "We could stand over there and observe."

"We could, but I need to be heading back, Jaime. Don't worry, they'll come and arrest him."

Jaime was disappointed but masked it. Thomas had done so much for her already today.

"Sure, let's go. C'mon buddy," she looked at Basil, who was taking a moment to sit down.

195

The three of them traipsed back towards the bus, all trying to process their eventful afternoon.

Chapter 47

Smiling at her son, Carol Carfax felt happy he had caught up with her to join in on a walk along the beach. She had been contemplating her friendship with Maggie and was feeling guilty. Not guilty for abandoning her, no. After meeting with her yesterday, Carol was convinced she would not care if she ever saw her again. Guilty for all the times she had put Maggie ahead of her family. Yes. She had insisted on Antigua every year since the kids were toddlers, then dumped them as soon as they arrived, desperate to catch up with her friend over cocktails.

Ashamed she'd had so many conversations with Maggie about how good life would be without their husbands, the graphic details they had gone into about how they might die. God. She shuddered, trying to recall if Maggie had ever mentioned whacking Greg over the head. Maggie was bitter and vindictive. Scary. And rude to those around her. How had she never noticed before? It was, she thought, disturbing the way she was… what was the word? Basking. Yes. Basking in her husband's death. It was like she enjoyed playing the part of the bereaved widow. All this pretend raging about affairs. This was not news. She had known this for a long time. Had she, Carol wondered, snapped? Was enough finally enough?

Now she'd had this thought, she wondered how well she knew this woman. Two weeks a year. What happened the rest

197

of the time? Sure - they would speak regularly, but Carol was not involved in Maggie's life like she was in her friends' lives who lived nearby back in Edinburgh.

Holding out her hand, Carol checked if she could feel any rain drops. No. The sky was dark, rain was inevitable, as was the possibility of thunder. But it was muggy. In a strange way, she relished the wind on her face, blowing her sarong around her body.

"When was the last time you spoke to Christy?" Connor was asking her, his face intense.

Embarrassingly, she had to give this some thought. "I saw her at breakfast this morning. We both did. Dad had to leave for his meeting, remember?"

"I meant *really* talked to her. Not just a few passing remarks at mealtimes."

Carol realised her son was right. When had he become so wise, so grown-up? To her and Caleb, they were both still spoilt brats. Then she became worried. "Is there something I should know, Con? Something she's told you?"

"I don't know, Mum." He shrugged. "I think she might be in trouble. I think she might need you. But I don't think she'll ask you for help. You've been a bit… absent."

Carol's heart sank. 'Absent' was a diplomatic way of putting it. She had ignored her kids for most of the holiday. And when they were home, well, they were away at boarding school all week. When they came home for the weekend, they sometimes stayed with friends or had friends stay with them. Caleb was always working. What was her excuse?

"What kind of trouble?" Carol asked.

"I don't know for sure. I tried to talk to her but didn't get anywhere. I think you should try."

Carol reached out and put an arm around his shoulder, ruffling his light red hair with her free hand. He didn't pull away. Sure, he was still immature at times, but it appeared that where it mattered, like looking out for his big sister, he was growing up. She still couldn't quite believe he had reached out to her in the first place.

"I'll talk to her, Con. Today. Leave it with me. And what about you? Everything okay?"

Running his hands through his short hair, he replied, "Fine."

"You've been spending a lot of time in your room. Maybe we should get out and see some more of the island together."

Connor turned towards her. "I'd like that. Can I ask you something?"

Carol nodded, feeling uneasy.

"I was wondering about the receptionist, you know. The one they arrested earlier."

"What about her? She was responsible for passing drugs onto guests. Good riddance, I say."

"It's… well, I knew her. Quite well."

Carol stopped in her tracks and stared at her son. "What is it you're saying, Connor?" Her face turned white.

Connor stopped also, staring out to sea. "It's nothing. I wanted you to know I knew her, but I'm glad she's been arrested. I'm glad she's gone."

Carol, now in full 'concerned mum' mode, making up for lost time, was weighing up how to handle this unexpected turn of events. She had resumed paddling through the lapping water, sandals in her hand, when she stumbled. As she righted herself, she noticed the water around her ankle felt icy, where it had been feeling warm.

Looking down, Carol Carfax saw the reason for her stumble. And for the icy feeling by her feet.

And she screamed.

Chapter 48

Thanking Thomas for all his assistance, Jaime stepped from the bus. Basil stayed put, as Thomas wanted to take him to his house and feed him. Plus, he said, his wife would love to meet him.

She felt drained. What a day it had been. Investigating a murder case was taking its toll and it was only day two. Heading through the lobby to her room, Jaime had a plan that needed to be executed. As she had sat on the bus heading back to the resort, she had realised in order to get into the clinic and obtain any information she would need an appointment. And that is exactly what she intended to get.

Entering the suite, she kicked off her shoes and plonked herself on the bed next to the telephone, retrieving the business card from her bag.

Dialling the number before her nerves kicked in, Jaime took a deep breath: no going back now. One ring, two rings, three rings…

"Good afternoon. Please state your name and extension number."

Jaime had given some thought as to how she was going to approach the conversation. She knew she would have to say it was an emergency. Time was of the essence here. She had decided to drop the councillor's name into the conversation. She was sure he would never have had any personal contact with a place like that. He would have been too careful. But, well, he was dead now. And it couldn't hurt her cause. Whoever answered the phone might recognise the name and give her what she wanted. The woman's abrupt manner took her by surprise.

"Er… good morning. Miss Jones here. I cannot remember the extension number Councillor Dickens gave me, and now, alas, there's no way of asking him. He said he had booked me in, and I can't remember when for." She held her breath.

The few seconds of silence on the other end of the line felt like minutes. Then, "Hold, please, Miss Jones." This was followed by Gloria Gaynor's 'I will Survive', tinny and out of place.

Jaime shook her head at the song choice. What were they going to come back and say? She needed to get inside.

"Miss Jones? I cannot seem to find an appointment for you."

Obviously the woman couldn't find an appointment for her. Jaime tried again. "Councillor Gregory Dickens assured me, before his untimely death, that you would do everything you could to assist me in my current situation."

There was a long silence on the other end of the line. Then the voice again. "I'm not sure I can help you, Miss Jones."

Bugger, I've blown it. Jaime was cross with herself. She needed an appointment to enter the building and attempt to snoop. There was no other way.

Masking her desperation, Jaime had one final attempt. "I'm afraid that won't do. This is an emergency. Councillor Dickens furnished me with more than adequate funds before he passed." Jamie wondered if she had gone too far. It sounded like she was attempting a bribe, which she was. Way out of her comfort zone now, she was expecting the other woman to hang up.

"One moment, please," came the voice on the other end, to be replaced with more surviving by Gloria.

A woman of few words, thought Jaime. Little Miss Efficient was an appropriate moniker.

After a few minutes and a full rendition, the voice returned. "Eleven am tomorrow morning." It was a statement, not a question.

Jaime nearly collapsed with relief.

"Fine," she responded, sounding grateful.

"Please ensure you bring a competent other. We don't allow anyone to leave unescorted. Insurance purposes, I'm sure you understand. And you'll need ID. We look forward to seeing you. Goodbye." Little Miss Efficient rang off.

Replacing the receiver, Jaime stared at it. 'Competent other'. That was unexpected. Well, at least she had managed to get over the first hurdle, an appointment, which wasn't looking promising, initially. Had the mention of Dickens' name helped? Or the suggestion of plenty of available funds.

Now she needed to find someone to go in with her. Thomas would be good. He already knew all about the place. But she remembered how he had not wanted her to go in before, and she felt bad about asking him to accompany her on a mission where the outcome was unknown, and he had already helped her out. There was always Henry. He would be willing. But she didn't want to owe him anything. Besides, could she trust him? He might be spotted by someone who knew him, and gossip could quickly spread. Damn it. She was stumped.

Feeling the need to check in with the crew, she grabbed her bag and slid into her flipflops.

Chapter 49

Walking into the bar, she spied Rob, Kate, Tony, Mario, Karen and Gabi sitting around one large table. With them sat an unknown man: short, rotund, balding with fuzzy grey bits of hair. The gravity on their faces led Jaime to assume the severity of Max's crime had been revealed.

"Hey, everyone. What's happening?" Attempting a nonchalant manner, she noticed the Carfax family sat not too far away with none other than Margaret Dickens. How odd. Why are they all sitting together, staring at the table? Something was off.

"Where have you been all afternoon?" Gabi's tone was nothing short of accusatory, and Jaime was taken aback.

"Nowhere interesting," she replied.

Mario stepped in. "Jaime, something's happened you need to know about."

Jaime braced herself, ready to show her surprise at Max's involvement with drugs. However, when the news came, her surprise wasn't feigned.

"It's Jean. She's been found dead. Murdered. This afternoon." Rob looked sullen.

Jaime's jaw dropped; she clamped it shut. Jean, dead? How?

"I know it's a shock. It has been to all of us." Mario continued, "But that's not all. Max's arrest was for possession of drugs. I'm told he bought them here and was intending to

203

smuggle them home. Mr Baxter has filled us in." He nodded in the direction of the unknown man.

Wanting information on Jean and whether Max had said anything about whether the councillor was involved, she was not quite sure how to phrase a question.

The rotund man spoke up. "Miss Jaime Jones? We've not met. My name is Stuart Baxter, and I am here as your attorney. I represent the interests of DebonAir employees, and you all need some reassurance right now." He smiled. "Inspector Fontaine and Detective Marshall do want to speak to you all this afternoon regarding the latest developments. As I was saying to your colleagues, Miss Blackthorn was found this afternoon on a part of the beach some way from the resort. Preliminary enquiries suggest a blow to the head, resembling the manner in which Councillor Dickens was killed. Death has been placed between two and three am, provisionally." He paused for breath.

"Who found her?" Jaime was picturing white mushy coconut stuck to Jean's bleached hair.

Stuart Baxter lowered his voice. "A lady and her son out for a stroll. In fact, she's sitting with her family behind us." He discreetly inclined his head towards the Carfax family.

"Of course, the obvious conclusion here is there is a link between the two deaths. That is what the police are working to establish. In the meantime, here is my card, and you must call me anytime if you are worried or have any questions. Officer Kennedy will fetch you one by one shortly. Now, if you'll all excuse me, a certain Mr Max Kleinbeck needs my assistance."

He stood, picked up his briefcase and headed off towards reception. As soon as he was out of earshot, Tony stated, "Well, of course it was Max. Has to be. It's no coincidence he's smuggling drugs, and there have been two deaths in as many days."

Karen was nodding emphatically. "What are the odds of there being a drug smuggler and a murderer on one crew? Zero. I'd say."

"You think a crew member is responsible for both deaths?" Jaime asked.

Karen shuffled her feet.

Kate responded, "Doesn't it seem obvious whoever killed one must have killed the other? I mean, they were killed in the same way, not far from each other and within a day. And we were under suspicion for Dickens' murder because of the beach access, and now Jean's dead, well, she was one of us. Naturally, we're under suspicion even more than we were before." Kate's face was flushed.

Jaime had to admit what she said made sense. But she was thinking about blackmailers. How they often ended up dead. She'd toyed with the idea already, but what if Jean was blackmailing the murderer? They'd killed once before, why not again?

Tony was following a different track. "Don't forget that lot sat over there," he stage-whispered, jabbing a thumb in the direction of the Carfax family and the angular-faced woman who was Mrs Dickens. "They had beach access, they knew Dickens, and they found Jean's body," he beamed.

"I'm sticking with Max. And don't forget the receptionist who was in on it with him. Between the two of them, they could have killed both. It must all be related." Gabi took a sip of water.

Everyone had an opinion. But Jaime was remembering the time of death Stuart Baxter had mentioned. Between two and three am. She couldn't help but be alarmed: she had been wondering around the resort last night, probably about the time Jean was being coshed over the head. Crikey, it wouldn't look good if someone had seen her. And she had been watching Max with his little torchlight bobbing all around the front of the hotel between 1.40 am when he had come down the stairs and 2.30 when he had headed back inside. She had watched him go upstairs and not return in the twenty minutes she had stood there, checking. There didn't appear to be any way he could have feasibly killed Jean, even if the time of death was extended either way, it didn't seem likely it was Max. He'd had other fish to fry last night.

And if the two murders were connected, which seemed likely, the chances were he didn't kill Dickens either.

Thomas' earlier words came back to her: being involved in drugs was not a crime that fitted the councillor.

Unless, of course, Max's partner in crime had helped him out. Edwina Kershaw had not been on duty last night. And Jaime was unaware of her whereabouts when Dickens was killed. Max could have given her his room key to access the beach and kill Dickens, but why? Why would either of them care about Dickens?

Jaime remembered the shock on Edwina's face when she had reported Dickens' murder to her. It had seemed genuine.

Turning to Mario, she said, "Why do you think Jean didn't go straight to bed?"

Mario shook his head sadly. "I feel guilty, JJ. But she was a bloody nightmare. Insisted on needing a brandy before she turned in. I walked her to the bar; there were a few lingering couples that I could see. I stood at the entrance as she walked to a table, sat and got out her phone for the umpteenth time. I left, glad to be rid of her. Jesus, I feel like shit."

Jaime felt for him. She could understand his guilt but also how horrendous it could be to babysit a drunk. At least they got her back to the safety of the hotel bar. Interesting she was checking her phone, though. It did suggest her meeting someone.

"Did she talk to anyone in particular at the club?" she pressed.

"Mainly danced with anyone and everyone."

Jaime smiled, imaging the scene. "There's nothing you could have done, Mario. She was a big girl." A thought occurred to her. Turning to Rob, she said, "Hey, Captain, you were in the bar last night. Didn't you see Jean come in?"

Rob's face coloured immediately. "No. I mean, yes, I went to the bar. But I left. Obviously, before she arrived." He picked up his drink and turned away from Jaime.

Before she could say anymore, a familiar, well-attired lady walked over to them.

"Afternoon. My name is Vanessa Fleet. To those of you whom I have not met before, I am the manager here at the resort. I wanted to say how sorry I am you have lost one of your crew in this…" she paused, struggling for the right words. Rob half stood as though he were going to her aid. She gestured for him to sit back down. "In this awful way. I know you have to speak to the detectives still, but once you are finished, I would like to do what I can to help, so please do feel free to spend the night here in the bar and order whatever you would like to eat and drink, on the house."

The collective thanks from the crew brought a smile to the manager's face, albeit a strained one. Jaime thought her attractive, well-poised, professional and kind. She tried to find some resemblance to Henry and thought perhaps the eyes were similar.

The crew were making plans to head to their rooms as soon as they could, change, then meet back in the bar for a night of freebies.

Tony was nudging Jaime. "Come down as soon as you're done, sweetie. Me and Mario won't need more than an hour to get ready. We're going casual all the way tonight."

Jaime decided she needed to hang out with the crew. She felt uneasy. They all thought it was wrapped up. But she knew it wasn't. She had spent much of her time pursuing Max, who she was convinced, was not a murderer. Just a low-life drug smuggler. Still, if she hadn't been spying on him the previous evening, she would not be able to eliminate him.

Hoping that the visit to the clinic tomorrow would confirm the idea that had been forming in her mind, she still wanted to find out if Tony and Mario were missing a room key. A good detective never left any stone unturned, even though they were convinced of who the culprit was.

And as well as herself and Max, she also remembered Christy Carfax was out late last night. No: too many loose ends, although hopefully, they would turn out to be red herrings.

She hoped Henry was not counting on a date with her tonight. There was one full day of this trip remaining, and there was still some sleuthing to do.

Chapter 50

The striking red trouser suit matched her nail polish perfectly. It gave her a dangerous look, which, Jaime was sure, was not an accident. With a wide gesture, the inspector indicated for Jaime to take a seat, which she dutifully did, noticing Detective Marshall had opted for a pastel yellow outfit today. It wasn't actually a trouser suit, though, mused Jaime. More of a designer boiler suit. Perhaps she was expecting some one-on-one combat. She had teamed it with deep orange nail polish and gold flats.

Fontaine was speaking. "We'll need to know your whereabouts last night. From when you returned to the hotel after dinner."

Jaime felt a knot in her stomach. These two already thought she hated the councillor enough to murder him, and that she'd had something to do with Ken's death all those years ago. Could she admit to her nocturnal activities? Confess to creeping around the resort in the wee hours of the morning? It wasn't like she had seen Jean, for goodness' sake. No. Jaime convinced herself she had to do the right thing. For her.

"I wasn't into Devine's. It wasn't my idea of fun. I'm not a great fan of dancing, so I opted out." Jaime felt sure she saw a raised eyebrow coming from Detective Marshall. She continued, "I said my goodnights in the lobby and Rob, Karen, Gabby and Max had also decided not to carry on the

209

party. I believe Rob headed for the bar and the four of us went to our rooms." She paused.

Fontaine stared at her for a full minute. "Then what?" she finally asked.

"I made myself a cup of tea and found an episode of *Murder, She Wrote*. My idea of fun. I must have fallen asleep as I missed the end, although I've seen them all before. Many times. The next thing I knew, my alarm was going off and I was making coffee."

The fact she had outright lied to the police did not bother her as much as she thought it would. After all, it wouldn't be the first time. She remembered back to the Arctic Circle ten years ago. The only concern here would be if someone had seen her creeping around, but she was sure no one had. Except Basil.

"Tell me about Jean Blackthorn." Fontaine tilted her head to one side, the picture of interest.

"I haven't flown with her before," replied Jaime. "On this flight, I worked at the back of the aircraft due to my lack of seniority. The CSD is based at the front of the aircraft and primarily deals with the first-class passengers. She sets the tone of the trip."

Fontaine was nodding. "How so?" she asked.

"Well, for example, they can relax uniform rules if they wish, decide how the service works on the aircraft, for example, will there be one drinks round or two, how many tea and coffee runs and so on. On some trips, the service can go on for hours. With a more relaxed CSD, the service will be minimal to enable the passengers to enjoy their films."

"And what type of boss was Miss Blackthorn?"

Jaime knew she would need to be honest here. Others had been interviewed ahead of her and hopefully, they hadn't all lied about what a bitch Jean was.

"She didn't work very hard on the flight. She didn't relax uniform standards, and she wasn't friendly. I suppose I've worked with nicer CSDs," Jaime concluded.

"Can you think of any reason why one of your crew would want to murder her?"

Jaime answered, "No. Being a stickler for the rules and a lazy boss are not motives for murder. Well, not in my book, anyway."

"And what would be a good motive for murder, Jaime? In your book?" The canary in the corner had decided to pipe up.

Jaime coloured. "I guess I'm not sure." Why did she always walk right into these traps?

A long red fingernail tapped on the polished surface of the table, Fontaine's trademark, it seemed. Finally, the detective asked, "Was anyone particularly anxious or worried when Miss Blackthorn failed to appear for the shuttle this morning?"

"I think most of us assumed she had..." Jaime paused, not sure how to phrase the idea that Jean acted like a first-class tart. "Found a friend for the night," she concluded lamely. She was positive she saw the glimmer of a grin on Inspector Fontaine's face.

"That will be all for now. We have advised all your colleagues to remain vigilant and aware. We have had two murders here and we don't want anymore. Thank you for your time."

Jaime pushed back her chair and left the office, feeling relieved to be away from the scrutiny of those two - trying to analyse why they made her feel guilty? They gave the impression they could see right through her.

Jaime headed towards her room to prepare for the evening ahead. She was remembering the first time the crew had been interviewed by Cagney and Lacey: the CSD making an observation about how easy it would have been for any of them to have witnessed the councillor accessing the beach if they had been on their balconies or taking a late-night stroll... She was also picturing the strange rendezvous between Jean and Gabi: Karen's demise since arriving and

211

her willingness to please Jean: Rob's obvious disdain towards Jean.

What she needed to do, was eliminate some of the red herrings that were dangling, throwing her off track. Tonight's free booze would loosen a few lips, and with that came information.

Walking through the reception area towards the staircase, she glanced out of the open doors, noting the dullness of the late afternoon. She spotted Stuart Baxter standing beside a gleaming BMW, briefcase in hand, chatting to non-other than The Stranger. Jaime stopped abruptly, causing a Dolly Parton lookalike to bump right into her. "Oh, I'm sorry," she mumbled, embarrassed.

The Dolly Parton lookalike beamed at her. "Now don't y'all worry 'bout it, sweetheart." She tottered off.

Pulling herself together, Jaime stepped over towards a pillar so as not to block the thoroughfare and was relieved to find Stuart Baxter and The Stranger still talking. Stuart Baxter was nodding, listening. The Stranger glanced at his watch and reached out to shake the other man's hand, turning back towards the lobby.

Jaime hurriedly slid around the post to conceal herself, wondering why, as she stood there, she felt the need to hide. She didn't know this man, and she had every right to be standing there. After a minute, unsure where The Stranger had gone, she decided to leave and without a backward glance, walked briskly to the stairs. Who was he? Why did he keep showing up? And now he appeared to have a connection with Stuart Baxter. Was this another red herring thrown in to distract her? She wondered if Tony or Mario might have an idea who he was. She would ask them later.

Chapter 51

Rushing to pull on her jeans, Jaime lost balance and fell back onto the bed. Okay, she told herself, more speed, less haste. Or was it the other way round? Either way, she decided a sprained limb was not the ideal way forward and took a deep breath. She was stepping into her wedges when the room telephone rang.

"Hello," she answered, wondering which of the crew was calling her and why.

"Hello back," a deep voice said.

Henry, she thought guiltily. After what he had done this morning, with the anonymous call to the police, resulting in the arrests of Max and Edwina, she had not spoken to him at all, although she was still embarrassed about the whole CCTV debacle.

"A good result earlier. Great job. I assume they didn't suspect a thing?"

"Not a bean," he replied, "It couldn't have gone better. I channelled my best local accent mixed with a tinge of John Wayne. I thought it was inspired."

Jaime laughed, wishing she could have heard the call.

"One of the reasons I'm calling," continued Henry, "Is, firstly, to check in with you after hearing the news about Jean Blackthorn."

"It's awful," commented Jaime. "And it does suggest a link between the two deaths and the crew."

213

"Right." Henry sounded thoughtful. "The hotel staff, including myself, have been interviewed. Your boss sat in the bar for thirty minutes, drinking a cognac, checking her phone every few minutes, according to the late-night barman. At 1.30 am, she left, out towards the beach. He assumed she was heading back to her room through the side doors, avoiding the lobby. Not heading to her death. He's mortified."

"I bet he is, poor man. You know, it couldn't have been Max. I mean, I was watching him throughout the crucial time." Henry was the only person she could tell this too.

"What about Edwina? She could have done it. Although it's a bit of leap from passing some drugs over a counter to hitting someone over the head. Oh, by the way, one of the staff told me earlier Caleb Carfax passed out in the bar on the night of Dickens' death. They had to carry him to a small nearby office to sleep it off on the sofa. They swear he never left until the morning. I guess that's an alibi for Dickens' murder."

Jaime was grateful for the information as it allowed her to rule out the Carfax father, helping her move forward in her current train of thought.

"Which brings me to the second reason I'm calling you," continued Henry, "Apparently, the police arrested one of your bus hijackers this afternoon in St Johns." He waited.

Jaime was taken off guard. She'd forgotten about this, what with all the other events of the afternoon. On the spur of the moment, she decided to pretend this was news to her - mainly because she didn't want Henry to feel hurt she hadn't mentioned it to him.

"What? How? Fill me in," she bluffed.

Henry obliged, telling her all about Thomas spotting him by chance. "But that's not all. It turns out his cousin put him up to it. Told him all about the crew arriving, what time, and one of them would have quite a bit of cash on them, namely Max."

This was news to Jaime - now she really was surprised. "How would this person's cousin know all this?"

"Edwina is the cousin." He paused for dramatic effect. "She knew Max would have the cash to buy the drugs from her. When Max had it stolen from him, she assumed he would have the means to access more funds as he wouldn't want to leave without his merchandise. Her cousin would split the cash with her. A double win, although a bit of a risk. His two friends have also been picked up, which wasn't difficult as the local cops knew who he hung out with."

Jaime needed a minute to take all this in. Recalling the bus attack, the words of the attackers came into her head – *we want the money*. It had seemed an odd way of saying it at the time. It wasn't a given the crew would have any cash on them. Indeed, it was unlikely. She also remembered Max pushing his bag under the seat, away from the attackers, whilst Tony was shoving his worldly goods right at them. It made sense now.

"We can talk through all this if you join me for dinner. It'll be fun, and we can see what we come up with." He'd taken her silence for shock.

Jaime was tempted. He had provided her with some great intel, and she had no reason to doubt his information on Jean's movements last night and Caleb's alibi. But she needed to pursue her own idea. The one that was niggling away at her. She strongly believed the answer to Dickens' death lay somewhere within the walls of the clinic. And Henry couldn't help her with this.

"I've promised to meet the guys, and I'm already running late. We'll do it, though," she said, hoping to sound convincing.

The pause on the other end of the line told her everything she needed to know. He was disappointed.

"No problem. But I will hold you to that, Jaime. And I know tomorrow is your last night on the island." He hung up.

Chapter 52

19:24

A cosy glow emanated from the lamp in the corner of the room. With her shoes kicked onto the floor, Winnifred Fontaine relaxed back into her chair, her feet resting on the mahogany table.

Letitia Marshall took a sip of beer and rested the bottle on a coaster. "Good call on the Chinese food, Win. That hit the spot. Just what I needed."

"I feel bad about your date," declared Winnifred. "You were looking forward to this one, and he's quite a catch."

"Don't worry. He's not going anywhere. Besides, we both know the score, and we're getting close. I can feel it."

"Yes, we are. Let's have a final recap before we call it a night. Do you have your notes?"

Letitia waggled a sheaf of papers. "Okay, let's concentrate on Dickens' murder. The adorable, sweet Margaret Dickens, known as Maggie, with Carol Carfax until midnight, then in a taxi, which took her to her door. They were both drunk as skunks. The poor waiter who had to bring them drinks all night confirmed they were strong cocktails and shots, and they were draining their glasses. It is unlikely either of them would have been able to smash Dickens over his big head. More likely, they'd have used a pina colada than a coconut."

"Shame," Winnifred chuckled. "I wanted it to be the obnoxious wife. Although I suppose that's a bit unfair on the

216

kids. They're already at a disadvantage in life from their gene pool."

Letitia nodded in agreement and drank more beer. "Next, our good captain. He was watching a film. That rules him right out." They both laughed. Letitia continued, "If only it were that easy. I checked, and Fracture was on HBO that night, although, as we know, he could have watched before to know the plot."

"Have you seen it?" Winnifred asked.

"Don't think so. Too busy going out on all these dates you keep setting up."

Winnifred snorted on her beer. "Don't blame me because you're so damn picky, Letty. Anyway, the kids and I watched it last night. Complex plot, but Tony Hopkins does kill his wife because she's having an affair."

"Interesting. Hope the kids enjoyed it."

"Oh, they loved it. They take after me. What I'm thinking is Captain Rob watched his film, got to thinking about his wife and suspected her of having an affair with Dickens. It enraged him, and he lured him to the beach and killed him in a fit of rage."

Letitia chuckled as Winnifred's beer bottle flew through the air as she enacted the killing.

"Great theory, Win, but if he was inspired by Tony Hopkins, it would be his lovely wife, Barbara, who was dead. Officer Kennedy has already told us about the nightcap with Vanessa Fleet and the skinny dipping. If his wife had an affair with Dickens, which is possible, the number of times she visited the island, I think Captain Rob is over it. He's moved on. With Vanessa."

Winnifred nodded. "I'm inclined to agree. Although the alibi is weak, I'm not seeing a strong enough motive."

"We're sure Dickens wasn't involved with Kleinbeck and Kershaw and their little band of merry drug smugglers. They're not the type to keep quiet about it and take the rap."

"Agreed. We know she got the drugs from her cousin, and he has already spilt the beans on where he got them from. We have the full chain, and none of it involves Dickens."

"You're right. I think it's safe to say none of the crew have an alibi, except Tony Hayward and Mario Vanetti vouch for each other."

"For what it's worth. Especially since Dickens' death allowed their planning permission to go through, according to our sources at the council, they have been trying to get that granted for months."

Letitia yawned. "Are you going to the Dickens' house tomorrow?"

"Yes, I have to update *her*, but I'll wangle a chat with the nanny. I bet she'll be dying to fill me in on her lovely boss. I shall return with as much juicy gossip as I can get my hands on. You never know when it might come in handy."

"Agreed," responded Letitia, nodding. "If nothing else, it'll be entertaining. Now – Caleb Carfax: his alibi checks out. The bar staff carried his passed-out form into a back office and onto a sofa for the night. He was checked on at regular intervals, and they're adamant he never moved."

"Wow. What a lot of drunks we're surrounded by. Okay. It still leaves the kids. The daughter is stunning. A snake like Dickens would not have missed that."

"You're right. Although the Carfax family don't seem to have had a connection with Jean Blackthorn at all. Unless she annoyed them on the flight over. Maybe took too long bringing their Champers."

"Oh, that would do it for me, for sure. Blackthorn's murder does point the finger more at the crew. At that time of night, it was a longshot to expect any of them to have an alibi."

"What we need to find is the person who has the penchant for coconuts. I mean, what is with that? Smashing a coconut over someone's head, hard enough for it to explode in their hair."

"Disgusting. If we hang out by the dessert section of the buffet tomorrow, we'll make a note of everyone who takes any coconut-related puddings."

They both erupted into laughter.

"Unlikely it was the captain, though. I wouldn't believe *his* story about spending the night with Vanessa Fleet, but her story matched his to the letter."

"I suppose they could be helping each other out with an alibi. It has been known."

"True. Let's not completely rule them out yet."

"We're going to need to find a solution to this, or we'll end up keeping the crew past their flying home day. That presents a bit of a headache. It would be easier if we had this wrapped up. And you know who will not be happy if we don't nail the culprit soon."

"Yes, I do." Letitia's eyes glazed over.

"Jesus, woman, calm yourself down. Maybe you should go on your date after all. Okay, we know who we're focussing on next. We need to confirm which of the ladies he was screwing - pardon my French. Kate Jackson, Karen Jeffries, Jaime Jones, Gabi Pascal, Christy Carfax. One or two of them, all of them?" Winnifred asked.

"Out of them all, I think Jaime Jones wanted to punch him over screwing him," Letitia replied.

"She's our killer, then." Winnifred's eyes twinkled. Then she added, "But on a serious note, she's possibly got form."

"That's right. Something very hard to prove, though. The Scandinavian police let it go. Moving onto the first officer, she would not be interested in sleeping with Dickens. Or any man, for that matter," Letitia concluded.

"Agreed. Which does rule her out if we're going on the information provided by one of Dickens' staff."

"Of course, Blackthorn could have slept with him and killed him, and then someone took her out."

"Okay, let's call it a day. We're both tired, and tomorrow is going to be a long day. We can spend all night going backwards and forwards, but we have a theory, and we're running with it."

They stood, disposed of their dinner remnants and beer bottles in the bin, switched off the lamp and headed out.

Chapter 53

Sitting on her balcony, enjoying the feeling of the wind in her hair, Jaime was taking a minute to think through her idea. She believed this entire business came down to the victims' nature. Dickens had been a womaniser, and Jean loved power. She was condescending, patronising and rude. She relished her role as head honcho and didn't appear to care if she hurt anyone's feelings. No, thought Jaime, scratch that. An image of the hideous Mrs Boynton came to mind in Christie's *Appointment With Death*. That woman went out of her way to make those around her feel uncomfortable. She sought out weaknesses, basking in the power it gave over people.

Jaime was convinced she was on the right track. But she needed proof. Something she could take to Cagney and Lacey. Her theory ruled a lot of people out. Tony and Mario, for example. It must put them in the clear if the motive revolved around the abortion clinic. But she couldn't ignore she had overheard them rejoicing at Dickens' death. Karen, Gabi and Kate were in the frame, as was the Carfax girl, although there was no obvious link between her and Jean.

Picking a cardigan off the chair, although not cold, the storm could arrive anytime, which chilled Jaime. She pulled the door closed behind her.

In the entrance to the bar, Rob stood with a bottle of beer, waving her over.

"Jaime. I'm trying to catch everyone as they come in. Officer Kennedy caught me a few minutes ago to tell me all the bus attackers have been apprehended."

Jaime attempted to look relieved. "Wow. Amazing news. I never thought they would get them." She tried to keep walking, not wanting to hear the same news over and over.

"Believe it or not, Thomas the bus driver spotted one of them in town. The police picked him up, and he was quick to land his friends in it."

"What a relief." Jaime tried to hide her need to move on.

"One of them was related to a member of staff here. The receptionist."

"Well, at least they're all behind bars. Thanks for letting me know." Jaime strode purposefully to the bar, feeling she had earned a drink.

"JJ. Over here."

Turning, she saw a pair of waving hands. Tony and Mario, in their 'casual' gear, which consisted of designer ripped jeans, white for Tony and faded blue for Mario and bright white shirts, opened to the navel with matching white vests underneath. Both wore tasselled loafers in caramel-coloured suede. *Well, if that's their idea of casual*, thought Jaime, *lord knows what they're going to think of my outfit*. Indeed, she had taken two minutes to throw on jeans and a Columbo t-shirt. (She loved the slogan 'Just one more thing' plastered above the cartoon-style picture of the famous detective and his Basset Hound - named 'Dog'.)

"Evening, you two. Bubbly?" She eyed the bottle in the cooler, standing beside the table.

"I believe Mrs Fleet said to have anything we like. On the house." Tony's manner was a little defensive.

"I told you it was too much," protested Mario. "It's distasteful, with Jean just murdered."

"Oh, hush and relax. It's not our fault she's dead. Jaime, we've got you a glass. Sit down. Did you bump into 'Captain Nob' on your way in?"

Jaime nodded, tilting her glass whilst Mario poured. "Unbelievable. That receptionist. What an evil cow."

"At least it's all over now. We can relax and enjoy our last full day." Tony settled back in his seat. "Although I suspect we might be screwed on the weather."

These two believed Max to be the killer, thought Jaime. Case closed as far as they were concerned.

"I can't quite believe it was Max," commented Mario. "He seemed like such a nice guy."

"You like everyone," said Tony mockingly. "He was a weirdo. And now it's been proved. He didn't give a shit about putting us all in jeopardy."

"True," agreed Jaime, referring to the drug smuggling.

"If he's got any sense, he'll keep his mouth shut."

Sipping her drink, Jaime asked, "Had you flown with Jean in the past?"

Tony and Mario glanced at each other for a second. Tony responded, "A few times. To be honest JJ, she tended to leave me to get on with what I was doing. She didn't interfere."

"And she'd never walk to the back of the aircraft. She would call and get someone to come when she needed some legwork doing," added Mario.

"You wouldn't label her a bitch?" asked Jaime.

"It's a name that's followed her around. And I've seen evidence of it. Just not in my direction."

"Mine neither. Although I think Karen was getting run ragged on the way out."

"Gabi didn't profess to like her much," said Jaime.

"Well, not surprising. Many less senior people who flew with her felt the same way."

Tony called out to the waiter for a second bottle and some menus. Jaime decided to go with the flow. They were still going to order the Champagne whether she was with them or not. She may as well enjoy it, she reasoned. And looking around, the remaining crew members were doing the same.

223

"It's got to be the seafood platter for two, Mario. I won't take no for an answer."

Mario shrugged, although Jaime suspected he had his limits where Tony was concerned. The waiter headed over, pad in hand, and they ordered. Jaime had decided on the surf and turf, suspecting Basil might like to try some lobster. If he didn't like it, there was always the steak, which she knew he liked.

"Whose room did you decide to camp in on this trip?" asked Jaime. "Whose was the best?"

"We didn't even bother checking this time," replied Mario. "We assumed they were all identical. We went straight to Tony's, and it's stunning. No point wasting time checking out the other one."

"You've not even seen it? I'd be interested to know if they're all identical. Mind if I take a peek if you're not using it?" Jaime didn't think Mario's room key was the one that let the councillor access the beach. Still, it was a loose end.

"Knock yourself out, hun." Tony gave no indication he was bothered.

Mario was pulling out his wallet. Jaime watched. Was he going to be able to produce the key? Apparently not. After some moments of fiddling in his wallet, he declared he could not remember where he had put it and would search the room later.

Chapter 54

"Here's to a great meal and the future." Tony raised his glass in a toast.

"Cheers," murmured Jaime and Mario. Jaime did think it in bad taste in the circumstances. Tony could be self-centred at times.

"You're upbeat tonight, Tony," Jaime said, hoping he had consumed enough alcohol to expand on his mood.

"Y'know Jaime, we have pulled off the deal of a lifetime. It's been a long time in the making, but let's say this could be the making of us."

"I'm not sure Jaime is interested in our business dealings, Tone." There was a slight edge to Mario's voice Jaime had not heard before.

Unfortunately for Mario, Tony was at that point where he was not going to take any notice. "Sure she is, aren't you, Jaime?"

Jaime nodded emphatically, hoping Tony would not listen to his partner. She was in luck.

"We got our hands on some prime beachfront land some time ago, and we've found out we've now got the planning permission we need to make it much more lucrative."

Jaime's ears pricked, realising she was getting an explanation for the snippet of conversation she had overheard with Henry and Basil the previous day when they had ducked behind some rocks on the beach.

225

"I know it sounds callous, Jaime, but we have been waiting for this for a long time," Mario tried to explain. "To be honest, Dickens' death helped us out." He looked mortified.

"So what?" Tony once again became defensive. "It's not like we killed him. It happened to come at a good time for us. He was opposing everything we put forward and persuading others to do the same. He didn't want any new developments anywhere near his properties, of which he had many. He didn't want their value to decrease. With him gone, nobody seemed to have an issue with our plans. Simple."

"Of course, we didn't kill him. Anyway, now we know it's Max and the receptionist, right?" Mario implored.

She was at a loss for words, not expecting to hear any of this information. She hadn't even had to ask. They had explained the overheard conversation. Did she believe them? With her new theory of the murder being related to an affair gone sour, these two were not at the top of her suspect list and coming clean about their business deal suggested a certain amount of innocence.

"Jaime, we didn't do anything wrong." Mario had taken her silence for uncertainty and was determined to get her to believe them.

"It does appear as though the case is solved," she lied.

"You don't seem sure." Tony sat a little straighter.

"I had a theory, that's all," Jaime said, unsure how far to go with this. How much could she trust these two? She decided to throw a few crumbs. "I thought it might be a revenge killing by a woman scorned, and Jean could have somehow found out and tried to blackmail the killer." She paused.

"Ooh, I like it." Tony was delighted with the idea. "Who do you have your eye on?"

But Jaime did not want to divulge any more information, not yet anyway. She wanted to trust these two, but did she trust her judgment? And Tony had a big mouth, for sure.

"To be honest, that's as far as I got. There's no shortage of possibilities."

"Well, from what we witnessed at Devine's last night, you might want to discount our first officer. She's not interested in anyone of the male persuasion."

Jaime glanced over to where Kate and Karen sat at the bar. Karen chatted, her hands waving around as she described a situation. Kate giggled. "It makes life easier," declared Jaime. "I suppose she could have still maybe been interested in The Dick as well?"

Mario snickered, but Tony was shaking his head. "No way, sweetie. A complete one-way street, that one. You know the saying, takes one to know one."

"So, you're doing a bit of detecting, are you?" Mario nudged her arm.

Before she could reply, two waiters headed their way, one carrying a modest plate of steak and lobster tail, the other battling with a three-tiered silver platter brimming with jewels of the ocean. Mario groaned. Tony clapped in delight. A few heads turned their way.

Grabbing a wedge of lemon and spearing it with a fork, Tony liberally squeezed it over the smoked salmon. "Dig in, hun. Before it's too late."

Despite his initial embarrassment, Mario did not need to be told twice.

Swallowing a mouthful of the succulent lobster, Jaime asked, "Do you think Rob was weird earlier when I asked him if he'd seen Jean in the bar? His face turned puce."

Tony waved his fork in the air, almost launching a mussel into the stratosphere. "Our adorable captain has been having drinky poos with a certain hotel manager. And very cosy they are getting too." He moved on to a prawn.

Jaime paused, fork halfway to her mouth. "How did you find out?"

"Mario gets on well with the bar staff. They'll tell him anything." Tony's sarcasm was not lost on either of his two listeners.

"That would explain his embarrassment. And why he's weird about his wife. And marriage. He's having an affair. Jesus, what a cliché. The airline captain sleeping around."

"Hold on a second. You've got that the wrong way round," Mario stated. "It was the Seychelles trip, wasn't it?"

Tony nodded, taking up the story - choking on the oyster he was slurping. "He brought his lovely wife, Barbara, and she was a blatant flirt. It was mortifying. She tried it on with me. Can you believe it? Well, I was more butch then, wasn't I?"

"Yes, dear. Much more manly," Mario answered, smiling. "I suppose it's my fault you're not anymore?"

"Definitely. I mean, who could compete with your muscles? Anyway, I heard she got one of the junior stewards interested, and Rob never knew. Can you imagine? And there were rumours at various other times about her. Thinking about it, I feel quite sorry for him. It could explain why he's such a prick."

"I guess a few drinks with Mrs Fleet is acceptable under the circumstances," concluded Mario.

"I'd say it was more than a few drinks, darling."

Jaime swallowed some Champagne, wishing she had trusted these two with her sleuthing much earlier on. But after overhearing their conversation yesterday, how could she have? They were her first suspects.

"Do you think Rob's wife could have slept with Dickens at some point?" she asked the pair.

"It's possible, but we never heard anything." Tony finished chewing a lump of crab.

Finishing their meals, Basil's share wrapped up, the three decided to call it a night. They rose to leave, Tony a bit unsteadily. Kate and Karen had ordered another bottle of wine. Jaime wished she could find an excuse to join them, but she suspected she would not be welcomed. They were very cosy together. Was Karen off men? wondered Jaime.

Climbing the stairs, a long rumble of thunder sounded.

"Tomorrow should be interesting when this finally erupts," Tony commented. "Mario, where are you? I need an arm support."

Jaime and Tony turned to see Mario trailing behind, fiddling in his wallet.

"Ha! I knew I had it somewhere. It was wedged behind my driving license. Here you go, Jaime. Knock yourself out." He handed her their spare room key.

Chapter 55

The oppressive darkness filled the room. She had been finishing her Laura Childs novel and had begun the Anne George Southern Sisters mystery since the constant rumbling, sporadic outbreaks of thunder, combined with flashes of lightning, had awoken her a few hours ago. It had been too early to go anywhere; she had snuggled under the duvet and revelled in her favourite pastime. With the rain lashing against the glass doors, she decided it was time for coffee.

Flicking on the tv in an attempt to drown out the weather, Hart to Hart came onto the screen, one of her all-time favourite shows. While she was waiting for the coffee to brew, she watched Jennifer don a disguise in order to get information from two of Jonathan's employees. *That woman will do anything to get information,* she thought, remembering the episode where she had taken on the persona of a romantic novelist in the deep south. *I do need to channel my inner Jennifer Hart.*

Pouring the brewed coffee, she mulled over how she was going to approach the clinic visit and who she was going to ask to go with her. Not wanting to ask last night without thinking it over, she had concluded it had to be Mario. He was dependable and had already shown he was not afraid to confront danger after kicking the attackers off the bus. Now she needed to persuade him. In her excitement at all the gossip she had heard from them last night, she had forgotten to enquire whether they had come across The Stranger.

Glancing at her watch, she noted it was time for breakfast. She was eager to get the morning underway. It was their last full day.

As expected, the restaurant was empty. Canopies had been placed over the open sections, and clear plastic had been rolled halfway down the sides in order to stop the driving rain from wetting the diners. Ceiling fans had been turned off, for which Jaime was grateful. She had put on a sweatshirt over leggings to ward off the chill the grey sky gave her.

Taking a larger table than needed - in the hope of being joined by the others soon, she ordered coffee, then strolled over to the pastry counter. The hot food bars were still being set up. The mini croissant looked appealing, as did the maple pecan plaits. She had brought *Murder Makes Waves* and Basil's breakfast, although it was unlikely he would be out and about. She hoped he was somewhere sheltering out of the rain.

A bolt of lightning made her jump, and there were nervous giggles from the few others who had arrived.

Sipping her coffee, nibbling a pastry, she indulged in her book. Jaime was intrigued and only looked up when she heard a nearby chair scraping on the tiled floor.

Kate was hesitating, hand on the back of the chair. "I wasn't sure if you wanted company or not?"

Jaime's hand reached out towards her coffee and noticed the cup was empty, as was the plate that held the pastries.

"Morning. I was passing the time until someone else emerged." She smiled at Kate.

The waiter was upon them, refilling her coffee.

"How are you feeling this morning? Late night, was it?"

Kate flushed. "A bit. I suppose we got carried away. But it turns out Karen is funny. And entertaining."

231

"Yes, I've flown with her before, and I do remember. She's not seemed herself on this trip, though." Jaime hoped for some information, but how much could she glean from Kate?

"She's got a lot on her mind. She's been through so much."

"The councillor's death must have been a real shock to her." Jaime thought she would ease her way in, not say too much in case she was way off base.

Kate's eyebrows rose. "Yes, it hit her hard. There were genuine feelings there. Or at least on Karen's side there were."

It was confirmed. Karen and Greg were seeing each other. "Hmm, must be tough. And to not get any real closure..." Jaime knew she was waffling, but if Kate noticed, she didn't show it.

"And for it to be the third time it's happened. Can you believe it?" Kate looked at Jaime curiously. "She's told you about Dirk and Simon, right?"

Jaime was sipping her refilled coffee but managed a slight nod.

Kate seemed to accept this and continued. "She's going to need some company this morning. This kind of weather always reminds her of Simon. I mean, how unlucky can you get? Still, I suppose it's not as bad as the shock of Dirk's alligator. I'm going to give her room a call and tell her where we are. She shouldn't be on her own. I'll get some breakfast on the way back. Won't be long."

Jaime stared after her. Simon? Dirk? An alligator? What the hell had Karen told her? Now she needed to know. Could she get Karen to talk to her if she made it to breakfast? She had to try and let the 'slut' comment go. The understanding approach might work. Karen didn't like her much right now, so it wasn't going to be easy.

Time for a pancake and some maple syrup before the show down. She jumped up and walked to the station, smiling at the chef. She spotted Kate heading her way.

"She's on her way down, Jaime. I'll get her some coffee poured." Kate's smile was wide and genuine.

Those two have certainly struck up a friendship, Jaime thought as she hurried back to the table, laden plate in hand. A few minutes later Karen arrived, possibly having been dragged through a hedge backwards. At least she's managed to clean away yesterday's make-up, thought Jaime. Striding towards the table, smiling at Kate, Karen faltered when she spotted Jaime.

Here goes. Jaime waved and smiled as warmly as she could, beckoning Karen over. It had the desired effect as Karen went ahead and pulled out a chair. Kate went into 'mother hen' mode and fussed around Karen, making sure her drink was as she liked it, getting her some sustenance.

Jaime decided to take full advantage of Kate's absence. "Karen. I know we haven't been getting on well in the last few days, but I wanted to apologise. I don't want to fall out with you. And I'm sorry for your loss," she added, hoping she hadn't gone too far.

However, Karen smiled. "It's okay, Jaime. I'm sorry too. I can't believe what I said to you. I'm embarrassed. I've been on edge since we arrived. I was looking forward to seeing him. But it wasn't to be. I don't know what I'm supposed to do to keep a man."

Lord, am I supposed to offer some advice? thought Jaime panicking. *Maybe you could find one who's available.* Instead, she said, "Kate's worried about you. She says this weather affects you?" Hoping she wasn't landing the other woman in it, Jaime hoped Karen might enlighten her on 'Dirk and Simon gate'.

Karen glanced over to where Kate was waiting for an omelette. "She's been amazing. Kind and caring. And she's listened to me, not judged me like most people do."

233

Judged you for what? Jaime wanted to scream. Curbing her impatience, she waited, hoping the other woman would continue. A flash of lightning caused Karen to almost drop her cup.

"It reminds me of Simon. He was playing golf when it happened." She stared at Jaime, who decided the best response was to nod with feeling.

"He'd finished with me the day before. His wife needed him, he said. Then this with Greg. The same scenario all over again. Dumped, and then they die. It makes me feel like the black widow."

Jaime thought Karen was enjoying the attention she was getting from Kate. But the investigation was moving forward. Karen's affairs with married men always resulted in her getting dumped and them dying soon after. Why didn't she elaborate on Dirk and his alligator? Jaime was consumed with curiosity.

But Kate was returning with a steaming plate and a side of toast. "Now," she fussed, "eat and restore some energy. I'll get you more coffee." She looked around for the waiter.

Deciding she had eaten enough and impatient to bump into Mario, she picked up her bag.

Bidding the two women goodbye, she strode out of the restaurant.

Chapter 56

Guests wandered aimlessly around. The weather was keeping them all inside, or they were trying to get last-minute bus tours around the island. Thomas must be busy, thought Jaime, glad she had decided against asking for his help. Leaving the lobby area, she strolled through the bar, which was fuller than usual for this time of day. Although only 9 am, people had decided rain, thunder and lightning meant you could start drinking earlier.

Spotting Caleb and Carol Carfax sipping on Bellini cocktails, she remembered Henry telling her about Caleb's argument with Dickens on the night he was murdered, although it appeared he had an alibi. Was it Carol Carfax's name she was going to find somewhere in that clinic? Could it be the reason for the altercation between the two men? Perhaps it would be Christy's name. The girl wasn't an innocent little angel. As Jaime had that thought, Christy herself walked towards her parents and took a seat. She noticed Carol reach out and place a hand on her daughter's arm.

Then she spied Tony and Mario. They were using one of the resort's board games, kept on hand for this sort of occasion. Backgammon. Mario was shaking the dice in the small canister provided and Tony was laughing at something. Relieved to come across them - she hadn't wanted to call their room and wake them up - she strolled over.

"Hi there. Who's winning?"

"He is at the moment," Tony pouted. "But don't worry, it won't last. It's luck, not skill."

"Whatever. I would like to point out I'm two games up."

"Have you checked out our spare room yet?" Tony asked.

Jaime had forgotten she had feigned an interest in taking a peek around Mario's unused room. "Just about to. To be honest, I need a favour."

Both the men paused and looked at her with interest.

"Are you still detecting, Miss Jones?" Tony's loud voice had the ability to travel all around the bar, even over the sound of the rain.

"Tell the world, Tony, why don't you? I don't think that man over there heard you." Jaime wasn't joking.

"Oops, sorry. I'm not good at this." He looked apologetic.

"Well, you can make up for it." Jaime sat close to the pair and kept her voice low.

"Remember last night when I said I thought the motive in this case was more likely to be about revenge, a woman scorned and all that?"

They both nodded, hanging on her every word.

"Well, I have a lead and it needs checking out, but I can't give too much away." Pausing, she took a breath. "I need to go into a clinic incognito, find out if anyone we know had an appointment there. And I can't go alone. I need someone to accompany me." Her eyes focussed on Mario, and he nodded.

"What kind of clinic? Where is it? Whose name do you think you'll find?" Tony had clearly missed the part where she had said she couldn't give too much away.

"Trust me when I say I will tell you, but not yet." The truth was she was afraid of Tony's inability to keep anything to himself, and she couldn't risk him alerting anyone to what she was doing.

Mario nodded. "It's fine, Jaime. Don't worry. You don't need to fill me in on everything. I'll go with you."

Jaime felt relieved.

"Like hell you will."

They both turned towards Tony's angry face.

He continued, "No offence, hun, but you're not the man the for the job. No way. Who's the leading light in the Pimlico Players? Who was cast as one of the ugly sisters in last year's panto, which was a roaring success, I might add? Who had an article written all about him in the Pimlico Tatler following his role as Stanley Kowalski? What was it they said, Mario?" Without waiting for an answer, he continued, "*Hayward's representation of this disturbing degenerate was totally believable.* You see, Jaime, there's no question I'm the star of this partnership. No offence, Mario, the special effects you produced were great, babe."

Not normally one to be taken off guard, Jaime's jaw dropped. She had no words. Mario's face had darkened, and his eyes had narrowed. He seemed to be trying to collect himself. Then he squeezed her hand - in sympathy for what she was about to endure, no doubt.

Tony appeared oblivious that he had almost pushed his partner too far. "You're in good hands with me, Jamie. Trust me. We'll get the information you need. I have years of training; my skills are finely tuned. Now, when do we need to leave? I'll need time to sort out my costume, not to mention hair and make-up."

Jaime was silently praying. What had she gotten herself into?

Chapter 57

Heading to her room to prepare for the big outing she was now dreading, Jaime spotted a familiar figure. Sitting alone, cradling a cup of tea, Christy Carfax stared out towards the ocean. Jaime made a snap decision and walked towards the lone figure. Not sure what she was going to say, she placed a hand on the back of the empty chair at Christy's table.

"Mind if I sit for a minute?" Jaime smiled broadly, hoping to come across as approachable. "I'm Jaime."

Christy's head jerked, and she blinked. "Oh, I recognise you," she declared, "from the flight." It was a statement, not a question, but Jaime nodded. "I'm Christy."

"I wanted to check on how you are. I think you and your family are staying in the new wing, along with us crew. We've all been grilled by the police about the murders. I guess you all have too?"

Christy relaxed. "Yes, we have. Those two are formidable. They scare me to death."

The two women laughed as Jaime agreed. She needed to find out if there was any way Christy could be a murderer. She thought not. Her theory pointed to someone else, but Christy was a loose end that needed tying up. The way forward here was to go down the 'camaraderie' route, they were both in the same boat.

238

"I was given such a grilling about my so-called relationship with Dickens when I barely knew him." She paused, hoping Christy would pick up the thread.

"Oh, me too -" Christy stopped, and her face reddened. Jaime's curiosity was piqued. Should she wait? Say something to relieve the tension? Part of her wanted to wait, see what Christy said next. The other side of her wanted to help the girl out.

"I wouldn't worry about it. I think it's part of their job to throw around accusations and see what sticks. It doesn't mean they suspect you." Jaime noticed Christy relax.

"I hope you're right. But they have discovered a lot about me. I'm not a bad person or anything; and none of my family even knew that woman from your team," she added.

Jaime wasn't sure she was going to get too much information from Christy in one meeting without gaining some trust. There must have been some connection between the teenager and Dickens, but it would be good to have it confirmed. Deciding to impart some personal information, something she would never normally do, she hoped it would be reciprocated.

"I know what you mean. They seem to have done their homework on me too. They found out I was married once. Years ago, when I wasn't much older than you, I'm guessing."

Christy's eyebrows rose.

Jaime continued. "It didn't last long. I was swept up in the idea of being married to an older man. It opened up a whole new world to me. We travelled all over: it was exciting. At first. Until I realised everything has its price." Jaime paused and noticed Christy nodding. She continued, "Soon enough, I discovered he had a temper and was possessive. Controlling. I hadn't noticed this before. Perhaps he had hidden it well, or I was blinkered. Either way, it didn't take me too long to realise I wanted out. As much as I enjoyed the lifestyle, I didn't want it like that. I would have to work hard for it, but it would be much more rewarding."

"What did you do? How did you tell him? Did he take it badly?"

Jaime paused, "Well, let's say he didn't have a lot to say about it."

"Wow. You're brave. Did you split up?"

"He's dead. Which is the part that interested the detectives."

"Why?"

"His death was unexplained. So, I was interviewed. I'm afraid it's enough for them to treat me as a suspect."

"Ridiculous." Christy was indignant. "You never remarried?"

"I don't think it's for me. I like the independence my life gives me. And there's plenty of time. I'm not that old. Detective Marshall discovered I didn't like Councillor Dickens, that we'd had a confrontation in the bar the night he died." Jaime decided that was enough information to impart and hoped her admission would be enough for Christy to feel comfortable.

Christy's fingers were drumming on the table, a grim look on her face. "No way. At least they didn't discover you were out with him that night. I mean, I thought there was no way they would find out about my date. I had been careful." Her eyes locked onto Jaime.

Jaime was trying her best to hide her shock. Out with Dickens on the night he was murdered. This was way more than she had bargained for. However, she rallied. "How did you meet him?"

"He's married to one of my mum's friends. I know what you're thinking. I must be some kind of slut."

"No, I'm not. None of us are perfect."

Christy's whole body relaxed. "It's good to have a real conversation with someone. You're not trying to come across all perfect. You've made mistakes and you own them. It makes me happy to think maybe there is a way out."

A way out, thought Jaime. Interesting phrase. "How come you agreed to meet him? If you don't mind me asking."

"It was a business arrangement. He said he needed a girl on his arm. That was it. He would pay well. And to be honest, I get bored of coming to this same place, year after year."

"Let me guess. Knowing what sort of a jerk he was from the odd occasion I met him, he decided he wanted more than an escort?"

Christy was nodding. "Right. And I was not into that at all. And I showed him what I thought of his proposition." She stopped for a few seconds. "Oh, it sounds bad." Her voice dropped to a whisper. "I don't mean… you know - that I killed him."

Jaime leaned forward and patted her hand. "I get it. I was about to punch him in the face until someone interrupted at the bar."

"Brilliant. I kneed him where it hurts. He went down like a ton of bricks." Both women burst into laughter, causing a few heads to turn their way.

"Good for you," Jaime managed a few minutes later. She liked this young woman and didn't want her to be a killer "I guess your evening finished early?" Jaime asked, hoping the question didn't suggest she suspected Christy.

"I left him at the party we were at and made my own way back. The cheeky bastard tried again after coming back here, calling my room, but I was having none of it."

"Good for you. I guess it was quite late?"

"Must have been around half eleven."

"But you didn't see him again?"

"No. I hung up on him. Went to bed and tried to forget about everything that had happened."

Jaime was thinking about the previous evening when she had been spying on Max. The car arriving outside the hotel, the exchange between the two people inside. Not one to assume anyone needed or wanted her advice - now, she felt it might be useful. "Be careful, Christy. I know it's important you find your own path and make your own mistakes, but men who use the services of escorts want more. And some will not take no for an answer."

Christy leaned forward. "I think I came close to finding out."

"The jerks of this world will always need to be put in their place. We need to be ready for them."

Christy's eyes widened at this last comment and Jaime stood to leave.

"Take care," she said. And meant it.

Jaime rushed away. Time had gotten the better of her, and she needed to get a move on.

Chapter 58

Officer Kennedy turned the page of his newspaper and stared at the columns. Sipping his coke, he realised he had been daydreaming and might have missed some important information.

The pounding of the rain was not helpful - any conversation he might have been able to overhear was now drowned out. The breakfast smelled delicious, although he had already eaten much earlier. He noticed the staff were keeping it running for longer today, probably trying to placate the guests who could not indulge in beach-type activities.

His quarry was seated at a small round table, sipping on a cup of tea, now alone, leafing through a magazine. Kennedy hoped he hadn't been spotted, although, from experience, he knew that was unlikely. He was good at blending into his surroundings. Today, he was enjoying the freedom being out of uniform afforded, and he had opted for his knee-length shorts and his well-worn ABFA t-shirt (Antigua and Barbuda Football Association).

William Kennedy was a man who wanted to impress his bosses. He thought it was high time for a pay rise and a promotion. So did his wife, Bel. In fact, it was pretty much all she talked about. He didn't blame her. She was ambitious for him because she loved him. And he wanted to make her happy. *C'mon, Will,* he admonished himself: *focus. Impress*

Fontaine and Marshall. Find the evidence they need. With a renewed vigour, he concentrated on the small round table to his left.

As he watched, a picture of Detective Letitia Marshall popped into his head. The admiration she had shown for him when he had presented his findings on Edwina Kershaw. He had been able to confirm she'd got an alibi for the night of Jean Blackthorn's murder. Her father had suffered from chest pains and she and her mother had called an ambulance. Bel's friend, Cassie, had been one of the attending paramedics and had confirmed Edwina and her mother had been present throughout the entire night. Alongside the information he had discovered about the Captain and Vanessa Fleet, well, let's say a promotion was surely on the cards.

Now, if he could only cement this with a hat trick. All he needed to do was nail this one in the act... Draining his glass, William Kennedy glanced over towards the round table and received a shock.

His quarry had gone. Vanished. *Holy snakes. How can I have missed that?* he chided himself, jumping up. Racing out of the restaurant, they were nowhere in sight. It seemed they had disappeared into the rain - along with his promotion.

Chapter 59

The gentle tapping on her door could barely be heard as the ever-worsening rain battered onto the glass doors. Grabbing her bag, she hurried over to open it.

"Hi, you two," she said to Tony and Mario, who were waiting outside. Mario smiled at her, looking more relaxed than earlier.

"So, what do you think?" asked Tony, twirling around to show Jaime his outfit.

What she thought was - it wasn't too bad. Plain blue jeans (no rips), powder blue shirt buttoned almost to the neck, deck shoes, no make-up and naturally wavy hair.

"You look…" she struggled to find the right words.

"Straight," suggested Mario. "He looks straight, thanks to my help. Now he shouldn't draw too much attention. Couples do go to these places together, right?"

Jaime had not had a choice but to fill Tony and Mario in on where they were going and why if she wanted Tony to play his part properly. And she had to admit, going as a straight couple might draw less attention to them as a single woman going with her flamboyant, gay friend. She congratulated both men on their efforts as they walked to the lobby.

"I'll get you a taxi," said Mario as they walked, "save you two getting wet. And I'll grab you an umbrella from

245

reception. I'll tell the driver you want them to wait for you, right?"

Jaime had already written the address down for him. "Yes, please," she replied, thinking how efficient Mario was.

"We need to stay out of sight," she said to Tony. "I don't want to alert any of the crew who might be around to the possibility we are going somewhere. They'll ask questions."

Tony nodded. "Of course, my dear. Whatever you say." He had adopted a deep voice, which sounded ridiculous.

Jaime laughed. "You can't do that," she exclaimed. "You'll blow our cover. Be normal."

"What the hell is 'normal' when it's at home?" Tony asked indignantly, but his voice had returned to its usual pitch.

"You could try something totally different and out of character," Mario said, rubbing his chin.

Tony and Jaime waited.

"What?" snapped Tony.

"Not talking." Mario burst out laughing.

"For goodness' sake, you two. Do not make me regret asking for your help."

They arrived in the lobby, and Jaime and Tony scooted off to a secluded sofa to await their taxi. Despite the dreadful weather, it was only a few minutes until Mario beckoned them to come.

He handed Jaime a large umbrella, standing aside as they passed through, whispering, "I'll be right here when you get back."

She mouthed her thanks and they rushed into the waiting car, which had been stood idling under the resort's canopy.

"All Saints is it m' dear?" asked the middle-aged driver, confirming what she had been told.

"Yes, please."

"Shouldn't take long, despite this." She gestured out the window. "Seat belts, please." Pushing her spectacles back onto her nose, the driver edged away from the entrance. As soon as they had driven out from under the canopy, the sound of the rain crashing onto the car roof was deafening.

"What's the plan when we arrive?" Tony had to shout.

Jaime was silent for a moment, then responded, "I'm not sure how this is going to work. Until we get in there, I won't know the set up. All I need is a name. If my hunch is correct, there will be an appointment booked for the woman he got pregnant, to push her into having an abortion. I could be wrong; he could have been handing her the business card to make her own appointment. But I suspect he was the controlling type, and he would have had the operation booked and paid for, leaving little room for backing out. Handing her the business card was to remind her." Jaime paused.

"How do you know she won't be here?" asked Tony. "Sat in the waiting room?"

"Because if I'm correct, there is no way this woman would even contemplate stepping into a place like this. She would have been incensed at the idea. And that rage is what got the councillor killed."

Tony shuddered. "Perhaps Mario should have come with you after all."

Jaime glared at him, then bit her tongue. It was too late now. She'd have to make the best of the situation. "All I need is to find a name I recognise booked into that clinic. Whether they turned up or not, there will be a record of the appointment. And if there isn't … I'm screwed. I'll have no evidence to back up my theory. Nothing to present to the detectives."

Tony blew out a long breath. "Okay, hun. We're going to need to be quick. In and out, no messing. One of us will need to cause a distraction whilst the other one flips through the filing draws and extracts the evidence. Shall I have a heart attack?"

Jaime hid her irritation. "Could it be something a bit less dramatic? The less attention on us, the better. Don't you think?"

"Hmm." Tony was not to be put off. "I could faint. At the thought of what you are about to go through. For the sake of our relationship."

"How about maybe you ask the receptionist a question? Or you could ask them to come outside with you so you can have a private word? Maybe ask them how long it will take, etc... You could free up the area for me."

"It could work." Tony sounded disappointed. "It's a bit tame."

"Tame is good. It just needs to work. But we'll need to be adaptable. There could be more than one receptionist. We don't know."

"Whose name are we going to find? Who do you suspect?"

"There is someone who fits the bill..." She trailed off, staring out the window.

Tony's eager face reminded her of her dog, Wolfe, when she was preparing his food. Noticing how grey the landscape was, compared to yesterday, she focussed on a quaint, pink cottage with water gushing down the gutters like a rapidly flowing river: front doors firmly closed and children nowhere to be seen. It was difficult to make out the outline of Betty's Hope as they whooshed passed. What she could see was foreboding in the grey light. The windscreen wipers on the taxi were battling against the downpour, looking as though they might take off at any moment.

A few minutes later, the car turned into a road Jaime recognised. She was feeling a strange blend of nerves and excitement, although she was comforted by the idea of having someone with her, even if it was Tony.

"You need to pull in towards those black gates," Jaime instructed the driver. "Line up level with the intercom and I'll speak into it."

The driver nodded and obeyed. A strange noise from next to Jaime caused her to turn around. "What are you doing?" she hissed at Tony.

"My breathing exercises. Channelling my inner calm."

"Well, channel in silence, please." She debated whether a short prayer might be in order but instead pressed the intercom buzzer.

"Can I help?" asked Darth Vader on the other end.

"Miss Jones here for my appointment." Jaime held her breath. She waited, but there was no response.

Tony jabbed her in the leg. "Look. The gates are opening. Oh my god. Oh my god. Oh my god. Oh m - "

"Shush." Jaime was going to lose it any second now. But there was no time, as a man was approaching the car window. Jaime wound hers down and poked her head out. "Miss Jones," she said, retreating before turning into a drowned rat.

"I will need some form of ID, ma'am." The request was polite but firm.

Jaime had been expecting this and produced her passport. The man studied it, careful to keep it out of the rain – handed it back, waved them through. Jaime wondered what the taxi driver was making of all this, but the woman seemed to be taking it in her stride.

"Are you okay to wait?" she asked the driver.

"Of course. No problem," was the reply as the driver pulled out a battered copy of Agatha Christie's *And Then There Were None*.

Fond memories came to Jaime upon seeing one of the greatest novels of all time. "Thanks. We'll be as quick as we can," she added, feeling her nerves rise once more.

Chapter 60

11:00

Getting out of the car and putting up the umbrella without getting too wet proved to be a far bigger ordeal than Jaime had expected. Tony refused to alight until she had walked around to his side and met him there. She tried to stop wishing Mario had come instead. It was counter-productive at this point. The car had pulled into the small rear car park, and there was not much distance to cover to the door. No turning back now, she thought, as a rumble of thunder made her jump.

The reception area was sparse. The walls were painted a pastel peach with hangings of various geometric shapes in black frames. There were the expected potted plants, three to be precise, and two cream faux leather sofas set at right angles to one another. They both breathed a sigh of relief to see that no one else occupied the room. A small reception area was on their left, and they could hear the low murmur of voices coming from behind a partition wall behind the counter. Looking at each other for guidance, Tony pointed towards the reception. As they reached it, a woman materialised from behind the partition wall.

Jaime stepped forward. "Good morning. My name is…" but she was interrupted.

"Miss Jones? Please take a seat and I'll sign you in. Sir, please make yourself comfortable."

Little Miss Efficient, I do believe, thought Jaime, remembering the crisp tone from her recent phone call.

Turning towards the sofa, Tony put an arm around her waist to guide her. She shot him a warning look that said *don't over play it*. They sat together - not directly opposite the counter - as the woman disappeared once more.

"I need to get behind the counter. It's where the paperwork will be," Jaime whispered. "And soon, before they whisk me away."

"There's more than one of them. I can hear them. What if there are loads of them? Crap. Now what?" Tony whispered back in a panic. He ran a hand through his hair, and Jaime noticed beads of sweat forming on his upper lip.

He's losing it already, she thought, feeling a bit panicky herself. *Okay, calm down. It's no biggy. We can always walk out of here and claim to have changed our minds. It must happen all the time.* She took a deep breath and strained to listen. Nothing. Squeezing Tony's knee, she rose and walked as nonchalantly as she could back over to the counter, then to the side of it, then around the back.

"Psst!" Tony half whispered and half shouted.

She held up her hand in a placating gesture, deliberately not looking in Tony's direction. As she was taking in her surroundings, there was the audible click of a door opening then closing and footsteps heading her way. Her heart was beating fast as she retreated to the further end of the counter and ducked out of sight.

Noticing the lack of files, paperwork or computer, she realised it would have to be a trip into the back office. The head of Little Miss Efficient popped into sight, and Jaime heard a gasp coming from the sofa. Turning towards the sound, she was in time to watch Tony slipping off the seat and onto the floor, ending in a heap on the jute rug. *Wow, he's not too bad*, marvelled Jaime from her cramped position on the floor, forgiving him for ignoring her and going for 'the faint' after all. It got the attention of Little Miss Efficient as she rushed around the other end of the counter and over to Tony.

Jaime watched as she tapped his face and called into her remote-controlled radio for someone to bring a glass of water. Jaime knew as soon as the water appeared, she had to take her chance and crawl into the back room. She would have at most, a few minutes whilst they tended to Tony before they would wonder where she had gone and start to look for her. And she had no idea whether the information would be on a computer, paper files, or not even in that room at all.

Footsteps could be heard; Jaime saw a pair of white pumps. *Please don't let there be more than two receptionists,* she prayed.

"What's happening, Sylvia? Oh, surprise surprise. We have a fainter."

"Bring the water and help me get him back on the sofa."

Jaime was not waiting around for the amusing spectacle of watching the two ladies try to lift Tony's limp form back onto the sofa. She was around the wall, through the slightly open door and in the back room. It was devoid of any more staff. She let out a long breath.

It was homely, with a small kitchen area containing a microwave and a coffee machine. There was one desk with one computer and a few stacks of boxes containing medical supplies, judging by the labels. Damn, she thought. A computer it is. Not the ideal scenario, but if it didn't need a password, she thought she could manage. Still on her knees, she crawled over and grabbed the mouse, causing the screen to come to life.

"Lift one arm and grab him under the armpit. Why have I got all the weight?"

"I'm lifting. I think his shoe has come off." The voices from the other room were loud enough for her to hear.

As tempted as Jaime was to crawl back out and take a peek, she resisted. Tony was getting into the role. Turning to the computer screen, she noticed the crowded desktop. Thank goodness, no password required. Somewhere there

252

must be a diary or appointments icon. Yes. There it was. Double-clicking it brought up a page labelled with today's date, and she could see her name there, under eleven o'clock. A quick scan showed four other names, none of which she recognised. Clicking on the little arrow brought up the previous day on the calendar, she scanned the names. None she recognised, again. *Don't be a waste of time,* she thought, clicking on the day before that: the only other day the appointment could have been for, the day after the councillor's death.

"Do you think I should get the smelling salts? He's not coming round."

"Waft a magazine in front of his face. A bit of air should do it. Why do they always bring someone who can't take it?"

"I know. Talking of bringing someone, where is she?"

Jaime knew she had to move. Scanning the list of names, finger poised over the mouse ready to return the screen to the homepage, she spotted it. A name she recognised. Booked in for 3 pm of the day after Dickens' death – a red line crossed through it. Her breaths had become short, and she had to concentrate on calming herself down.

But she could barely hide her elation. *Yes, yes, yes! I knew it.* Her arms wafted in the air as she did a little victory wave. Then, back to reality, she crawled to the partition wall, through the door and behind the counter, peeking around.

Sylvia stood up. "She must be using the bathroom. I'll go check on her. We don't need two fainters on our hands." She turned towards the entrance and pushed through the glass door.

Other than that door, there was one more, and it was facing the sofa Tony was slumped on. It must lead to the operating rooms, thought Jaime. She needed to get back into reception but how was she going to do it with Little Miss Efficient still present? She couldn't just pop up from behind the counter.

Crawling back once again, she peeked into the back room. The door she had heard opening and closing earlier was located to the left, next to the pile of boxes. It was her only means of escape, and she knew Tony was going to have to come round soon, although she had to admit, he was doing a terrific job.

Feeling like a toddler who has yet to learn how to walk, knees feeling sorer by the second from her crawling around, she hobbled over to the door and turned the handle, opening it a crack. Peering through, she saw a small corridor with a couple of spotlights in the ceiling, three doors to her left and one to her right. That had to be the one leading back into the waiting room. Tiptoeing into the empty corridor, she stood, smoothed her clothing, glancing in horror at her bright red knees and strode to the door. Opening it, trying her best to look confused, she was confronted by Little Miss Efficient rising from the sofa as Sylvia came through the entrance door.

"That's odd, she's not in there," she was saying, then stopped when she saw Jaime opposite her.

"I can't seem to locate the loo?" Jaime tried for her timid, 'help me' voice, hoping it was believable.

"We thought you'd vanished into thin air," responded Sylvia. "The bathroom is on the left as you come in." She indicated the door behind where she stood.

"Your friend has fainted, Miss Jones. We're trying to revive him. We're becoming a little concerned."

"Oh," Jaime waved a hand in the air flippantly. "Don't worry. It's happened before. He just needs a minute. Leave the water and I'll sort him out. I'm so sorry." *Come on, Tony, this is your cue to wake up. Don't milk it for too long.*

"If you're sure. It is something that happens quite a lot here, I have to say. Come on, Penny, let's get organised for Miss Jones and prepare her forms to fill in." Then to Jaime, "We'll be a few minutes. Call if you need us." They retreated around the counter.

Jaime hoped the computer screen had had time to go back to sleep. The last thing she wanted was to be accused of spying and have them call the police. There wasn't any time to waste. She sat next to Tony, and the second the two women had left, nudged him. No response. She nudged again, harder. Still no response.

"Wake up. They've gone. We need to go."

Nothing. Jaime stared at him, aghast. *Oh my goodness, he's not acting. He's really fainted.* In a panic, fearing what would happen if the two women came back to collect her, she turned to face Tony and gave him an almighty smack across his cheek. Her hand stung from the contact. However, it had the desired effect as Tony's eyes popped open. Looking confused, his hand rising to his flaming red cheek, he shuffled to sit upright.

"What's happening? What's going on? Have you managed to get the name?"

Resisting the urge to smack him again, she replied, as calmly as she could manage, "I'm done, and we need to get out of here. Now!" she added through gritted teeth.

Tony pushed himself off the sofa, falling into her. "My cheek hurts," he whined.

Jaime, who was still thinking about being led off to a back room, pushed him upright, grabbed his hand and yanked him towards the door.

The rain had not lessened any, and even with the umbrella, they were going to get soaked. But there was nothing for it. Opening the door, and taking the umbrella from the large pottery vase, they headed out at a run, holding hands as they pelted back to the waiting taxi. Diving in the back, Jaime placed the umbrella on the floor and signalled the woman to drive off. Smiling brightly at the guard through her window, she was relieved he had opened the gates for them to exit.

Only when they were passing by Betty's Hope did her pulse return to normal.

Chapter 61

11.39

The ride back to the resort consisted mainly of Tony whining about his painful cheek. He said he found it hard to believe it happened when he slid to the floor. Jaime insisted it must have occurred then, even though Tony was convinced he had the outline of a hand imprinted on his face. At first, he had tried to pretend the faint was great acting, then had decided, upon seeing Jaime's sceptical face, to admit it had been real but only because his blood sugar must be low. This was the first Jaime had heard of his blood sugar condition but decided it best to let it drop.

He had asked her several times what she had discovered, and although she felt as though she should share her findings, she held back. Tony was one of the biggest gossips she had ever met, and this was a dangerous matter. Jaime was convinced she had discovered a killer, and there was no way this information could be allowed to leak out until she had passed it on to the proper authorities: Cagney and Lacey.

Yes, she would no doubt be chastised for what she had done; interfering in an investigation, withholding evidence, and who knew what else. But she knew she would have to deal with that.

Progress was slow as the taxi crawled along: the floods formed on the roads making the journey treacherous. Several times as they headed back to the resort, Jaime turned to stare out the back window. It was difficult to see as the rear wiper worked intermittently. Not being able to shake the feeling they were being followed, she could make out the shapes of several cars behind, but that didn't prove anything.

She leaned forward to address the driver. "Have you noticed any particular cars following us at all?" she asked.

The driver, who was concentrating on the road ahead, at first didn't answer. After thirty seconds or thereabouts, she replied, "Hard to tell. I can't make out much at all, sorry."

Jaime sat back and turned round again. The driver was right. It was impossible to make out any details through the lashing rain and the spray from the road surface. What had made her think they were being tailed? *Nerves*, she reasoned. *I'm on edge.*

"Are we being followed, Jaime? Is the killer stalking us? Oh my god, I need Mario."

Jaime wished she had never said anything. Tony looked like he was going to faint again.

"It's my imagination." She smiled. "I read too many books. Mario's waiting for us - he said he'd be in the lobby, remember?"

Pulling into the canopied entrance of the Reef Royale sometime later, Jaime paid the driver with a generous tip for hanging around for them and her expert driving in such awful conditions. Tony jumped out of the cab and ran into the hotel, no doubt in search of Mario. Lingering, Jaime scanned any cars pulling in behind them. There was a four-wheel drive, which contained a young couple. This was followed by a small tour bus, its window wipers moving too fast to cope, and then came a local taxi, which was interesting. Watching intently, no one emerged. It could be empty, she supposed. A hand grabbing her wrist made her jump.

"Come on inside. Mario wants to hear all about it, don't you, Mario? I told him my faint was wonderful, the best. Had everyone fooled, even you." Tony gave Jaime a warning look.

Mario, who was hovering in the background, winked at Jaime. "I can't wait to be filled in. You need to tell me everything. It's been torture sitting here, waiting."

A thought struck Jaime as they headed towards the bar area. "Whilst you were waiting, did you happen to notice if any of our crew left the resort?"

"No. But I got up and walked around a few times. You'd have to be crazy to head out in this storm. The hotel staff have been circulating, asking everyone, for our own safety, to stay inside the resort, and preferably our rooms. Until the worst of it passes."

The bar was about empty, the advice of the staff being heeded.

"Do you think the crew will be having lunch?" asked Tony. "I'm starving."

"We can look. But first, I need to know what you discovered."

"Jaime's not telling. She found something, though," Tony stated accusingly.

"It's not that I'm not telling," Jaime protested. "I want to tell the detectives first. It's important they get this information and can act on it without the killer being alerted."

"So, you found the killer's name?" Mario's eyes lit up.

A voice from behind the group startled them. "What are you three plotting?" There was no mistaking the Brummie accent.

"Karen." Mario was the first to collect himself. "You're looking windswept."

Indeed, it was true. Karen looked as though she had braved the bad weather, however, brushed the comment aside.

"Is this a secret meeting?" she persisted.

"We're heading for some lunch," Tony entered the conversation, obviously trying to sidestep Karen's questions.

"The restaurant's pretty much closing. They're pushing people towards having room service so they can finish erecting the storm shutters." Karen must have come from there.

"Room service it is. Come on. Thanks, Karen. We'll catch you later." Tony grabbed Mario's arm, followed by Jaime's and marched them off towards the stairs.

As they reached the bottom of the staircase, Jaime broke free of his grasp.

"I need to find the detectives. I'm going to have a quick check around."

"We'll come with you."

"Let's eat first. We can do it after lunch," Tony whined.

Mario frowned at his partner. The last thing Jaime wanted was to cause a rift between these two.

"You two go on ahead. I'll give you a call when I've located them." Seeing Mario's concerned expression, she added, "I'm not leaving the resort or the public areas. Go on. I'll be fine."

Reluctantly, Mario allowed himself to be dragged away by his partner, who gave Jaime a cheery 'toodle-oo' as they departed.

Chapter 62

Knocking at the detectives' door, Jaime waited for a beat, then tried the door handle. Locked. Damn. She put her ear to the door and listened. No sound. No one was in there. She must get her information to them.

Deciding to find Henry or Vanessa, she walked along to their offices. Both rooms were locked. Jaime was becoming frustrated and worried. Where was everyone? A loud clap of thunder made her jump. She knew she was on edge. Heading back to the lobby, she would check out the bar and the restaurant again. One more lap of the public areas – surely she could find someone. There were a handful of people in reception, queuing at the desk. She could hear one lady demanding a full refund for an outing that was not going to take place. It's not going to be much of a fun job today, thought Jaime, thinking about the poor receptionist.

Moving through the wide passageway towards the bar, she circled all the way around, noting the occasional couple, some drinking, some utilising the board games. Jaime thought how ironic most people elected to play board games when they were bored. The restaurant was now closed, all the rain shutters were up, and staff were hurrying around, tidying tables and sweeping the floor, no doubt anxious to be finished and on their way. Jaime wondered what they would do later for the evening meal. Would they be able to reopen and feed the hungry throng of guests?

Back to the problem at hand: there was no one in authority around she could pass her information onto nor indeed any of the crew. They must have taken the resort's advice and gone to the sanctuary of their rooms.

Standing at one of the large, floor-to-ceiling windows, Jaime stared out at the angry ocean. For a moment, she imagined being caught in those ferocious waves, gasping for air, being pulled down, down into the murky, dark depths. Forcing all thoughts of Ken to one side, her mind turned to Basil. She tried to picture where he might be. Failing to find him earlier that morning to give him his treat, she wondered if he was sheltering somewhere dry. Was he being taken care of by someone? Or was he standing out in the rain, cold, wet, shivering, frightened? The image was too much to bear, and she knew she had to go out and see if she could find him. If he needed her help, she would never forgive herself.

Hoping beyond hope he was okay - after all, he was a smart dog - she pushed through the swinging glass door to the canopied but unoccupied outdoor bar area. Not having packed any waterproofs, there was no reason to go to her room and change. She was going to get soaked and was resigned to the fact. Striding out towards the beach, she felt the cold drops of water on her back as soon as she stepped out from under the protection of the canopy. Forcing the unpleasant feeling away, her eyes scanned as she walked.

The place was deserted. All the sunbeds had been stacked into neat piles along the back edge of the beach. The umbrellas were down but stood forlornly looking out to sea, swaying back and forth. It didn't take long for Jaime's hair to be plastered to her head, her skirt clinging and heavy. If anyone saw her, they would think she was off her rocker. She turned to walk a little way along the beach, away from the direction of the resort, although so far, she was pleased there was no sign of Basil at all. The claps of thunder were formidable and forced her to stay away from any loitering trees.

261

After fifteen minutes or so, Jaime was satisfied Basil was not anywhere nearby, in which case, she decided, he must be sheltering somewhere. Turning back towards the resort, she was contemplating how she would get to her room without anyone seeing the dripping mess that she was. Hopefully, there would be no one around. She would have to hurry up the staircase as she would be creating puddles all over the floor the minute she stepped inside.

Straining to see ahead of her through the driving rain, Jaime's step faltered. A figure was heading towards her. *How odd*, she thought. *Some other mad person out in this weather besides me.*

Jaime slowed as she neared the figure. Now she could see who it was. The dark hair hung in ragged clumps and dripped over the sweatshirt. The figure stopped within a few metres of Jaime and stood, hands on hips, breathing heavily.

"Fancy seeing you here, Jaime."

Chapter 63

Jaime's heart skipped a beat. Although it was Gabi's name she had seen on the computer in the clinic, and it was Gabi she had suspected of murdering the councillor and Jean, it was still a shock to be confronted by the woman herself.

Playing dumb, Jaime asked, "What are you doing out here in this storm?"

Gabi leaned towards Jaime. "I think you know what I'm doing here, Jaime. You do know, don't you?"

It was hard to swallow: this woman was a murderer. She sounded calm. Normal. Although Jaime knew from the novels she'd read, most murderers appeared 'normal'. A low rumble of thunder could be heard over the sound of the rain. Jaime was unsure how to respond. Should she come clean? Or should she keep feigning ignorance? Knowing a murderer stood not two metres away, with not another soul in sight, was not a situation anyone would relish. However, the decision on how to respond was taken out of her hands.

"I've been watching you. Sneaking around. Trying to get information from people. then today, your visit to the clinic." There was a pause.

Jaime's mouth opened and closed like a goldfish. Gabi had followed them earlier. She could have kicked herself for not being more discreet.

"You have no idea how revolting he was." Gabi's voice had turned ice cold.

Jaime shivered. This did not seem like the same woman she had been conversing with the past few days. She was showing a different side to her personality, and Jaime felt in imminent danger. "I know how revolting he was. Believe me." Jaime raised her voice to be heard above the rustling trees and howling wind.

"What do you want me to say, Jaime? What gave me away?" Gabi sounded tired.

"Just small things, I suppose. You not drinking any alcohol, even though you professed to merlot being your favourite tipple. The way you disappeared before your interview with Dickens, then lied about it. Your rendezvous with Jean in the lobby and how uncomfortable you seemed in her presence. She was blackmailing you." Jaime paused, wanting Gabi to continue. Murderers always wanted to brag about how clever they were; surely she was no different?

"Nom de Dieu," cursed Gabi. Looking intently at Jaime, she continued. "I've been coming to Antigua for years. As have you. You know what a sleaze he was. But I could handle him. Give him the brush off. Ignore him - like I assume you did."

Jaime nodded, knowing no matter what, she must not antagonise her.

"Well, one trip, about three months ago, I was in the bar with a few colleagues. We'd had a lot to drink. I was feeling low. Problems at home. My husband and I had been trying to conceive. Tests showed no direct cause from either one of us. Well, it was doing our marriage no good, and we were arguing about everything. I went on the trip feeling depressed, such was the amount I was drinking in the bar." Gabi was lost in her narrative now, unaware of Jaime's presence. Her eyes had taken on a far-away look, as though she were somewhere else and not stuck in the ferocious storm.

"My colleagues wanted to go to bed. I wanted to carry on drinking. Finally, they left me there. I don't blame them. I can

264

be obnoxious when I'm drunk. As soon as they went, I ordered another drink. It was brought over by the councillor. I guess he had been watching me and I'm sorry to say, I was not unhappy about that.

"A few drinks later, and we found ourselves on the beach. You can guess what happened next." She paused, wiping her drenched hair from her face. "When I awoke, I had a hangover from hell and vague memories of what had happened the night before. I was ashamed. I didn't leave my room for the rest of the trip."

Staring at the dark sand for what felt like an eternity, Gabi finally continued. "It was two weeks later when I found out I was pregnant. At first, I was ecstatic - it was like a miracle. My husband was over the moon, and our relationship improved one hundred per cent. I guess I had blocked out the night with Dickens. The euphoria only lasted a week, though. I began to have doubts. It was highly likely it was Dickens' child I was carrying.

"I was out of my mind thinking about it. I went to see a… a psychiatrist?" She looked to Jaime for confirmation it was the correct word. Jaime nodded, so she continued. "I needed to unburden my guilt. She said what was done was done. I didn't plan it. And the possible result was the gift of bringing a child into the world. If it made my husband and I happy and complete, if I could forgive myself the infidelity, all could be well.

"I was content; I am a mentally strong person, and I convinced myself that my husband was the father of this child. Miracles could happen, and this was a miracle baby."

Jaime, wiping the rain from her face, had forgotten she was listening to a murderer's confession in the middle of a raging storm. "When did things change?" she asked.

"I was scheduled this trip here. I was going to go sick, not wanting to face Dickens. But then I thought, why should I stay out of his way? Merde! If only I'd stayed at home…

Don't misunderstand; I didn't come here with any plan in mind except that I wouldn't hide away.

"That bloody doctor with his loose lips. I wish I'd never gone to see him after the bus attack. He told Dickens I was pregnant. They are all connected out here. All mates together. It seems nothing is sacred. I should have killed him too." Her face contorted into an ugly mask, mascara streaking down her cheeks.

Jaime took a small step back.

"Dickens called my room when I failed to show for my interview and demanded to see me."

Jaime nodded. If she was any detective worth her salt, she'd be recording this.

Gabi continued, "He insisted we meet. Said he had something for me. I had no idea what it was. Of course, I didn't want to meet him, but I couldn't shake him off. He suggested we meet at midnight, which I agreed to. I didn't want to be seen with him. He wanted it to be somewhere away from prying eyes and suggested the private beach. I didn't have a problem with that."

Jaime knew the councillor had spent his evening with Christy Carfax, which was why he wanted to meet Gabi at such a late hour.

"We met by the access gate. I used my key card. We walked a distance along the beach away from the balconies, and he grabbed my arm, demanding for me to admit the child was his. I denied it. He said he didn't believe me. I told him I couldn't care less, and from now on, it was none of his business. He said he was going places politically, and he could not afford to have any illegitimate children cropping up anywhere in the future."

Before she could stop herself, Jaime found herself saying, "Unbelievable. Who the hell did he think he was?" and meaning every word of it. She was outraged. Yes, Gabi was wrong to have gotten drunk and slept with Dickens. But it shouldn't ruin her entire life. Men like him needed teaching a lesson.

Gabi continued, "He told me he'd got an assistant to call the clinic as soon as he had spoken to the doctor. He got out an envelope full of cash. I counted it later, $20,000. An extra incentive to get rid of my child. I was incensed. The presumptuous prick. How dare he treat this as though it were a business transaction? I had to wonder how often he had been through this before. He handled it with such ease."

"The business card was still in his hand when I found the body. Once I discovered what the place was, I was convinced that was the reason he was killed," Jaime stated.

Gabi's eyes widened. "I think I made my decision there and then. I 'accidentally' dropped the card as he was trying to hand it to me. He tutted and bent to retrieve it. I reached and grabbed a coconut from near my foot and whacked him on the head with all my strength. He keeled over, and the coconut exploded. It was disgusting. I hit him again and again. His head hit a rock."

Jaime gasped. Even though she knew what was coming (she had discovered the body, after all), it was still a shock. Shuffling back further, her left foot caught the edge of a sharp stone, and she winced in pain, not daring to look at the damage and take her eyes off Gabi. "You know, it's not first-degree murder, Gabi. It wasn't premeditated."

"I felt calm afterwards. I could get on with my life again. I walked back without a second glance. My only regret was when I later realised the access to that part of the beach was so limited. It put the crew under direct suspicion. But I figured the police would assume someone had climbed the rocks or approached from a boat. An absolute bastard like that had to have so many enemies." She paused to catch her breath.

"Could you not have taken the money and pretended to go along with him - never come back here again?" Jaime asked.

"It was the principle, Jaime. Can't you see that?" Gabi implored. "Everyone is better off without him, even his own wife and children."

Jaime realised she'd had this thought only a few days ago. Turning the conversation to the cabin service director, she said, "And Jean. She was blackmailing you, but not for money, right?"

"She knew, Jaime. She came to my room the next day and said she had seen Dickens and me at the beach access gate. God knows what she was doing there. I think she was following him around like some little lovesick puppy, and when she saw us together, she assumed we were carrying out some illicit affair. After the body was discovered, she put two and two together."

"I suppose if one of us had happened to be out on our balcony or taking a late-night stroll, we could have seen the councillor entering the beach…" quoted Jaime.

Gabi stared.

"Jean's exact words when we were first interviewed after Dickens' death. She was hinting to the murderer she had seen them. She had done exactly that. I thought it was familiar when she said it. Then I remembered a scene from *Death on the Nile*. The victim's maid says something similar when she is attempting to blackmail the killer. I knew then why Jean had been killed."

Gabi half smiled. "She said she knew everything but didn't want money. I tried to give her the $20,000 Dickens had given me, but she pushed it away. She didn't even threaten to go to the police. She picked up the photograph I have by my bed of me and my husband, smiled, put it back down and walked out of the room. She scared me. She was evil."

"I assume it was what you were discussing in the hotel lobby? You looked uncomfortable - Jean looked triumphant."

"She was following me around. Dropping comments and hints, wanting to torture me, make me squirm. It was a silent threat to my marriage, and I could not have that. You do see, don't you?" she implored.

"She was a Mrs Boynton character."

"A who?"

"Never mind," replied Jaime, marvelling at how Agatha Christie's work had helped her out. Two despicable human beings had been removed from the world, and no doubt, many people would be happy never to see either of them again. She stared hard at Gabi, the rain dripping off the end of her nose.

A loud rumble from the sky caused both women to glance up. The rain was not easing off, if anything it was faster and harder.

Gabi's confession continued. "After the meal at Ricardo's, she was easy to manipulate and agreed to meet me later. I had to hang around and wait for her to return from the club. I changed in my room, then went and hid on the beach. I nearly died when the captain turned up with some woman. But they didn't stay long and didn't spot me.

"The bitch thought she had won; she was going to make me beg her not to tell. That was what she wanted. Well, she hadn't won, and she got the same treatment as him. I kept bashing with the coconut until she went down. And it was well deserved. The world does not need a Jean Blackthorn in it. And I didn't make the same mistake of using the private stretch of beach again." She studied Jaime's face as if trying to read her expression.

Jaime understood the feeling of being pushed too far. There were some people in this world who drove women to the point of killing them. She knew, when she realised what 'Choices' was, someone had been pushed to breaking point.

Neither victim had any morals. They were both cruel and used people. Dickens wouldn't be dead if he had left Gabi alone to get on with her life. He would never have heard from her again. And Jean, if she'd had an ounce of compassion in her, she would have helped Gabi, not tortured her.

269

This was surely the end of the killing for Gabi. She had been protecting herself, hadn't she? Jaime would speak to Cagney and Lacey, and try to get them to understand Gabi's motives, as she did. If it wasn't that an innocent person might be wrongly blamed for these murders, Jaime might have been tempted to walk away. She wasn't in any danger from this woman now.

But Jaime was wrong.

"Why couldn't you leave well alone, Jaime? Why did you have to investigate? It could have all been over with now. They would have assumed it was Max and beaten a confession out of him."

"I don't think so, Gabi. We were all under suspicion. And it's not a great feeling to go through life being under suspicion."

A sudden movement from the other woman caught Jaime's eye. She froze. The wind had whipped up around them, and Jaime sensed the danger. The need to run. A flash of clarity showed her she had underestimated this woman because as she looked down, she saw in Gabi's hands a dreaded coconut.

It seemed, Jaime too, must die.

Chapter 64

Jaime was amazed at this woman's unending supply of the tropical fruit. She moved backwards slowly like you're told to do if you encounter a wild bear. Jaime stared at the weapon, wondering how much damage it could do when the potential victim was expecting it. She saw the look on Gabi's face. Her eyes were glazed, and Jaime guessed all sanity had evaporated. She needed to turn and run. Why the hell didn't she have her bag with her? Her canister of pepper spray would have come in useful right now.

Gabi stood between her and the resort, she would have to run in the opposite direction. In the split second it took her to have these thoughts, she had turned away from the mad woman and was beginning to sprint along the beach, feeling glad the heavy rain had firmed up the sand. Frantically, her head turned in every direction. A person, a house, anything, but there was nothing and no one around.

The driving rain prevented her from seeing far enough ahead to make anything out. The fear and panic were making her breaths ragged, and she struggled to get enough air into her lungs. Half of her was expecting the coconut to come soaring like a missile at her head. Knowing her luck, Gabi had probably been a member of the French shotput team.

Jaime knew if she was going to create enough distance between her and Gabi, she must stay calm and focused. Her legs pounded on the sand as she ran. Her skirt was a huge

271

hindrance as it clung to her legs, hampering her stride. She wanted to look back and see how much distance there was between her and certain death. Knowing it was the wrong thing to do, temptation took over, and she dared to risk a glance. Still holding the large fruit clutched to her body, Gabi was running flat out. She wasn't gaining on Jaime, but she was not far behind either. For a pregnant woman holding an awkward object, she's not doing too badly, thought Jaime begrudgingly.

Then she saw him. Running as fast as his four legs would carry him. A ball of hair hurtling along the beach towards Gabi, gaining on her. The sight caused Jaime to falter. The falter caused her to lose her balance, and she flew forward. Knowing she was about to faceplant did nothing to stop it. A bit like one of those dreams when you know you are about to fall off a mountain, and there's nothing you can do. Her face smacked into the hard sand, and now she wished it was not quite as firm.

Laying rigid, trying to work out what had happened, there was no tell-tale crack from her fall, but her hand flew to her nose, feeling for any signs of blood. There was none. Panic swelled within, and her breaths were even shorter and sharper. Hardly daring to turn around, she heard a scream: high-pitched, painful, followed by a long, deep growl. Forcing herself to look, she held her breath.

Gabi lay on the floor, arms outstretched, the coconut had rolled away, and Basil stood, one paw on her right arm, teeth bared, ready to take a giant bite of flesh. Jaime manoeuvred onto all fours and crawled the distance over to the dog, muttering soothing words, trying to calm him down. Reaching him, she stroked his back and felt the tension in his rigid body.

"It's alright. Good boy. You've done a great job. Good boy," she uttered.

Basil relaxed, and the growling ceased. He sat and touched her cheek with his wet nose.

"You're such a good boy, Basil. You saved my life." A tear trickled down her face.

The two of them sat for a minute, calming each other - taking stock of the situation. Gabi, meanwhile, lay motionless on the sand, eyes closed, breathing shallow. The teeth marks on her wrist looked angry, and already there were signs of the bruise to come.

Shouting could be heard in the distance. Both heads spun around: Basil growled once again. Jaime stared in the direction of the distant commotion and saw a group of people, rain macs on, hoods up, heading their way. She couldn't make out who they were, then she heard,

"Jaime. Jaime. Are you okay? Oh god!"

"Miss Jones. Wave if you can."

Jaime was startled. She recognised the voices of Henry and Inspector Fontaine, who had ditched her heels and was sprinting along the sand like an Olympian. Relief washed over her.

"It's okay, Basil, it's help. They've come to help."

Basil stopped growling.

As the first two approached, there was a stirring from Gabi, She groaned, attempting to move. Jaime had had enough of this woman. Scooping Basil up, she stood, wobbling, then moved away in the direction of the runners. Henry was the first to reach her and embraced her, almost suffocating Basil in the process, who didn't seem to mind. Fontaine was talking into her radio, asking for medical assistance.

"Be careful," warned Jaime, shouting over the wind. "She's dangerous. She tried to kill me."

"Don't worry, Miss Jones. We know all about her."

Jaime's eyebrows lifted a notch in surprise.

Henry said, "Inspector Fontaine had her under surveillance until Officer Kennedy lost her earlier, and they called me to help them look. I told the detectives you were doing some sleuthing, and their concern made me panic."

273

"She killed Jean too. She tried to kill me. I could be dead right now if Basil hadn't shown up."

Henry frowned. "Jesus. If another guest had not seen you come out into this rain, we wouldn't be here now. What happened?" He patted Basil on his head. Not waiting for a reply, he said, "I think we should get you two out of this rain and warmed up. You may be in shock. Let's leave this to the authorities now."

Jaime was more than happy to get off the beach, although the rain had finally eased, now more of a drizzle. Turning one last time to survey the scene, she saw Detective Marshall was securing the area, and despite the injury to her wrist, had Gabi in handcuffs. Other officers were lifting her to a seated position, and for now, Gabi was complying. She was otherwise unharmed.

As she was being led away, Jaime's eyes stopped on one man in the group, who, although wearing the same dark mac as the others, was dressed more casually underneath it, in light trousers and soaked canvas pumps. A gust of wind caught his hood and half blew it down, his hand flew out to retrieve it and pull it back. But Jaime caught sight of the light, fair hair, and as he half turned, the piercing blue eyes. She caught her breath. It was him again. What on earth was he doing here? Was he part of law enforcement? She had to know and was about to march over when she felt Henry's hand on her shoulder, attempting to guide her away. Detective Marshall strode towards them, having left her prisoner in the capable hands of the officers. "Do you need medical attention, Jaime? Are you hurt?"

Jaime shook her head. She had recovered from her fall and felt fine.

"We'll need a statement. Why don't you wait for us in the bar area? Have a hot drink. We shouldn't be too long." Detective Marshall gave her a warm smile.

Jaime was surprised at the detective's suddenly friendly attitude. Deciding to capitalise on it, she asked, "Who's that man? The one with blonde hair?" She waited.

Marshall half turned, then stopped, probably realising she didn't need to look to know who Jaime was referring to. She merely said, "You'd better get out of those wet clothes. You'll get hypothermia." Then headed back to the scene, and Henry managed to propel Jaime away.

"Henry, who's the man with the fair hair?" Jaime was pointing over towards The Stranger.

Henry shrugged. "No idea. With the police, I guess." He was only interested in getting Jaime out of the wet.

Jaime was desperate to know who this person was. There was something she had realised, though. She had seen him before and not around the resort alone. No, she had seen him on the way over to Antigua on the plane. Sitting in sky-class, which is where he would be sitting if he was keeping an eye on Max. That must be why he was in Antigua. He must have gotten word about Max's criminal activities, somehow. Then two murders occurred, and he was right in the middle of things. Surely this was the mysterious owner of DebonAir? Charles Debon, himself.

Chapter 65

They had managed to find a table in the rapidly filling bar. Upon arriving at the sanctuary of the resort, Jaime had gone to her room to dry off and change clothes, leaving Basil to be fussed over by the hotel staff. Then she had taken his lobster and steak treat to him and sat with him as he ate.

Now, relaxing in a cushioned chair in the bar, she was in danger of becoming the centre of attention.

"How did you know? I mean, she was one of us, you know, a regular person?" Kate was looking at Jaime in awe.

"Speak for yourself, love. There's nothing regular about me," Tony smirked and winked at Mario. He continued, "I was integral to uncovering the killer. I helped Jaime find out who had an appointment. Tell them about my acting skills, JJ."

Jaime laughed relieving some tension inside her. She was glad Tony was taking back the limelight. "You'll tell it better. Go ahead," she responded.

Tony spent the next twenty minutes regaling them with the story of his acting prowess. Mario reached over and squeezed her hand. "I'm sorry we left you alone, JJ. We should never have done that."

"It's not your fault I went out into the storm alone. It was stupid. I should have known better,"

"It's going to feel odd going home minus three crew members," Rob observed. "Max and Gabi are going nowhere anytime soon, and Jean's body won't be released for a while yet."

"I wonder if she had any close family?" remarked Kate.

"None that I know of. She wasn't married. Never had been," responded Mario.

"Well, I for one, don't feel too sorry for her. We can't forget she was a nasty piece of work. She asked for all she got," said Tony.

"She sought people out and spied on them, trying to get secrets she could manipulate them with." Karen's flushed face spoke volumes to Jaime. She knew Karen would never admit to what Jean was holding over her, but the way in which she had pandered to Jean on the aircraft suggested there was something. And Karen had definitely perked up.

"Damn right, she did. Seems she should have left the mad French woman well alone." Tony was intent on putting Jean down.

Mario held up a placating hand. "She's dead. Okay, she wasn't the nicest person in life, but she's paid the ultimate price."

There was a moment's silence.

"Well, I for one, say well done, Jaime. If it wasn't for your perseverance and not accepting it must be Max, we'd all have been flying home with The French Assassin. She could have murdered every last one of us before we touched down at Heathrow."

"Perhaps a little over the top, babe," Mario chided his partner once again.

Jaime turned to Tony and Mario and said, "Inspector Fontaine and Detective Marshall were trying to locate Gabi. It was when Officer Kennedy lost her; she jumped in a cab and followed us to the clinic. Checking if we were on the right track, I guess."

Tony was jumping in his seat. "I told you we were being followed, Jaime. I could sense it. I said so, didn't I? Jesus, I was probably going to be next."

Unbelievable, thought Jaime. She was debating asking the others if they had seen The Stranger around at all. If they thought he could be Charles Debon. But if it was, a part of her wanted to keep it to herself. To be one of the few airline employees who had seen him. Irrational, but there it was.

"You should start a detective agency, Jaime. I think you have a knack for it." Kate seemed sincere. "You noticed so many things the rest of us missed. But how could you rule out Max and Edwina?"

Jaime didn't want to admit to spying on Max in the early hours of the morning to the rest of the crew, although she had shared this with Tony and Mario. She sensed they might think her a little bit mad. Instead, she said, "When I saw the business card with the body, with the word 'Choices' on it, and Thomas discovered what type of place it was, I joined the dots, knowing what kind of man *he* was." She crossed her fingers, hoping no one would ask any further about the card.

"Why kill him, though? Karen asked. "She could have said no. Just walked away."

Jaime sipped her drink. "I suppose if a woman feels threatened enough, there's no limit to what she might do to protect herself: her way of life."

A long silence followed this whilst they contemplated Jaime's words.

"A detective agency…Oh, now that's not a bad idea. We can do it together. Mario can be the muscle." Tony, reverting to the earlier suggestion, glanced sideways at his other half, who pretended to be indignant.

"I do have a brain as well, you know."

Jaime relaxed now she had finished telling the crew what had happened. Reaching over for a salmon blini, she popped it into her mouth. Delicious, she thought. The canapes, coupled with the bottles of Champagne, were a welcome treat.

Vanessa Fleet sailed into the bar with a huge smile on her face. To Jaime, she looked ten years younger. It reminded her that Henry was still hiding the fact that this was his mother. Vanessa hovered next to Rob with a hand on his shoulder.

"I hope you are all doing well. I'm relieved this whole business is over." She turned to Jaime. "I hope you're okay. That little dog of yours is a hero."

Jaime was once again forced to the forefront but managed a smile.

Mario raised his glass towards Vanessa. "We can't thank you enough for the drinks and canapes. They are delicious."

There was an awkward silence in which Vanessa's mouth opened, then closed again. In true manager style, she rallied. "I'd love to take the credit, but someone has beaten me to it. I am not responsible on this occasion."

The crew glanced at each other - at Captain Rob - then seemed to collectively decide their benefactor did not lie in that quarter.

"Well, Champagne is Champagne, and it's bloody good - bottoms up, everyone." Tony raised his glass.

Rob stood, placed an arm around Vanessa's waist and bid the crew good night, arranging to meet them for their flight home in the morning. As soon as they were out of earshot, Tony opened his mouth to speak. However, whatever comment was going to pop out, it was stopped by Mario, who stood, took Tony by the wrist and pulled him to a standing position.

"I think we will follow their lead and go and enjoy our last evening here. We hope you all enjoy yours, too." He looked straight at Jaime. "We bid you all goodnight." Mario bowed, and the two of them headed out of the bar.

Karen reached over and poured the remnants of the bottle into the remaining three glasses.

"We're planning to eat here in the restaurant now it's reopened. You're more than welcome to join us, Jaime."

Jaime smiled at the two women. "I'm glad the storm has subsided, and things are returning to normal. I've made plans for tonight, so thanks but no thanks."

"Not with the customer relations manager? It is, isn't it?" Kate waited for a response from Jaime.

"Of course it is," Karen chipped in. He's had his eye on her since we landed. Well, you go for it and have fun."

"Thanks. You too."

As she drained her glass, Jaime stood to depart. She noticed Karen look in Kate's direction and wink. Kate's reaction was to blush. Jaime decided she was relieved she had alternative plans for the evening. Playing gooseberry was not her idea of fun. Waving to them, she silently wished them both well.

Chapter 66

Nipping back to her room, Jaime wanted to grab a sweater and apply some lip gloss before meeting Henry. He had not wanted to take no for an answer this time, but she was looking forward to the evening – now she knew he wasn't a murderer, of course, although there was still the small matter he was concealing: the truth about his mother.

Walking into her room, it was hard to miss the large bouquet of red roses in the middle of the coffee table. Gasping in surprise at their beauty, she pulled out the accompanying card. No name, but a brief message:

Congratulations Super Sleuth.

Jaime smiled. So, he was a real romantic. Not only dinner but flowers as well. Not wanting to be late, she applied lip gloss and left the room.

Reaching the bottom of the stairs, she headed across the lobby and along the small corridor to Henry's office and tapped on the door. It swung open. He must have been waiting right next to it. He was wearing a plain light blue shirt, open at the neck and a pair of faded jeans. He had shaved and put on a splash of exotic cologne. Understated but handsome. He pecked her on the cheek by way of greeting.

"Shall we?" Holding out his arm in a chivalrous fashion, she took it, laughing.

Jaime was relieved when Henry opened a side door from the hall and led her straight outside, around the edge of the

281

main building, towards the service entrance where a taxi was waiting. She didn't relish the prospect of all eyes on her as she headed out on a date.

"The Cove Cafe, please." Henry had chosen where they were going to eat.

On the way to dinner, Henry pointed out various places of interest, it was getting dark, and the lights sparkled, shining on the colourful buildings and the water. The recent downpour had freshened everywhere, and the smell was of damp earth and fragrant shrubs. They approached the harbour, and the taxi came to a stop outside a quaint little one-story bungalow with fairy lights around it – stunning but not at all like a restaurant.

"Are you sure we can eat here?" Jaime asked, her curiosity getting the better of her.

"Wait and see," Henry grinned. They ascended a couple of stairs and through the open doorway. An attractive, middle-aged lady was standing behind a tall lectern. She looked up as they approached, her face lit up.

"Henry. My angel! How are you?"

"I'm fine, Rene. And you?" He pecked her on the cheek.

"Business is good. Despite the earlier storm, there were no cancellations. We are booked up for the entire season."

Jaime felt disappointed. Surely Henry had not had time to make a reservation? They had only arranged to eat out together a few hours ago.

"May I introduce a friend of mine, Jaime Jones. Jaime, this is Rene." The two ladies smiled at each other and shook hands.

Jaime liked the other woman. She had a warm yet professional manner, a cool, firm handshake and warmth in her eyes.

"Let me walk you both to the bar where you can enjoy a drink while we prepare you a table."

"Thanks, Rene."

Walking through an open doorway into the restaurant, Jaime gasped at the simple beauty of the place, scanning the small veranda with a bar and a three-piece band who were strumming blues tunes. The whole place stood outdoors with a wooden roof intertwined with ivy. Large comfortable wicker chairs were placed around low tables covered by simple, crisp, white cloths; small tea lights added to the ambience along with more fairy lights around the tops of wicker screens. Large palms waved in the now much calmer breeze and shielded the diners from each other. The restaurant was right next to the harbour, the boats were lit up: large and expensive. Rene pulled out two stools for Jaime and Henry.

"Enjoy your drinks. Victor will take care of you." She ruffled Henry's hair and walked away.

"What can I get for you?" the barman asked.

"Would more Champagne be too much for mademoiselle?" Henry's attempt at a French accent made her smile.

"Absolutely not," she declared, thinking she could never tire of the drink.

"Champagne it is."

Victor busied himself with preparing the gleaming ice bucket and showing them a bottle of Moet, to which Henry nodded.

Jaime could contain her curiosity no longer and had to ask.

"How often do you come here, Henry? And how come we can get a table when the place is fully booked till the next millennium?" She had visions of him bringing in a different woman every week and a long-standing arrangement for a table for two on a certain night.

He seemed to read her thoughts. "It's not what you think. This happens to be the best restaurant on the island, and I wanted you to see it. The owner also happens to be my mother's best friend and my godmother. When I was

283

growing up, my mother worked a lot. She often hadn't the time to cook. So, we would arrive, and Rene would get us a table from the storeroom, set it up on the beach over there, and we would eat like royalty.

"Often, I would come alone, armed with my homework or a book to read. My mother is the manager of the Reef Royale." He looked at Jaime awkwardly.

"Of course she is, silly!" responded Jaime, trying to break the tension. "How could a hot detective like me have not discovered that? Why didn't you say Vanessa was your mother days ago? You had ample opportunity."

"I guess I find it a bit embarrassing to admit I work for my mother. It might seem as though I have this job because of her."

Jaime rolled her eyes, and they both laughed. "It made me seriously mistrust you."

"I realise that now," he responded. "I'm an idiot."

Jaime rested her hand briefly over his. "How lucky to be able to eat here whenever you like. It's so tranquil, so beautiful." She envied this way of life whilst feeling sad for the lonely little boy who sat in these romantic surroundings, dining alone.

"I suppose I am lucky - although these days I have to remind myself there should be more to life than work and career." He looked into her eyes.

Jaime turned away as the moment was broken by the pop of the cork. Victor poured the gold liquid into their glasses. Henry handed one to Jaime and took one himself.

"To what shall we toast?" he asked.

Jaime smiled. "To solving my first case."

"First case? Please tell me you're not going to make a habit of this?" They clinked glasses, taking a sip.

They were escorted towards the beach and a quiet little alcove surrounded by palms. The table was simply laid with a small candle. The bottle was placed between them. They could have been the only people around for miles. Jaime could not imagine a more stunning setting.

"Mademoiselle. Sir," announced the waiter. "Our specials this evening are locally caught, broiled lobster and fresh oysters to start."

Jaime was delighted, and both nodded. The waiter retreated, and Henry refilled their glasses.

"Oh," Jaime gasped. "How rude of me. I've been swept off my feet this evening, I forgot to thank you for the beautiful roses."

Henry, whose glass was halfway to his mouth, stopped dead and stared at her.

"What?" she asked as the realisation hit her. "You didn't leave them in my room, did you? They're not from you?"

Henry managed to collect himself and grinned. "I guess I'll have to up my game."

Jaime wished she had not mentioned the flowers, but she had assumed they would be from Henry. Now she'd put a dampener on this beautiful evening. *Bugger*. But the nagging thought was, who had sent them?

The rest of the evening passed in a whirl, both trying their best to put the flower incident behind them. The oysters were divine, fresh with a squeeze of lemon; the lobster rich and tasty, and the second bottle of Champagne was as delightful as the first. Henry was open and funny, happy to talk about himself, although peppering her with questions about England.

Their coffees arrived, and they carried them as they wandered down the beach a little to enjoy the view. It was Henry who broke the silence.

"I would like to thank you, Jaime, for reminding me there is more to life than working."

She smiled at him. However, looking into his attractive face, a different image came to mind.

The image of a tall, fair-haired stranger with remarkably blue eyes...

285

Chapter 67

Sitting alone, sipping on her second cup of coffee, Jaime was waiting for her guest to arrive. She took the last bite of the Eggs Benedict and savoured the flavour. Surveying the restaurant, she spotted the Carfax family sitting huddled around a table for four, the adults drinking coffee and Christy and her brother, orange juice. The mother and father chatted, and they all laughed at something said. Jaime thought they must be relieved now the murders had been solved.

"Hello there."

Jaime jumped and looked up. "Hi. Thanks for coming."

"Are you sure? You nearly had a heart attack." Thomas' eyes crinkled.

"I'm sure. I was lost in thought. Let's get you a cup of coffee and some breakfast, then we can head out."

Thomas ordered himself the American pancakes and a side of beef sausages, she fetched a cinnamon bun, so Thomas didn't feel self-conscious eating alone. They conversed as they ate, and Jaime filled him in on the clinic caper of the previous day. He stared at her during various parts of the story, especially when she had crept into the back room and accessed the computer.

"Y'know, Jaime, you've got more guts than me. I don't think I could've taken the stress of waiting outside."

Jaime patted his hand, which was resting on the table. "You would have been fine. But I knew you would have been booked up. And you and Tish have already done more than enough."

They spent a pleasant half hour chatting about life, Thomas proud of his children's achievements. She told him about her houseboat and the antics of her two 'children', Ellery and Wolfe. Thomas laughed when he heard how Ellery had accompanied her to the local takeaway and stood on his two back legs to peer over the high counter, for all the world looking like he was perusing the menu taped to the wooden surface. The poor man had jumped out of his skin at the sight of the large Doberman, and Jaime had had to suppress her amusement and pull him back down, chastising him half-heartedly at the same time.

"Who takes care of them when you're away?" he asked.

"I'm lucky to have my neighbour. He's right on the next mooring and looks after them. It's the most minimal disruption for them, and they all adore each other. He has a spaniel named Tubbs."

Scraping the last morsel of buttery pancake into his mouth, Thomas sighed. With his eyes shining, he asked, "Shall we go?"

"Absolutely," she replied, and as they stood, she noticed him wrap an uneaten sausage in his napkin and put it in the pocket of his lightweight jacket. She smiled. *I knew he was the man for the job.*

They strode out to the beach. Everything felt much fresher after the storm the previous day. The sand was damp but clean, and the palm trees sparkled. There were members of the hotel staff out and about clearing debris in the form of branches and palm fronds.

"Now, this is where we have been meeting," she explained. "But as you know, he'll find you pretty much anywhere. Especially if you need him. And, of course, now he does know where you live."

As they perched on a rock and waited, she told Thomas about the capture of Gabi and Basil's part in it. He was overwhelmed by Basil's bravery but not surprised.

"I knew he was special," he declared. "There is something about him."

"Hey! Here he is,"

Basil appeared on cue, tail wagging, delighted to see them both. Jaime made a fuss of him, then edged back whilst Thomas took over. As he fed Basil the breakfast treat he had brought away for him, Thomas informed him Tish had purchased a bed which would be in the kitchen whenever he wanted to use it.

"Perhaps you could even come on some of my outings with me?" Thomas suggested.

Basil finished chewing the last of the sausage and looked at them both in turn.

Satisfactory, the look seemed to say.

Chapter 68

The first-class lounge was full. Most of the leather reclining chairs were taken, as were the stools around the bar. The diminished DebonAir crew sat sipping drinks and chatting as they waited for their flight to be called. A fresh crew had been flown out on another carrier to work the flight home.

Jaime found herself glancing around the lounge. She kept coming back to the idea that the man who had appeared all week and who had been there at the end, helping to apprehend Gabi, was Charles Debon. It made the most sense. The reason he stayed in the background, playing it low key, the reason he was onboard in the first place, watching Max - then once he had been taken into custody, turning his attention to liaising with the police about the murder of his CSD.

The man had the reputation of being hands-on in looking after all aspects of his business. Jaime hoped he would be flying back with them. Afterall, business was about concluded here on the island, and there was not much more he could do. She thought back to the time she had witnessed him spying on Max. It made complete sense. But why the interest in her? Why had he been watching her? She had seen him several times, most notably in the bar when he had stared at her with a look of... what was it exactly? He must have suspected her. Why not? The detectives must have shared their theories. Damn, was her job in jeopardy?

289

Taking a sip of the Sancerre, she tried to analyse her feelings. Perhaps she shouldn't have interfered in the investigation. He clearly knew what was going on, with Max, at least.

"Down it, hun. They've called us," Tony nudged her shoulder.

"Don't be crass, Tone," interjected Karen. "It's a bloody expensive wine. You don't 'down' top-notch wines."

"Some of us will down anything that comes our way," Tony bantered.

The plane took off on schedule, with the crew relaxing in their first-class seats, which turned into full-length beds, utilising the buddy seat which was designed for a dinner guest if you desired. Each seat had its own sliding partition offering complete privacy from those around. There was a fifteen-inch tv screen with a choice of movies to watch. Jaime, though, had other ideas for entertainment as she dug into her bag, pulling out her final book, Carolyn G Hart's *The Christie Caper*. Perfect.

She was handed a menu to peruse along with a pre-take-off glass of bubbly. Glancing through the choices, she was horrified to see a coconut sorbet featured in the dessert section. Shuddering, she turned her attention back to the savoury items. The smoked salmon followed by the Pasta Puttanesca - Jaime made her choice quickly. Then maybe a glass of Bordeaux with the cheese board.

After surveying the cabin, which she sensed was quite empty, she sat back and sighed.

Take-off was smooth, and it wasn't long before a crew member materialised, taking orders for lunch and offering more drinks. Kate's head popped through Jaime's curtain, which was the only way in, as the partitions were always in the 'privacy' position, to avoid the potential embarrassment of the passenger having to look rude, as though they didn't want to converse with those around them.

"We're heading over to the bar. C'mon. We may as well make the most of the facilities." Kate grinned.

She ought to be concerned about Karen's track record of dead ex-partners, Jaime thought. "Coming," she replied, retrieving her half-empty glass.

The bar was small but had enough seats to accommodate them. Rob was already in situ, along with Tony and Mario, who were asking their colleague for cocktails. They turned as she approached.

"You must request a trip with us both soon, Jaime. We can help you solve your next mystery."

"How do you know there's going to be one? I can't magic a crime to solve because you fancy it."

"I bet you're one of those people who mysteries follow around."

Jaime felt uncomfortable. There had, to her knowledge, only been two mysteries in her life, this one, she had solved. The other, ten years ago, onboard a cruise ship heading for the shores of Greenland, remained a mystery - to the authorities. A body had never been recovered.

"Shame you can't see anybody. How are you supposed to know if there's anyone you fancy?" It was Mario this time, looking around the cabin. Tony's sass was rubbing off on him.

Karen replied, "I was thinking about what Rob said when we arrived in Antigua. It feels so long ago now."

Rob raised his eyebrows. "What did I say?"

"You know, about Charles Debon being on board. If he was with us on the flight out, there's a chance he'll be on the flight home too. And what a perfect opportunity to say hi."

Jaime felt her face flush. She was feeling hot and was relieved no one was looking her way.

"Good point," replied Tony, staring at the man in 4A, who had, for some reason, decided to lower his privacy partition. "What about him?"

Five sets of eyes followed his to the seat in question, where a portly man in his late sixties was scarfing a packet of peanuts, washing them down with swigs of whiskey.

"No. Definitely not," stated Karen.

"And why not?" demanded Tony, no doubt not liking to be disagreed with.

"Charlie boy must be hot. He must be. In all my fantasies, he's ridiculously sexy. Please don't spoil that."

Even Rob managed to laugh.

"I thought your fantasies had changed during this trip, Karen." Tony didn't miss a beat.

Karen frowned. "Time to eat, Kate." She slid off her stool, pulling Kate along with her.

It was quite eerie looking around the cabin, not knowing if seats were occupied or empty.

"I guess we'll have to accept we'll never know what he looks like," Mario sighed.

"It's the way he wants it," commented Rob. "He had his work cut out for him on this trip, what with Max and his criminal activities to contend with – and a murdered crew member and a murdering crew member."

They all nodded solemnly. Jaime felt the need to change the subject.

"Any plans to spend time with Vanessa soon?"

Rob's eyes crinkled. "She's going to take some time off and head over for a visit. I need to get my life in order. That capable boy of hers is going to take the reins for a while."

"Talking of Henry, Jaime. Any plans for you two hooking up again?" Tony sipped his Dirty Martini.

Jaime answered irritably, "No. He's a nice guy, but not for me."

"But you sampled the merchandise before you decided, right? It would be criminal not to check out something so damned attractive."

Mario nudged Tony a little harder than he had perhaps meant to, sending a slosh of cocktail over his skinny suit trousers.

"Bloody hell, Mario, what the..." Tony caught himself in time, remembering where he was. "I need to wash this off before it stains." Jumping off his stool, he headed for the toilet, forward of the cabin.

Jaime smiled at Mario. "Thanks," she said.

"He means well. He does care about you. He wants everyone to be hooked up. He ought to be a matchmaker."

"That would suit him well," commented Rob. "Well, I think I'll head off to lunch. See you all soon."

As he walked away through the curtain which had been drawn across to separate the bar from the cabin, Mario commented, "Well, he's a lot nicer when he's in love."

"You're not kidding," laughed Jaime. "I think I'm going to head back too. I'm feeling peckish. You know, Mario," she added, "I'm glad you two were on this trip. And I'm sorry I suspected you for a while."

Mario laughed. "I wouldn't have had it any other way. Enjoy your meal."

Jaime slid through the curtain, noticing the crew had switched the lighting to a shade of deep purple, enough to navigate around the cabin but also dim enough for those who wanted to sleep. She needed some alone time.

Arriving at her seat, Jaime saw her table was out and set, the table lamp switched on. It was cosy and inviting. Sliding in, she spotted the smoked salmon already there, complete with lemon, capers, black pepper and thinly sliced bread.

"I took the liberty of ordering your favourite wine to accompany the salmon. A chardonnay."

Jaime jumped as she stared in the direction of the voice, her mouth open. Sitting opposite her, filling the buddy seat with his tall frame, was the fair-haired, blue-eyed man who had been occupying her thoughts. The Stranger.

Close up, the eyes were more intense than ever, the skin around them faintly lined. And the voice, deep and seductive. Jaime's heart was beating wildly in her chest, and she could not find any words. She just stared.

"You don't mind me joining you?" The man faltered.

Jaime shook her head and managed to utter, "No."

The man smiled, relaxed again and sure of himself. "How about a toast? To you, Jaime Jones and your detective skills."

He raised his glass, at the same time sliding one over to her. As she reached out and took the glass from him, their fingers brushed, and Jaime felt such a jolt of electricity pass between them she almost spilt the wine. Looking over at him, she was sure he had felt it too.

"Cheers," he said.

"Cheers," responded Jaime taking a larger sip than usual. The crisp, cold liquid did the trick, and she regained some composure. "I feel at a bit of a disadvantage," she said.

The man put down his glass, his hand resting on the table, dangerously close to hers. "How so?"

"You seem to know a lot about me, and yet, I don't even know your name."

"Well, that's easily solved, Jaime." He held out his hand. "I'm Charles. Charles Debon. It's a pleasure to finally meet you."

THE END

Join Jaime Jones as she stars in her next high-flying
adventure.

With love and gratitude for my family.

Many thanks to my friends at the South Hams Author Network for all their advice and for giving me the final push I needed!

About the Author

Figgy Mack is the author of the Up in the Air mystery
series featuring sleuthing flight attendant Jaime Jones.
Figgy spent many years working on long-haul flights for a
well-known airline. She has also been a driving instructor,
owned and ran a café / wine bar and taught secondary
school students.

She is currently hiding out in a cabin in Devon with her
husband Phil, where, when not travelling or losing at chess,
she is working on her next Up in the Air mystery.

www.figgymack.co.uk
Follow Figgy on Facebook

Printed in Great Britain
by Amazon

32288371R00172